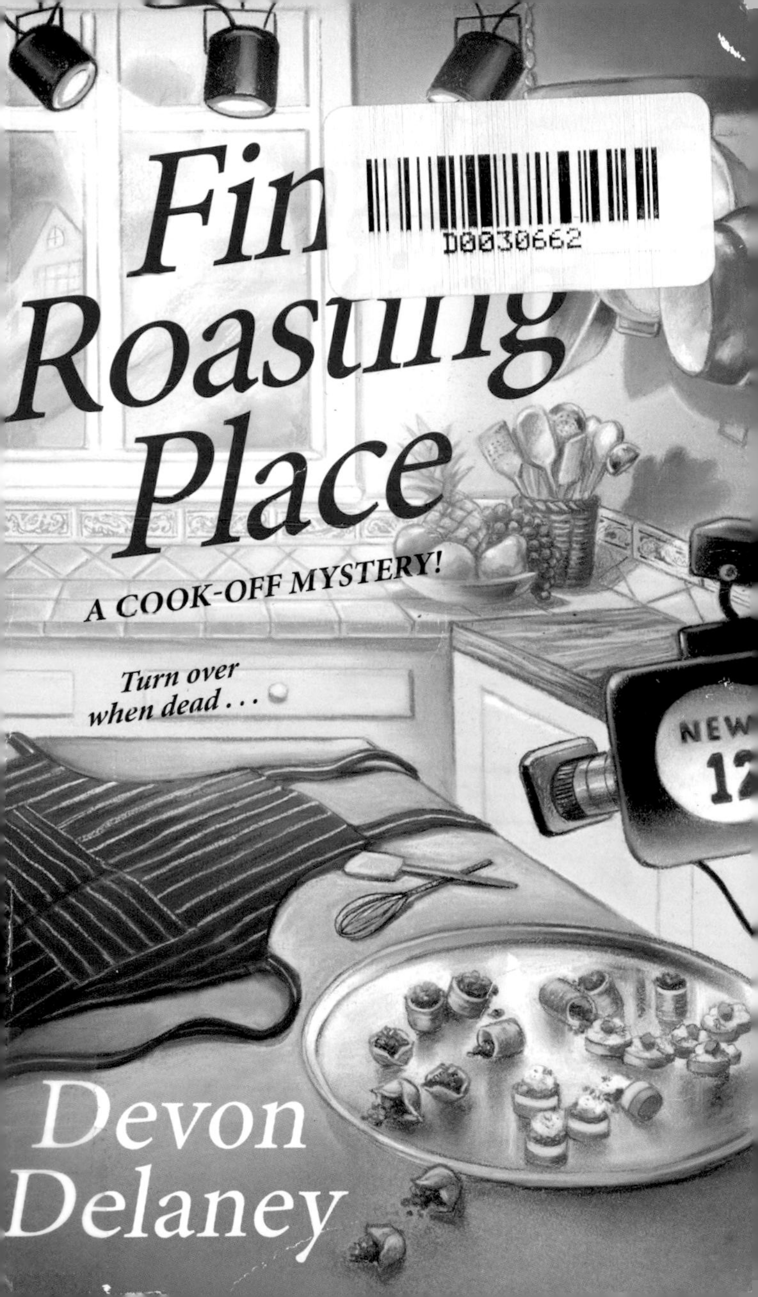
Fin
Roasting
Place
A COOK-OFF MYSTERY!
Turn over
when dead . . .
NEW
12
Devon
Delaney

KENSINGTON
U.S. $7.99
CAN $8.99

Don't Miss the First Cook-Off Mystery!

ISBN-13: 978-1-4967-1445-9
ISBN-10: 1-4967-1445-8

ANOTHER RECIPE FOR MURDER

Sherry stopped pacing. "Dad, what was going on at the cook-off yesterday, and I don't mean during the cooking portion? Afterward." She heard a groan on his end of the phone. "I saw you involved in a conversation with Carmell Gordy, one I would almost categorize as heated. And the same goes for your interaction with Brett Paladin. How do you even know those two? Granted, most of the town knows of you, but they don't all *know* you." She paused long enough to suck in some oxygen. "And to make matters worse, you had me stow away a punch tool before we went through the station's metal detector because you knew they wouldn't inspect my cooking equipment bag. And one like it was used to take Carmell Gordy's life. Maybe even that exact one. To compound matters, the tool didn't come home in the bag, unless you know where it is."

"That tool has one hundred and one uses. Better than a Swiss Army knife. Cuts string, opens cans, threads string through a tight spot, clears clogs. I could write a book about its versatility. I never leave home without it." Erno's laugh was as bittersweet as grapefruit rind. "Sherry, I didn't kill that woman. May appear bad, but I wasn't involved in any way with Carmell Gordy's death."

"Dad, I didn't mean to get you worked up again. We'll fix this. Detective Bease came on strong, but that's his job. If I have to, I'll start digging around. There's a reason someone hated Carmell enough to want her dead. We have to figure out what, why, who, and where." The words she dreaded saying escaped her mouth faster than steam from the first puncture of a hot baked potato. "Dad, you do have a plausible alibi, right? I can't, in all honesty, say I was with you while the murder took place. . . ."

Books by Devon Delaney

EXPIRATION DATE

FINAL ROASTING PLACE

Published by Kensington Publishing Corporation

Final Roasting Place

Devon Delaney

KENSINGTON PUBLISHING CORP.
http://www.kensingtonbooks.com

KENSINGTON BOOKS are published by

Kensington Publishing Corp.
119 West 40th Street
New York, NY 10018

First Printing: October 2018
ISBN-13: 978-1-4967-1445-9
ISBN-10: 1-4967-1445-8

eISBN-13: 978-1-4967-1446-6
eISBN-10: 1-4967-1446-6

10 9 8 7 6 5 4 3 2 1

Printed in the United States of America

Chapter 1

"You'd think winning recipe contests was a matter of life and death. Two of the contestants stormed out of here in such a huff I didn't get to try their appetizers." Erno Oliveri put one arm around his daughter, while snaking his free hand toward the plate loaded with crab-stuffed mushrooms. He popped one in his mouth. "If your recipe beat these beauties, you must be a great cook." He released his daughter and went back, double-fisted, for more.

As Sherry touched her warm cheek, she envisioned her face glowing radish red. "Thanks, Dad, but you're exaggerating a bit. I don't think anyone was in a huff. And if you think I'm such a good cook, why haven't you had more than one taste of my Spicy Toasted Chickpea and Almond Bites?" Sherry untied and removed her new *Watch Sunny Side Up with Brett and Carmell weekdays at 8 a.m.* apron. She folded the cloth to the size of a dinner napkin. "I have to say, the way you've been scarfing down my competitor's food, I'm glad you weren't one of the judges." She used the compacted apron to swat her father's head with loving restraint.

Sherry set the cloth on the polished acrylic table she and her fellow cook-off competitors had displayed their competing dishes on. The spills and splatters each cook had produced during their thirty-minute time allotment had been mopped up, and Studio B was ready for whatever broadcast segments were coming up next.

"Congratulations, Sherry, great recipe," the woman who had crafted the crab mushrooms said as she headed toward the building's exit, appetizer platter in hand. Her kind words couldn't mask the sagging frown on her face.

As she passed, Erno's hand jutted forward to hijack one more bite. He was a moment too tardy; the plate traveled beyond his reach, and his hand remained empty. His arm collapsed down to his side, and his chest deflated.

"Yours were great, too," Erno called after Mushroom Lady. He turned back to face Sherry. "Forgive me. I'm not a chickpea fan, but obviously your appetizer was perfectly executed." Erno's gaze followed the exiting tray of fungi across the TV studio and out the door. "Farewell, delicious ones, I'll miss you."

"Dad, you're so transparent. Can you get your mind off the crab long enough to help me gather my stuff, please?"

A block of a man with a headful of wavy salt-and-pepper hair approached Sherry as she placed her baking sheet inside her rolling carryall. She lifted her head and smiled at the imposing News Twelve station owner, Damien Castle. She began to utter a greeting before she realized he was talking on his cell phone. Sherry swallowed her "hello" and continued packing her cooking supplies.

"I'll be there. Yes, of course. I haven't missed one yet, have I? Thank you for being so accommodating." Damien put the phone in his breast pocket, lifted a mixing bowl off the counter, and handed it to Sherry. "Your cook-off win today is the biggest thing to happen at News Twelve since the governor's motorcade stopped by unannounced to use the men's room last month. We had to interrupt our broadcast because his entourage created such a stir." Damien pursed his lips and handed Sherry her serving spoon from the pile of rinsed silverware.

"Thanks, Mr. Castle. I love these smaller cook-offs." Sherry arched her eyebrows skyward as she reconsidered her comment. "I didn't mean this was a small cook-off in any negative sense."

Sherry sucked in a deep breath, in hopes of washing away any lingering taste of the foot she had put in her mouth. She blew a wayward lock of hair from her face. The hairstyle she had begun sporting recently was taking some getting used to. She hadn't worn a shoulder-length cut, without clips or barrettes, since she was in her twenties. "Certainly was one of the most fun appetizer competitions I've been a part of in a long time. Your TV station went above and beyond to make all four of us contestants feel well taken care of."

Erno cleared his throat with a rumble rivaling a food processor set on full power. Sherry heaved her slumping shoulders back and gulped down the emerging words she had been about to relay, rather than continue rambling. Instead, she watched her father relocate to the edge of the room, where he found a seat.

Sherry resumed collecting the kitchenware she had brought from home. Some contests provided all the supplies needed to complete a recipe while others required participants to bring supplies needed for success. Sherry preferred the former, but was resigned to the growing popularity of the latter. It was a more economically sound way for the sponsor to run the contest, but, for Sherry, always a juggling act to get supplies to and fro.

"Please, call me Damien. I may own this place, but I don't put on airs. On airs, on-air. That's quite punny if you think about it."

The chuckling man took a step away from Sherry, only to be replaced by a woman in a pinstripe blazer and pencil skirt.

"Damien's right. You proved once again you're Augustin's most decorated home cook. Thanks for entering our contest. You elevated the level for all the others who tried and failed to beat you. For your information, there were close to one hundred and fifty recipes our staff whittled down to the final four, from the chefs who competed this morning, so you should be proud to come out victorious." Carmell Gordy edged backward until she was shoulder to shoulder with Damien.

"Thank you, Carmell." Sherry thrust her platter of appetizers toward Carmell. "Would you like to try some? I don't think you got a chance to try them during the cook-off." Sherry's second attempt to lure the News Twelve personality into a taste-test was thwarted with a wave of Carmell's elegant hand.

"I'm careful about what I eat." Carmell patted her concave core with one hand while clutching a vibrant green smoothie in the other. "Television anchors think they can sit behind a desk and hide extra pounds, but savvy viewers know when you've let yourself go."

"Hard to break my urge to want to fill bellies." Sherry set the platter back down. She wedged the tips of her fingers just inside her straining waistband and sighed as she struggled to fit more than one finger in. She untucked her shirt and yanked the hem over her stomach bulge. "I'm thinking of taking up Zumba. Lately I've been doing too much cooking and not enough sweating. I need to get back in shape."

Carmell glanced past Sherry. With no real intention of taking up the dance aerobics exercise du jour, Sherry was glad her comment was ignored.

Carmell rotated on her heels for a close encounter with Damien. "Are you behind in your e-mails? I'm waiting for a reply. There's time sensitivity involved." The words hissed from Carmell's mouth like escaped steam from a pressure cooker.

Damien winced and pulled out his phone. He began talking into the device.

"Ugh. He's not fooling me. He puts on that act when he wants to avoid a conversation, especially one involving me." Carmell craned her neck toward Sherry. "Did you hear his phone ring? I didn't. Did you see him dial out? I didn't."

Sherry scraped her shoe along the ground. "It could be on vibrate. We were told to shut our phones down when we came in the building."

"He owns this place. He plays by his own rules. I've heard his phone ring during a broadcast plenty of times. And if he's talking to someone right now, I'm the queen of England." Carmell took a noisy pull on her straw. "Time to get back to the anchor desk. We have a segment coming up on Augustin's Andre

August Dahlback Festival. As you probably know, he's the legendary founder and namesake of the town of Augustin. If he hadn't brought those first onion bulbs over from his native Sweden and made this land the prosperous center of the onion universe, who knows what this town would be famous for today? Tune in for more information." Carmell's sweeping wave brushed Sherry's shoulder as she turned and walked away. "Bye, bye."

Sherry watched Carmell hop over the camera cables crisscrossing the floor of the studio before slipping through the studio doors.

Damien returned his phone to his pocket. "I've got to run. Need to stay ahead of the next mini crisis brewing. Sorry I can't offer more cleanup assistance." He helped himself to a cluster of Sherry's chickpeas and almonds and marched away in Carmell's footsteps.

A young man in an oversized flannel shirt trotted over. On his head, a haphazard man bun fidgeted from side to side with each step he took. A shorter man, who reminded Sherry of a beet, bottom heavy and red-faced, tailed him.

"Carmell Gordy sends me on a wild-goose chase to find a certain kind of treat for her dog, and now the picky canine won't touch the pricy biscuit. What he did eat was the receipt. Now I can't get reimbursed." Man Bun stuffed the pouch of dog treats in one of his multiple cargo pants pockets. "What am I doing all this for? Certainly not for the big bucks. Interns don't make a dime. Her pooch hates me and, considering all I do for him, he could be a tiny bit grateful." The taller man locked gazes with Sherry. A broad smile bloomed, revealing gleaming white teeth. "Hi, I'm Steele Dumont, esteemed station apprentice.

My job description is, if someone wants something done and no one else wants to do it, I'm your man."

"Nice to see you, Steele. I know of you, although you probably have never heard of me. I work for your grandmother one day a week selling her pickles at the farmer's market. She mentioned I might see you here. Such a small world, right?" Sherry returned the smile. "I was in the appetizer cook-off this morning. I think I saw you darting around the studio behind the scenes. You're hard to miss." Sherry observed Steele's man bun, which was sprouting free-spirited hair. "And now I'm on my way out. Good luck in your job."

"Much appreciated. Got to go, too." Steele spun around toward the shorter man. "Brett, do you need me to grab any supplies from the closet before I get too involved in settling Dog Treat-gate with Carmell?"

"Nope, all set. I'm on in ten after Carmell finishes her segment, so right now I'm heading to my dressing room for a touch-up. My rosacea is acting up again. Stress-related, I'm sure." The man who had served as the moderator of the morning's cook-off, Brett Paladin, brushed his glowing cheek with the back of his hand. "Hard to believe, but I could use a bite to eat, too."

"I didn't get a chance to tell you how much I've enjoyed watching you over the years. I watched your very first broadcast. If I'm not mistaken you anchored a show called *On The Front Burner With Brett.* That same year you visited my high school and gave a talk in our English class. I was star struck." Sherry visualized a statuesque powerhouse of a man whose authoritative voice had kept the interest of twenty-two willful teenagers for an hour. All these years later, standing next to him, the bridge of her nose was the same height as the top of his head. She had to decline her chin to make eye contact.

Brett massaged his well-fed stomach. "Thank you. Loyal viewership means the world to me. I remember how difficult it was working solo. A partner like Carmell is an invaluable asset." He tossed a glance toward Sherry's plate of food and held up what appeared to be a large cookie. He took a hearty bite. Half of the remaining cookie collapsed to the floor. "I make these energy breakfast cookies myself. I think they're good enough to market. Would you like a taste? I'd value your opinion."

Sherry's stomach warned, "No more room until I've digested the crab mushrooms, mini sausage sliders, and phyllo spinach quiche the other contestants had me sample."

Sherry attempted to send a signal of refusal with the wave of her hand, but it was ignored. Brett broke off a chunk.

"Okay." The word leapt out before she could squash it.

The cookie landed in her hand. Brett's lips parted. The cookie entered Sherry's mouth. After a moment of mulling over the flavor and texture, she transported it down her digestive highway. She gulped hard to squelch a rising belch.

"Well? Pretty good, right?" Brett's grin was so expansive, his ears lifted. He took a bite of the remaining cookie.

"If I could give you one suggestion."

Brett's shiny smile went south faster than mayonnaise sitting in the summer sun.

"If you add a spoonful of almond butter, the batter

will be moister and bind the baked product better. And maybe add more flavoring. I suggest turbinado sugar. Oh, and some chopped almonds for crunch. Oatmeal would give the cookie a desirable chewy texture, and a sprinkle of sea salt would deliver a tangy, bright note." After analyzing Brett's creased forehead, Sherry added, "I see great possibilities, though."

Sherry's rising shoulders dropped when a man carrying a clipboard jogged over to a scowling Brett. Clipboard Man's crew cut was so flat on top Sherry imagined she could rest a stack of pancakes without concern for toppling. He pointed out a spot on a sheet of paper to Brett before proceeding on. Brett grumbled and massaged his temples with his fingertips in a small circular motion.

The building heat of heartburn churned in Sherry's chest. "Boy, a typhoon of constant motion around here. People rushing in, people rushing out. Gives me an uneasy feeling."

The way Brett studied the room from one corner to the other, she knew he wasn't fully invested in listening to her.

"That guy can't make a decision to save his life, and he's our producer." Brett exhaled with such force that crumbs came flying out of his mouth. "Truman Fletcher's clipboard is what really runs this place." Brett's voice reverberated throughout the room. "Where's your dad?"

"How did you know my father was with me, Mr. Paladin?"

Brett's facial hue deepened. "Call me Brett, please. Only Dan Rather deserves the honorific 'Mr.'" Brett laughed at length, without drawing in air, until the color drained from his face.

Brett finally vacuumed in a breath. "I recognized Erno Oliveri in the back of the room, off-camera, while you were cooking. It wasn't hard to pin him as your father. The resemblance is quite strong. I rushed onto the cook-off studio floor this morning, so I didn't get a chance to say hi. To be honest with you, I thought the kitchen segment was solely Carmell's. Didn't get that assignment until five minutes before shoot time. Not sure how that girl has the wherewithal to make changes for others at the last minute, but if Truman Fletcher okays something, it's as good as done." Brett gestured toward the mountain of a man in chino pants and an oxford shirt, sleeves rolled up, examining his clipboard.

"I had no idea you and Dad knew each other." Sherry shifted her weight from one leg to the other. "Dad's right over there in the back of the room." She pointed him out, seated along the dimly lit edge of the studio. Erno was partially obscured by the massive lens of a TV camera. "I'm almost done here. In a minute I'll take you over to him."

After Sherry stored the last of her utensils in her rolling suitcase, she strained to close the zipper, but, a few failed attempts later, she gave up. Sherry turned to Brett. "Follow me."

"Watch the cables." Brett steered Sherry by the arm as they headed over to Erno.

As she neared her father, Sherry's footstep snagged a thick plastic-encased wire, and she lost her balance. Brett's reaction wasn't fast enough to keep her from pitching forward toward a monstrous camera. Her ribs took the brunt of the blow.

Carmell Gordy emerged from Erno's side and steadied Sherry by grasping her shoulders. "Are you hurt?" Carmell's lips were as puckered as a week-old apple slice. "You were almost breaking news. I wouldn't want to have to report that the cook-off winner was a casualty." Carmell released her grip, and Sherry teetered for a split second.

"Thanks. I'm clumsy. Old news there." Sherry righted herself. The intensity in Erno's eyes was that which the little girl in Sherry had seen on a few occasions growing up. That uncomfortable energy he transmitted meant a punishment was about to be doled out.

"I'm going." Carmell's clipped tone was fortified by the harsh tapping of her heels as she strutted away. She stopped and turned her head. "Oh, Brett, Damien took you off the Founder's Day feature we're shooting tomorrow. Did he tell you?"

"Yep. Can't count on much around here lasting more than a few minutes." Brett scuffed his shoe on the floor.

"What was that all about?" Sherry leaned over and put her hand on Erno's shoulder. "You and Carmell could have toasted my appetizer almonds with the heat generated between you two."

"Just a friendly chat." Erno avoided Sherry's glare. "We'd met prior to today and were catching up on lost time."

"I brought Brett Paladin, Carmell's co-anchor, over to say hello." Sherry stepped aside to let Brett slide between them. "He was asking for you."

"Good to see you, Brett." Erno shook Brett's hand.

"Good to see you too." Brett spoke with such urgency his words blended together as one.

"How do you all know each other?" Sherry pointed from one man to the other. She crossed her arms on her chest.

Brett rocked forward onto his toes. "Most anyone in town knows your father, I'd say. Probably best our acquaintance wasn't broadcast ahead of time, what with your being a contestant and all. Of course, my knowing your father had no bearing on the contest judging." Brett checked his watch. "I've got to get going. Nice to spend time with you both, and have a good day."

Brett removed his blazer and slung it over his arm. He ran his hand through his pile of hair, before marching away.

"Ah, there you two are." Damien Castle rushed toward Sherry and Erno. He was able to navigate his short journey without once lifting his face from his phone screen. "We need to get you on your way. Station security doesn't allow visitors, even as esteemed as you two, to stay much beyond your allotted segment time. I've been sent to find you because you haven't signed out at the reception desk. The other three contestants are long gone."

Sherry and Erno returned to the table in the center of Studio B. Sherry snapped up the handle of her carryall. "We're all set."

"Don't forget this." Damien handed Sherry her cook-off trophy. His massive hand obscured the base of the shiny statue. "Do you have your grand prize check?"

"Right here." Sherry pulled a small envelope from her pants pocket and waved it in the air. "All two hundred and fifty dollars' worth. A nice surprise that'll fund my next recipe experiment. Thanks so much." Sherry held the trophy up to eye level. She spun it until the inscription faced her. She read the words aloud. "'Augustin's Local News Twelve TV, You Watch Us Watch You.'" Sherry clutched the bronze replica of an oversized spatula in the crook of her elbow, before realizing she also had to juggle a tray of leftover appetizers, along with her supply bag.

"Can I help you?" Before Sherry could respond, Damien snatched the suitcase handle with a swipe of his hand.

"Thanks." Sherry tightened the crook of her elbow to keep the trophy from slipping through. The base of the shiny statue rested on her hip and shifted with each step she took. At the same time, she clutched the tray of remaining Spicy Toasted Chickpea and Almond Bites.

"Right this way." Damien motioned Sherry and Erno toward the studio exit. He pocketed his phone long enough to turn the lock securing the door shut to unauthorized personnel. "Oh, I almost forgot. If you wouldn't mind leaving the trophy with the receptionist, we'll have the engraver put your name at the base of the spatula handle." Damien let the door slam shut after Sherry and Erno stepped through. "Do you prefer we inscribe your name as Sherry Frazzelle or do you have a middle name you'd like to include?"

With Damien's question delivered, Sherry stopped short. Erno clipped her heels. The front row of toasted appetizer took flight from the platter and winged its way across the hall.

"Sorry, you caught me off guard. I'm in the process of getting my name legally changed back to my maiden name, Oliveri. This'll be the first time I'll officially be an Oliveri again." Sherry corralled some stray chick-peas with her foot into a neat collection before side-stepping them. "So, if you wouldn't mind, I'd prefer Sherry Oliveri." Sherry turned toward a door on her right. "This way?"

"No, that's the control room. The brains of the operation." Damien scooted around Sherry to take the lead again. "Down this hallway. We have to duck through the main studio to get to the lobby."

Sherry noticed her father examining the next door they approached. "This way, Dad."

"Is there a men's room around here?" Erno asked.

"Right over there." Damien indicated the direction with a head tilt as barking erupted from the other side of the door.

"Bean, keep quiet." Damien tapped the toe of his shoe on the door. "Carmell's Jack Russell makes himself at home in her dressing room while she does her show. I need to check her contract. I might want to rescind the perk, citing continual noise violations." His words had an edge as sharp as Sherry's favorite paring knife. "Erno, head that way, and you'll see a men's room symbol on the door. We'll wait for you in Studio A. Be as quiet as possible when you come in. They're on live now." Damien pointed to the illuminated "Quiet Please" sign at the end of the hall.

Erno shuffled past Sherry and was enveloped by the dark corridor.

"I hope my dad can find his way." Sherry stared into the dingy abyss in front of her before glancing over her shoulder. "His vision isn't as sharp as it used to be in low lighting. I guess if the governor found the men's room, Dad can too. Minus the entourage."

Damien was too busy checking his cell phone and murmuring to himself to acknowledge Sherry's attempt at humor.

Chapter 2

"What was that?" Sherry's feet refused another step. She braced her quivering arms against her sides to steady them. She bent her knees and assumed the "ready to bear heavy weight" stance. As her hands lurched backward, a few more legumes and nuts were ejected from the platter she carried. "Did you feel a tremor?"

Damien's phone squealed. He scrambled to click a button that ended the shrill alarm. "A tough storm is about to pass over us. I'm getting a tornado warning on my phone. Heavy thunder, intense lightning, and hail possible, imminently . . . well, strike that, right now." He brushed his finger across the phone screen. "There's an ominous blob on the local radar. We're in the bull's-eye for the next ten minutes."

Sherry checked the hallway behind her. No sign of Erno. An army of chilling goose bumps advanced up her arms.

"Listen, I've got to run to the control room and make sure operations are running smoothly. Sometimes a surge of electricity creates havoc at a low power station like ours. I'll get your equipment case to the receptionist where you can collect it on your way out." Another muffled boom echoed through the hall. "Head straight through those doors and wait in the back of the studio for your dad. Best place is behind the camera operator, Kirin. You won't be in the way back there. And please, no talking."

Sherry jutted out her lower lip. Waves of silent pleas left her brain, begging Damien to stay with her, but his phone was his primary concern.

Damien took off in the opposite direction and was soon out of sight.

"If my ex-husband's connection with me had been as strong as Damien's is to his phone, Charlie and I would still be married," Sherry whimpered.

Sherry was left alone, with the challenge of opening the door to the main studio with full hands. Fort Knox didn't have such impenetrable doors. A quick survey of her surroundings confirmed there was no one else around to help solve her problem.

Sherry's first thought was that, if she had once solved the dinnertime quandary of satisfying her meat and potatoes–craving ex-spouse when her refrigerator contained only one portobello mushroom and a cup of leftover black rice, this dilemma should be a piece of cake. Her second thought was that maybe her spontaneous cooking experiments were another reason why her ex-husband, Charlie, had been dissatisfied with their marriage.

"Why am I even thinking of Charlie at a time like this? You're on your own, girl."

Sherry set her serving plate and trophy on the floor and leaned on the door latch. No movement, whatsoever. After another rumble of thunder shook the walls, she pounded on the metal door, but was rewarded with only a muffled thud and a sore hand.

Sherry set back her shoulders, guided her trophy and plate to the wall with her foot, and stared down the unforgiving barrier in front of her.

"Let me help," a boisterous voice chirped.

Sherry rotated around, arms poised to strike, and whacked Steele Dumont on his forehead.

Steele let out a gasp. "Sorry. I didn't mean to startle you." He waved a laminated card across the sensor. The door unlocked with a resounding click.

"I didn't hear you coming." Sherry puffed out her cheeks, picked up her food and hardware, and walked through the open door. "My dad should be heading this way in a few minutes. Will he be able to get through without some sort of pass card?"

"There's always someone coming or going. He won't have to wait long before he's let in." Steele closed the door with slow precision. He put his finger up to his lips. "One more minute and the segment's over, so if you'll wait over there, please."

Steele indicated a spot next to the giant camera being operated by a woman in a backward-facing baseball cap. "If I don't get Carmell's change of lipstick to her dressing room by the end of the next commercial break, there'll be hell to pay." Steele's rubber-soled desert boots screeched without mercy on the linoleum floor as he reversed directions.

Sherry took her position in the shadows at the back of the live set. As a result of her holding her right bicep cocked in support of her trophy for an extended length of time, a twitch was developing. *Might as well try to relax and enjoy the show until Dad shows up. I wish he'd hurry up.* Sherry turned her attention to Carmell seated at the anchor desk centered on a slick wooden riser. The woman in pinstripes, garnished with a gemstone statement necklace, delivered the words on the monitor with the smoothness of vanilla pudding.

"As you can imagine, making a better life for his family was what motivated Andre August Dahlback, a sack of onion bulbs slung over his shoulder, to settle in this part of Connecticut, and aren't we all better off for his having done so. Augustin's Founder's Day celebration is the brainchild of the town historical society. The festivities promise to deliver as many layers of fun as one of Mr. D.'s onions." Carmell's head bobbed up and down, as she appeared to agree with her own assessment. Her eyes, the color of kale and the shape of a crosscut carrot slice, enticed the camera lens to move in for a close-up. "After the commercial break, *Sunny Side Up with Carmell and Brett* will be taking a turn from our, thus far, food-themed show to explore the top five habits people have that unknowingly offend others on a continual basis."

Carmell drummed her fingers on the desk. "Wow, I hope our producer isn't sending me a message with that story."

The camera's red light faded to black. Sherry studied Carmell as the anchorwoman froze her toothy smile until the set lights lowered. As the lights lowered, so did the angle of Carmell's lips. She pulled her cell phone from under the desk, held the device up to eye level, and shook her head. At the same time, Steele hopped up on set, only to be redirected with a wave of her hand.

"Brett, four minutes. Be on set in four minutes," an overhead speaker called out.

Sherry was fixated on Carmell, who was pounding her fist on the wooden desk. Carmell's lips were moving as if she was talking to herself.

"I'm going to roll this bad boy back a few feet to frame a two-person shot. Watch your feet," warned the woman steering the camera. "Kirin" was embroidered on the side of her cap. The camera operator stepped down from her perch and hauled the equipment backward. The woman hopped back up on her elevated seat and began extending and retracting the impressive lens.

"Kirin, is that your name? Can I offer you a snack? I was in the cook-off this morning, and I have some leftovers." Sherry tipped the plate to show off the contents.

"Yes, I'm the notorious Kirin of Studio A. I didn't shoot you over in Studio B. My counterpart, Lucky, owns that territory. I see by your trophy you won first prize. Congrats." Kirin pointed her elbow toward the shiny spatula statue without taking her hands off her camera's controls. "I suspect there was no giant game show check to go along with the win. Between you and me, this place is a bit strapped for cash." She let out a puff of air. "Thanks for the snack offer. If you don't mind, I'll wait until after the next segment. We're about to resume shooting, and, if my hands are greasy, controlling this monster could get dicey."

The words "strapped for cash" landed in Sherry's ears with the subtlety of Bananas Flambé.

Sherry pursed her lips. "They're not greasy, but it's your decision. I'm on my way out. I could leave a sample with the receptionist out in the lobby. Kirin, I noticed the apron they gave me for the cook-off was printed with *Sunny Side Up with Brett and Carmell,* but

Carmell told me the show's name was *Sunny Side Up with Carmell and Brett.* What's the correct order of names?"

"Both ways have been correct, but Carmell is on top currently. Brett's been the morning anchor here for twelve years. Carmell is in her second year. The youngster swept in like a twenty-three-year-old tsunami, and we're all holding on to her coattails for dear life at this point. She made a suggestion, and the show title changed in an instant. Pretty amazing. I swear she has some invisible force making her quite powerful." Kirin shrugged her shoulders. "If you think the show's name change sat well with poor Brett, think again. Damien Castle is her puppet. Don't even get me started on Truman Fletcher's role in all this."

A thunderous boom turned heads. Kirin mumbled an indecipherable collection of words as she peered into the camera's massive viewfinder. The overhead lights surged with an impossible glow before flickering and dying out altogether. A despondent curse was exclaimed. A resounding crash and a dull thud echoed through the room. Sherry dared not move, visualizing the spaghetti-like maze of thick cables on the floor, the towering microphone boom at head level, and a landscape of television monitors conspiring to stage a mechanical coup in the pitch black.

"Attention, people." The room din ceased. "Remain calm. The storm has knocked out power. We're not sure why the generator has failed, but we're trying to locate Mr. Castle to get some answers."

An almost inaudible voice added, "The penny-pinching owner has sure done it this time. You get what you pay for."

Kirin began humming to herself. Sherry wished

she knew Kirin well enough to ask her to refrain from humming her eerie tune, which, in the enveloping darkness, was as unwelcome as grit on spinach leaves.

"I can't hold these anymore, so watch where you step. I have to put my platter down. My arms are on fire." The lights burst on as Sherry set the platter down.

"Dear God." Kirin leapt away from the camera, grazing Sherry's foot with her combat boot. "Someone help Carmell."

There was a piercing scream and pounding footsteps. Sherry blinked hard to acclimate her eyes to the light. As her eyesight adjusted, she witnessed the monitor come to life. On the screen, she was able to make out the anchor desk amidst a flurry of background activity. Sherry pushed her face closer to the screen, in hopes of clarifying what a pile of clothing was doing in the middle of the camera shot. Upon further inspection, she was able to make out a head and a set of shoulders amongst the clothes. Behind the desk, someone had his or her outstretched arms blocking full visual access to the scene. Orders were being barked.

"This area must be cleared out. We need space."

Sherry grabbed Kirin's arm. "Is that Carmell Gordy slumped over?" Sherry blinked hard in hopes the scene would present itself in a clearer light. "What's the liquid dripping over the edge of the desk? Reminds me of the red wine syrup I make to go with poached pears."

The tips of Sherry's fingertips went numb as a cold shiver overtook her body. The arm Sherry had a death grip on was shaking.

"She might have spilled her smoothie. Wasn't her

smoothie green, though?" Sherry jumped back when she caught sight of someone approaching her from the side. She released Kirin's arm. "Dad, there you are. Thank goodness."

"Sherry." Erno threw up his arms. "You could have picked a more visible spot to wait for me."

"This is where they told me to wait. I had no choice. What took you so long? I was really worried you wouldn't be able to find your way back when the lights went out."

"Listen, I couldn't make out what's happening, but something terrible may have happened to Carmell Gordy," Erno said.

Sherry's eyes darted back to the television monitor. People were crowding the periphery of the anchor desk, ignoring the directive being given to clear away. Sherry no longer saw any sign of what she thought were Carmell's head and shoulders. She lifted her vision from the monitor to focus on the live commotion.

"I can't figure out what's going on. One minute I'm waiting for you and watching the end of a report on the upcoming Founder's Day celebration; the next I can't see my hand in front of my face because all the power's out. When the lights came back up, the scene was more panicked than the grocery store the day before a February blizzard. We're obviously in the way here. Let's get going."

Erno massaged his chin with one hand. "Reminds me of an old saying . . ."

"This isn't a good time for your pearls of wisdom, Dad. We need to get out of here." Sherry huffed and squatted down to retrieve her trophy and plate of food. She regretted not finding plastic wrap to secure the spicy treats on the plate, but she hadn't, so a steady hand was required to hold them in place.

A clock on the wall caught Sherry's eye. "Eleven forty. We've got to get to the store. You did leave a sign on the door saying you'd be opening late today, didn't you?"

"I might have forgotten that detail. But we'll be there soon. The needs of the hooked rug community must be met." Erno wagged his index finger in the air.

"Let's go. We'll check back later and find out what happened." Sherry headed toward the exit sign with Erno in tow. After two rocky steps, she turned. "Would you mind carrying this? It's not going too far. We're leaving the trophy at the receptionist's desk to be engraved." She tottered over to Erno and presented him with the trophy wedged in the crook of her elbow. "And watch your step." She nudged a snakelike cord with her shoe.

As the father-daughter duo reached the edge of the room, someone shouted, "Keep nine-one-one on the line until the ambulance gets here."

Sherry dodged the door as it swung open. A man and a woman in uniform raced in.

The woman officer lowered her weapon and turned toward Sherry. "If you two wouldn't mind staying outside in the main lobby, please. We need to collect your names and contact information. But I need you to exit this room without delay. EMTs are unloading their equipment."

Unable to will her legs to move, Sherry stood frozen in place. She managed a head rotation, following the officers bolting across the room.

As they neared the anchor desk, one exclaimed,

"Step back, people." The small group of onlookers cleared away, revealing Carmell's head resting on her desk. The overhead lighting picked up the glimmer of shiny metal sticking out of the back of her neck. In an instant, the thought of a pop-up timer embedded in a turkey breast danced through Sherry's brain. She shook her head to clear her thoughts. No, not a pop-up timer. She gasped when she was struck with the familiarity of the wooden handle attached to the protruding silver object. She speared Erno in the ribs with the plate she was carrying.

"Hey, what was that for?" Erno rubbed his core.

"Carmell's neck. How did that . . ." She spat out each word as if they were charred and bitter.

"Sherry, you're not making any sense."

"Don't you recognize that?" She thrust her finger toward the scene.

"No way, can't be." Erno covered his eyes with his hands. He lowered his head and moaned. "How in the world . . ."

"Has anyone seen Damien?" Brett scurried through the studio doors propped open by the attending emergency personnel. He cupped his hands around his mouth to amplify his question. "Damien's gone, Truman's gone, who's running this place?" As Brett passed Sherry and Erno, he pulled up short. "Have you seen Damien Castle? We could use some leadership around here right about now. He and Truman have gone AWOL."

Brett rubbed his palms together. Sherry cringed at the rough scratching sound.

"Damien was the one who brought me to the studio after the cook-off to wait for my dad before the lights went out, but I haven't seen him since. He never came inside the room. He left me at the door because he said he had to check on the control room. He was concerned the storm might wreak havoc on the station's power." Sherry twisted her torso as tightness overtook her back muscles. "What's going on?"

Brett passed a glance Erno's way before sighing. "Someone's tried to kill Carmell."

Sherry's elbow collapsed, and the remainder of her chickpeas and almonds landed on the floor. Erno grabbed her arm before the plate went down too. Sherry examined her father's pinched eyebrows and tangled lips.

"I've gotta keep moving. The police want your names. After that you're free to go. Seems like a waste of time to me. It's Steele they should arrest on the spot." Brett turned and moved one loafered foot in front of the other before tumbling to the floor.

"I'm sorry. Those darn chickpeas are slippery." Sherry extended her hand to the fallen man.

Brett turned his head away. He whimpered as he rubbed his backside. "Have you been dropping your appetizer all over the building?"

"Maybe." Sherry observed her plate, which was empty. "Dad, can you help him up?"

Erno didn't move.

"I'm fine." Brett stood and brushed off his backside. His face was the deepest hue of rose color Sherry had ever seen on human skin.

"You've ripped your pants." Sherry's cheeks burned. "Let me pay for any repairs."

"It's fine; it's fine. Not important." Brett smoothed

his tussled hair and took off, his sight fixed on the floor beneath him.

Sherry and Erno left the studio and headed toward the lobby.

"Are you Mr. and Mrs. Oliveri?" A police officer with a notepad approached. The woman's hair was tucked up inside her peaked hat. Her broad torso seemed enhanced to Sherry, as if she might be wearing a bulletproof vest.

"You're the officer who pulled me over once. We met again at the Hillsboro Cook-off awards dinner that went terribly wrong." Sherry's vision blurred as her mind drifted back to the events of her most memorable cooking contest to date.

"Yes, ma'am." The officer stood poised to write.

"We're not married. We're father and daughter." Erno braced his stance by locking his knees. He liked to appear statuesque and attentive when addressing uniformed personnel. Respectfulness was one of the old-fashioned qualities she loved about her father.

"I see." The officer made a notation. "Sherry Oliveri and Erno Oliveri. Correct? Sir, do you have a wife named Sherry Frazzelle? She is listed alongside you two."

"Sorry for the confusion, but, when I mailed in my recipe for the News Twelve appetizer cook-off a few months ago, I entered as Sherry Frazzelle. Now I go by Oliveri." Sherry glanced at the unadorned spot on her left ring finger, which was the prior home to a sapphire and diamond wedding ring.

"Ma'am, we need your legal name." The officer tapped her pen on her pad.

Sherry nodded. "Yes, Sherry Oliveri. Drop the Frazzelle."

"My daughter's name is not yet legally Oliveri." Her father tipped his head to the side.

"In two days I'll receive the court papers from my lawyer, and my name will legally be Sherry Oliveri, but yes, today, Frazzelle."

"Okay, fine. I'll check off all three names and add an asterisk on both of the Sherrys." The policewoman scribbled on the paper. "And you are Augustin residents?" She peered over her paperwork and received a pair of nods. "The visitor logbook has these phone numbers recorded." She flashed the numbers they had written down on their way into the TV station.

"Those are correct."

"You'll be contacted if need be. You're free to go." The officer marched away before any reply was made.

Sherry and Erno continued down the hall before stopping at the "Visitors Must Sign Out Before Exiting" placard. The woman hunched over the sign-out book straightened up. She turned and offered Sherry the pen. "Signing out?"

"If you're done. Thank you." Sherry's mouth dropped open. "Patti Mellitt. What a surprise it was when I found out you were today's cook-off judge. A nice surprise, I might add."

"The even bigger surprise was when I found out the appetizer I judged as the winner belonged to the one and only Sherry Frazzelle. I enjoy blind taste-testing the most because when the winner is crowned, I get to put a face with the chosen dish and see the spontaneous, happy reaction." Patti smiled and eyed the trophy secured in Erno's arms. "Not the grandest prize you've ever won, I'm sure."

"My daughter sees every win as her grandest win. That's the mark of a true champion." Erno peered around Sherry. "Hello, Ms. Mellitt." He set the trophy on the receptionist's desk.

"Thank you, Patti. By the way, I go by my maiden name now, Oliveri." Sherry kicked a dust ball with her foot. "I should tattoo the name on my forehead for all to see."

"Too bad, Frazzelle was a fun name to try to pronounce." Patti flashed a sly grin. "We need to catch up sometime. We've been through some rough times together, you and me. There's a kind of bond between us now and forever. Not a good time, though. I'm late. Always a deadline to meet. I'm going to check back and see what's happened to Carmell, but my rumbling gut is warning of the worst." Patti reached around to the back of her neck. "What was sticking out of her neck?"

"If it's what I think it was, we sell them at Dad's store. If I had to guess, I'd say it was a punch tool that hobbyists use to make hooked rugs. They have extremely sharp tips, and I can imagine the damage one could cause when used as a weapon." Sherry balled up her fist and mimed a plunging blow.

"Can we please get out of here?" Erno was halfway out the door when he called out the request. "My head is killing me."

Chapter 3

Sherry lugged herself through the front door, where she was welcomed by Chutney. She set down her load before scooping the dog up. With his advancing age, Chutney was losing the ability to hear activity at the front door, so he didn't often greet her there, but she had been gone for hours, so he had most likely been camped out in anticipation of her return. Sherry was never sure who was more excited to see whom. The enthusiasm of his greeting was enough to temporarily reenergize her.

"Let's get you outside, buddy. I can't wait to tell you about my morning." Sherry hooked the leash to Chutney's collar. On her way out, she made a quick check of her cell phone. There was one new voice mail. She must have missed the call as she had forgotten to turn her phone on after leaving the television station. Before she could play the message, Chutney yanked his end of the leash, and the phone was almost launched sky-high.

"Okay, okay. Your message is more urgent than the one on my phone. I understand." She plunged the phone in her pocket and slipped out the door. The furry twelve-pounder bypassed all the enticing smells he normally investigated and got down to business.

"Hi, Eileen." Sherry flashed a wave to her neighbor across the street.

"Hey, Sherry. I watched you on News Twelve this morning. Great job!" Sherry's silver-haired neighbor used her hands to form a makeshift megaphone, resulting in an over-amplification of her compliment.

Sherry's head bobbled in all directions as her eyes searched for disturbed onlookers. She put her finger up to her lips.

"I'm still excited for you. Let me take a breath to calm myself." Eileen raised her arms in an arch over her head and lowered them. "That's better. Toward the end, I was afraid the crabby stuffers might overtake your spicy toasted whatchamacallits. I screamed at the television so loud when you won, the Tates next door thought I was being accosted. They barged in and scared me half to death."

"Sorry about that." Sherry steered a reluctant Chutney in Eileen's direction. "Thanks for watching, though."

"What happened right after your cook-off? I was in the middle of the segment on the Founder's Day celebration, and the channel went black. After that, it never came back on the air. I figure it had to do with that crazy storm that blew through. It was a fast mover, but did some damage. With that channel out of commission, I was forced to come outside and pick up the branches that fell. You know I only watch local. National channels are always carrying such horrifying breaking news. Murder and mayhem and such. Gives me nightmares." Eileen, bundled up in a fuzzy sweater, hugged her arms across her body as she swayed side to side.

"Not sure what happened there. I'll let you know if I hear any updates." Sherry's hand drifted up to her temple. She rubbed a tender spot, hoping it wasn't the beginning of a headache. "I'll see you later, Eileen." Sherry let Chutney lead her past a few more houses before heading home.

By now, Chutney had latched on to aromas transmitted to the surrounding shrubs by various animals. The dog's pace slowed as his twitching snout dealt with each scent. Sherry's sensitive nose detected a stagnant tang. The air, after the morning storm, was sour and heavy with residual moisture. The breezes whipped her hair into a frenzy. She tugged on Chutney's leash to remind him the intention was to exercise his legs.

A raven perched on a branch above them squawked out an ominous warning that they'd entered his territory. His black iridescent feathers were a sharp contrast to the colorful autumn leaves. The majestic maples and oaks that lined the neighborhood's sidewalks were succumbing to the season's near-freezing evening temperatures, and most had no green leaves remaining. It wouldn't be long before the New England autumn suppressed the air temperature in the daytime, too. Time to put her vegetable garden to bed. Another chore to attack on her to-do list, only this year the task was unintentionally simpler. She'd had to replant her garden midseason after it was ravaged and stripped nearly bare by critters. She would save what plant seeds she could salvage from her surviving plants and hope for better success next season. When it came to the success or failure of her vegetable garden, Mother Nature was commandeering the ship, and Sherry could only go along for the ride.

When Chutney's mission was accomplished, Sherry headed back to her house. She gave her dog an early afternoon snack, which he gobbled up in nearly one mouthful. For herself, she made an almond butter and fig jam sandwich.

"I'm sorry, boy. This is my afternoon at the Ruggery. You know I usually take you, but not today. I've got too much on my mind. I wish I had a pal for you so you wouldn't get lonely." She knelt down and scratched Chutney's neck with vigor.

His back leg flexed and flailed in the air, stopping the moment the massage did.

"I'll be back before dark."

The penetrating brown eyes beamed upward. A bitter note gurgled up in her throat.

"Don't give me the evil eye," she scolded.

Chutney made his way over to the hooked throw rug by the front stairs and curled up in a ball. His eyes were closed in an instant.

"Your indifference only compounds my guilt." Sherry sighed, collected her purse and keys off the front hall table, and closed the reclaimed wood door behind her.

Once in her car, Sherry let curiosity get the best of her. She played the voice mail she'd been ignoring.

"Detective Ray Bease here. I've contacted your father, and he has agreed to answer a few questions about . . ." The voice on the phone faded. There was a strong cough, followed by a throat clearing and a possible phlegm expulsion. ". . . the murder at the television station this morning. He explained that you will be at the Oliveri Ruggery by one-thirty p.m. and insisted you be present when I stop by. I'll try to arrive before three."

The emotionless words battered Sherry's ears harder than if the detective had screamed them. She flinched and dropped the phone on the passenger seat beside her.

"Murder."

Sherry started the car and drove to her father's store, oblivious to her increasing speed, until she saw a police car parked on the side of the road. She removed her lead foot from the gas pedal, flexed her rigid ankle, and let the car slow to the legal limit.

Along the parkway, the continual shower of red and gold leaves, along with the bombardment of acorns, combined to distract Sherry from seeing the exit for Center Street. She swerved at the last second and made a traffic maneuver she hoped there were no witnesses to.

Sherry steered the car up to the front of the symmetrical two-story building painted dove gray with burgundy trim. A raised wooden sign displayed the building's "9" above the austere rectangular plaque bearing the name "The Oliveri Ruggery." A pang of pride warmed her heart, as was the case each time she saw her family's business establishment.

The multi-paned windows were lined up in a perfect grid across the welcoming façade. The slate roof was shaded with varying darks and lights and put a regal cap on the Ruggery. The center entry boasted an intricate paneled door that always held Sherry at pause before she turned the knob. She enjoyed rubbing her fingers across the busy grain of the wood as she considered the majesty of the tree used to construct the store's enviable entrance.

Sherry turned her car into a narrow driveway that ran between her father's store and an upscale pub named Wine One One. In the shared back lot, Erno's well-loved car, normally parked with military precision, was parked askew, leaving her no choice but to pull in at an angle.

She slid out of the car and trotted to the back door. She yanked on the door's brass knob. No movement. She tried again, this time pulling so hard her knuckles blanched. "We need to get this old guy fixed." Sherry surveyed her surroundings for possible assistance. "Or is it locked? Can't be. Dad never locks up during business hours." She knocked on the door and waited. Silence. She threw up her hands and turned to begin the trek to the front of the building when she heard the ages-old hinges groan.

Erno's eye was visible through the narrow opening between the door and frame. "Sherry, thank goodness. Come in."

"Why is it locked?" Sherry pushed the door open wider and entered.

As soon as she cleared the threshold, Erno slammed the door behind her and flipped the dead bolt. Sherry watched him test the knob. When the door refused to budge, his grip relaxed.

Sherry's father was quick to avert his gaze from Sherry's probing stare. He turned and made a move away from the door. She followed him through two of the store's arched doorways to the main showroom. Sherry's nostrils flared as she was rushed by the distinctive smells of the store. The hint of oily lanolin combined with the musty odor emanating from the fibers of the rugs' wool tantalized her senses.

"Dad?" Sherry stepped behind Erno and put her hand on his shoulder.

"Talk of break-ins recently. Merely taking precautions. You know what I always say, easier to replace something that's lost than something that's stolen."

"Whatever you say, Dad." The clock on the wall chimed. Detective Bease wasn't expected for a while, so she wanted to get as much work done as possible in the meantime. She set her purse under the checkout counter. "I'm glad I brought my sweater. Why is the temperature so low in here?" She wrapped one arm around the other.

"I guess I forgot to turn the heat up." Erno went over to the thermostat in the corner and rotated the dial. The boiler in the basement rumbled to life, sending vibrations through the wide plank floorboards.

"Dad, you okay?"

"Fine." Erno's voice was bland and lifeless. "I guess the events of the morning shocked me some."

"I know what you mean. I haven't had a chance to process what happened, or maybe I've been avoiding thinking about it altogether."

"Let's not then. What are you working on today?" Erno asked.

"For starters, I haven't finished dividing the skeins of that beautiful robin's egg-blue yarn we dyed last week. While there are no customers in the store, I'll be in the yarn room finishing that. Sound good?"

Erno was staring out the window, holding his wrists behind his back, shoulders rounded forward. Sherry sauntered toward her father. Not wanting to startle the man, she uttered in a near whisper, "I love the display."

On the wall near the window was a floor-to-ceiling latticework frame that supported many examples of the hooked rugs the Oliveri family was so passionate about. The room's ten-foot ceilings provided abundant room to show off the store's gems. Richly colored yarns were woven into designs ranging from simple to elaborate. Clients brought in a photo of their pet, their favorite flower, or a nature scene, wishing to have their fond recollections represented on an area rug, giving Erno and his craftsmen a starting point for their creative process. More ambitious hobbyists hooked their own rugs, with supplies purchased at the store. Prices were hefty, but the labor and supplies were of the highest quality, so customers, after recovering from the initial sticker shock, seldom complained when they saw the final result.

Erno wheeled around with a slight blush. "Thanks, honey. This is one I had made for Marla, but your sister hasn't been able to visit since the last cook-off you two were in." He pointed to a small oval rug hanging at the top of the frame.

Sherry walked over to the rug that depicted purple cabbage heads, orange carrot bunches and, butter-yellow summer squash. She ran her fingers across the yarn that was as soft as peach skin. "Gorgeous. If she doesn't claim that beauty soon, guess who will?"

Sherry smiled at the joke she made at her sister's expense.

Erno frowned and lowered his head.

"Call me if a customer comes in. I'll be out here." Sherry stole one last glimpse of Erno and made her way to the room that housed the rainbow of beautiful wool.

After spending a good amount of time separating various yarn bundles, she'd accomplished her quest. Sherry emerged from the yarn room with four bundles cradled in her arms.

"Dad, I think this dye lot is closer to sea foam than robin's egg. What do you think?" She halted midway across the worn wooden floor.

A woman in white pants and an aqua silk shirt, with a multicolored scarf swaddled around her neck, was huddled with Erno near the checkout register. They gave themselves more distance when Sherry approached. A distinct flush swept onto her father's face. The fold above the bridge of his nose deepened, and he hiked up the sleeves of his oxford shirt. All gazes converged on Sherry.

"Excuse me, Dad. I had a quick question about . . ." The words fought one another as they left her mouth. When she lost track of what she was saying, Sherry held up the yarn as if the wool could better speak for itself.

"Sherry, this is Beverly Van Ardan."

The woman with the golden updo put out her gloved hand, but retracted it when Sherry couldn't free up her arms.

"Sherry works for me twenty hours a week, in the afternoons, which is why you've never seen her here."

"How wonderful to have a daughter in business with you. We Van Ardans pride ourselves on promoting family values through business." Beverly's gaze lingered until Sherry severed the connection. "Of course, Sherry needs no introduction. She's the most famous home cook in Hillsboro County." Beverly paused, and silence settled in. "But you probably have no idea who I am."

Sherry decided the woman wasn't expecting a reply.

"I live in the city, but venture out for special visits to my favorite rug store when I have a room in the apartment that needs a facelift. Your father is a master craftsman, as you must well know, and I dropped off my specifications for his next great masterpiece." Beverly gestured toward a pile of papers on the counter. "There's a reason this is the oldest business establishment in Augustin and possibly all of New England. It's called excellence."

Erno's expression was stoic and unwavering, Sherry noted, odd for someone who a moment ago had received more compliments than a perfectly executed croquembouche.

"Mrs. Van Ardan is one of our most loyal patrons." Erno intertwined his fingers. "I appreciate her business as much as I appreciate all of my loyal customers."

"And, with that being said, I'm off before my driver leaves without me." Beverly pulled her wallet from her purse. "How much of a deposit do you require?"

Before Erno could respond, the brass bell over the front door tinkled. In walked a woman wearing a loose-fitting royal-blue blazer and matching skirt. On her cap was a gold badge.

"Excuse me, Mr. Oliveri. I'm verifying the story the limousine driver parked outside gave me. His meter's expired, and he claims his passenger is in your store." The woman in uniform eyeballed Beverly. "I told him I wouldn't give him a ticket if the story checked out."

"Thank you, Leila." Erno waved the back of his hand toward Beverly. "Mrs. Van Ardan was leaving. No deposit required, Beverly. I trust you'll be back."

"Thank you, sir. Don't want to lose you any business by antagonizing your customers, but a meter's there for a reason." Leila spun on her rubber-soled pumpernickel-brown shoes. She offered a flip of her hand as she left the store.

"Augustin's finest parking enforcement officer. Actually, our only one. No one else wants that job, I can guarantee that." Sherry snorted as she tried to suppress a giggle. "Nice to see you, Mrs. Van Ardan. Have a safe trip home."

"I'm known as Beverly, dear. I'll be sure to visit on the days you're here if you'll share your schedule with me. But I do hate driving in the afternoon, what with all the voluminous school buses, unwieldy delivery trucks, and whatnot. So, on second thought, unless you switch to mornings, I may not see you much." The woman flowed through the door with her scarf wafting behind her.

Before Sherry could comment, Erno plucked the yarn out of her hands for inspection. "You're right; this isn't robin's egg blue. You have a good eye." Erno winked at his daughter and handed back the soft wool strands. "Check to see if there's enough in the batch; otherwise we can set a new dye lot in motion before the end of the day. I'm running to the men's room. Can you watch the front end for a minute?"

No sooner had Erno disappeared to the back of the store, but the doorbell tinkled again. Detective Ray Bease, in wrinkled, baggy khakis, lace-up dress shoes, an oversized blazer, and weather-beaten hat, sauntered through the door. Sherry's heart rate quickened. She forced her eyes up to his after a head to toe assessment of the man's outfit. Sherry clasped her hands together in a tight grip and stepped over to the register.

"Detective Bease, it's been a while." Sherry lost her bearings as flashes of an award dinner, an interrogation, and a scolding flooded back and drowned her brain. "Not mentoring an up-and-coming detective these days?"

"I'm always being threatened with that possibility, but, for now, I'm flying solo. I don't have to tell you I prefer it that way." The detective held a steady gaze on Sherry's eyes.

"What can I do for you?"

The detective removed his hat and set it on the counter. "May we sit down? My legs are killing me."

He tilted his head toward a long wooden table near the rug display, where a half-drawn canvas lay on the table and photographs were strewn.

"Please." Sherry pulled two chairs across from each other, and they each took a seat.

"Thank you. I do yoga in the morning before work now, but my legs haven't adjusted to the increase in activity yet. My blood pressure's down, so the torture's been worthwhile. This is my first full caseload assignment since the doctor prescribed more downtime. Too much free time can make a man crazy."

"Funny, I did notice your posture is much straighter. You resembled the letter *C* last time I saw you. Now you're closer to a *D*.

"Not sure if that's a compliment, so I'll take it at face value." Ray set down his briefcase and pulled a vibrant green pen from his breast pocket. Sherry made out the words "Green Mountain State" running along the edge.

Sherry pointed to the pen. "I see you're still collecting state pens. I have a cook-off coming up soon in Vermont. Maybe that's a good omen."

"The verified existence of omens would make my job a lot easier. I wish I believed in them." The edges of the detective's lips curled up the tiniest amount. "First things first. Your name is on my list of those at the scene as Sherry Oliveri, not Frazzelle. Double-checking that." He retrieved a folded sheet of paper from his breast pocket.

Sherry sat up a little straighter. "That's right. Since last I saw you, my divorce is, for all intents and purposes, a done deal. I wanted to put the period on the end of my marriage, and that's what the name change is about. I'm certainly not going to miss correcting people's pronunciation of Frazzelle; that's for sure. But, you know what that's like." She cocked her head. "Right? How many times have you said 'Bease rhymes with grease not bees?' I learned that about you the first day we met."

"Speaking of the last time I saw you, I guess you decided against my invitation for a bite out? That was months ago, and, as the country song says, 'if my phone ain't ringing it must be you who ain't calling.'" Ray clicked his pen's retractor multiple times.

"You know the last we left off we had worked fairly well together to snag a murderer, but let's face facts; getting past your flagging me as one of the main suspects in a murder investigation has been a process."

Ray nodded his head. "Duly noted."

"Why do you need to talk to Dad? There isn't anything he knows that I don't."

"Verification and corroboration. Sorting fact from fiction. My job is to reconstruct the incident, sift through clues and suspects, and identify the murderer."

"I understand, but that's my dad we're talking about. He doesn't factor in beyond being at the scene and supporting me while I cooked."

The detective gave Sherry a side-eye glance and cleared his throat.

Ray sighed. "I don't want to say 'here we go again,' but if the phrase fits, there's no denying. If he has any eyewitness accounts he can share, I would be appreciative."

"My dad's in the restroom. He'll be out in a minute."

Ray pulled his tablet computer from his briefcase. He aligned the bottom of the rectangular device to the edge of the table. He swiped his broad finger across the computer screen.

Sherry's mouth drew up into a smile. "Tech savvy, I see. That's quite an accomplishment, given your inclination toward more antiquated methods of recording information." Sherry studied the Vermont pen he set on the table.

"You make it sound like I'd prefer using a quill and an inkwell. There's no harm in putting pen to paper, but at work I'm howling in the wind on that point." Ray poked at a button on his computer. He arched his back, groaned, and shook his head. "There we go. Temperamental little bugger. I also may have forgotten to charge this sucker. I never had to worry about that with my notepad and pen." He scrolled to his document. "Carmell Gordy, age twenty-five. Cause of death: severed spinal cord, bled out. Pretty straightforward."

"That's awful. So young, with what should have been a long life ahead of her. Who would do that to someone? And how did he or she get away with the crime with all those people around? Fact is, I was literally in the dark when whatever happened, happened. I guess that answers my 'how did he or she get away with the crime with all those people around' question. Under the cover of darkness."

"That has yet to be verified. You're merely speculating at this point. Be careful with that. Is there someone to verify your whereabouts at the time of the murder?"

"I was standing in the back of Studio A. I was waiting for Dad to return from the bathroom. There was a camera woman, Kirin, right next to me. We didn't move a muscle while the lights were out. I was afraid of tripping over the miles of cables or crashing into the heavy equipment all around me." Each word Sherry spoke crashed into the next as she sped the pace of her story up. Ray had yet to take notes.

As her father entered the room, Sherry hoisted

herself up with such force her chair toppled over. "Dad, do you remember Detective Bease?"

Erno shuffled toward the detective's outstretched hand.

"Detective Bease, nice to see you."

"Name's pronounced Bease, rhymes with grease not bees." The detective's hands hovered over the computer.

"Right." Erno peered over his shoulder at the clock on the wall. "If you don't need me, I'll be in the back."

Ray stood and walked around the table and righted Sherry's chair. "Sir, if I could ask you a few questions about this morning, please."

"Dad, you don't have to answer any question you don't want to." Sherry joined Erno.

"I have nothing to hide. Go right ahead. . . ." Erno's voice trailed off to a whisper.

"Would you like to have a seat?" Ray asked.

"Nope."

"Okay." Ray directed his attention to his computer and read aloud. "The murder weapon was identified as the sharp metal tool, which, when used as properly intended, is threaded with yarn and punches holes in canvas to create a hooked rug."

Sherry closed her stinging eyes and mashed her teeth together until her jaw ached. When she let the light in again, nothing had changed. It wasn't a dream or a nightmare she could awaken from.

"The Oliveri Ruggery is the sole retailer of these specialized tools within a one hundred and fifty-mile radius of Augustin," the detective said. "The point is moot, though, because a punch tool can be mail ordered from purveyors in other locations without difficulty."

"Of course. Obviously, Dad has no connection to the murder weapon other than the mere coincidence of his line of work."

"But, the particular punch tool plunged in Carmell's neck was labeled 'do not remove from O.R.' on the wooden handle. I'm going to hazard a guess that O.R. stands for Oliveri Ruggery." Ray reached down the table and pulled a partially completed canvas closer to him. "For example, this piece of material has a sticker in the corner. Reads: 'O.R. sample, do not sell.'"

A barrage of sizzling hot needles pricked the back of Sherry's neck. She reached around and kneaded the hotbed of irritation with both hands as if preparing bread dough.

"I have questioned others who were at the station, trying to get an eyewitness as to your whereabouts prior to and during the time the lights in the TV studio went out. There's a distinct gap as to your location at that time. Would you be able to tell me where you were between the time Sherry finished her cook-off and when you signed the logbook as you were exiting the station?" Ray flexed his fingers inches above the computer as if he were playing air piano.

Sherry put her arm around her father's lower back. "I'll tell you. It's no mystery. He went to the men's room in the hallway between the studio where the cook-off was held, Studio B, I think, and the main studio, where the morning show originates. During the blackout Dad stayed put wherever he was. Thank goodness he didn't go blindly searching for me in a building he was unfamiliar with. There are no windows in that place, just darkness. He didn't have his phone with him, so no flashlight app. All phones were switched off anyway, mine included, per station rules. By the time we could get them powered up, the lights had returned."

"Mr. Oliveri, is your daughter's statement accurate?" With no answer forthcoming, the detective took his gaze off his computer screen and zeroed in on Erno.

"Dad! Dad!" Sherry screamed. She watched in horror as her father wilted like a fresh spinach leaf in hot water. "Get some water, Ray. Now."

Ray jumped up and threw his arms in the air. "Where?"

"Never mind, help me get him in the car. The emergency room's close."

Ray gathered Erno up, with Sherry's help, and they guided him through the back door into Sherry's car. They laid him, conscious but drowsy, across the back seat.

"I'll ride with you." Ray opened the passenger-side door.

"No. Stay with him for a minute while I get my purse and lock up the store. You've pushed him too far, Ray. If anything happens to him, I blame you." Sherry spat the words at the detective with as much force as she could muster. She was somewhat satisfied when he winced.

Moments later, Sherry returned with her purse and the detective's briefcase.

"My computer?"

Sherry nodded.

"My hat?" Ray asked.

Sherry shook her head. "Detective Bease, your hat's safe inside. You'll have to come back when we reopen." Sherry slammed her car door and started the engine. Giving the man only seconds to move out of the way, she set the car in reverse, spraying pebbles with her spinning tires.

Chapter 4

"Dad, we spent six hours in the emergency room last night. You're not all right. This time you have to listen to me." Sherry savored each word as if she were eating the last ounce of Kobe beef left on Earth. "The diagnosis should have been extreme stubbornness, not a panic attack."

Sherry moved the phone away from her ear and shook her head. She paced from the kitchen to the living room and back. "If you won't let me stay with you, will you promise to call at least twice a day? And keep the phone charged and your tummy full. No alcohol, no caffeine, plenty of water."

"I'm on the sofa watching an old Western. I have a watery cup of herbal tea and half a piece of your chicken in lemon rosemary sauce beside me, which wouldn't normally be my first choice for breakfast. The chicken didn't microwave too well, needed thawing first, I guess. Texture's off, but the taste is pretty good." Erno's voice grew faint.

“Did you say the chicken tastes like wood?” Sherry’s voice rose to a shrill siren.

“Good. Taste was pretty good.” Erno’s reply was labored.

Sherry stopped pacing. Her shoulders sloped forward. Her throbbing back screamed for attention. “Dad, what was going on at the cook-off yesterday, and I don’t mean during the cooking portion? Afterward.” She heard a groan on his end of the phone. “I mean, I saw you involved in a conversation with Carmell Gordy, one I would almost categorize as heated. And the same goes for your interaction with Brett Paladin. How do you even know those two? Granted, most of the town knows of you, but they don’t all *know* you.” She paused long enough to suck in some oxygen. “And even worse, you had me stow away a punch tool before we went through the station’s metal detector because you knew they wouldn’t inspect my cooking equipment bag. And one like it was used to take Carmell Gordy’s life. Maybe even that exact one. To compound matters, the tool didn’t come home in the bag, unless you know where it is.” She heard a whimper on the other end of the phone, but couldn’t stop the words from tumbling out of her mouth. “Why do you always carry that with you, anyway?” She squinted and wondered if her heart had relocated to her eardrums, the beating was growing so loud.

“The tool has one hundred and one uses. Better than a Swiss Army knife. Cuts string, opens cans, threads string through a tight spot, clears clogs. I could write a book about its versatility. I never leave home without it.” Erno’s laugh was as bittersweet as grapefruit rind. “Sherry, I didn’t kill that woman. May appear bad, but I wasn't involved in any way with Carmell Gordy's death." Erno began coughing.

"Dad, I didn't mean to get you worked up again. We'll fix this. Detective Bease came on strong, but that's his job." Sherry shook her head and thinned her lips. "If I have to, I'll start digging around. There's a reason someone hated Carmell enough to want her dead. We have to figure out what, why, who, and where." The words she dreaded saying escaped her mouth faster than steam from the first puncture of a hot baked potato. "Dad, you do have a plausible alibi, right? I can't, in all honesty, say I was with you while the murder took place."

"As a wise man once said, 'not all alibis are created equal.'"

"Who would that wise man be?" Sherry heard a base hum come through the phone. "Dad, don't worry. Call me later so I know at least one of us is feeling better."

"Will do, honey. And thanks again for watching the store for the next few days. Do I have to pay you time and a half for your extra hours?"

"You know the doctor recommended more than a few days off. Stay put, and we'll negotiate later." Sherry ended the call. As she did so, she noticed the voice mail alert was active. With another tap of a key, she played the message.

"Hey, Sher, I may be your ex-husband, but I'll never break the habit of following your cooking contests. How did the cook-off go? I forgot to record the show, so when you have time, give me the blow-by-blow or, better yet, invite me over to watch the replay because I know you set your DVR. Have a good one."

"He's right, I did. I don't think Charlie will believe

another cook-off ended with a death. I can't even believe it myself." Sherry carried her phone into the living room and flopped on the sofa. Sherry dropped the device on the cushion and patted the pillow next to her as an invitation for Chutney to join her.

"Yesterday was quite a day of ups and downs. Mostly downs. I won a grand prize for my cooking. Jump for joy." She stroked her dog's neck. "I was in the same room where a murder took place. Pure shock. I spent the better part of the evening at the hospital hoping my father would survive. Rock bottom."

Chutney settled down on her lap. The body heat the dog radiated relaxed her thighs, which were tight from pacing for hours while Erno was tested for ailments ranging from heart attack to dehydration. "At least yesterday is in the history books."

Sherry moaned as she picked up her phone. She dialed her sister, Marla. It was an hour earlier in Oklahoma, so she hoped she wouldn't wake her, but, on the other hand, part of her hoped she did.

"Hi, Mar, how's it going? I'm calling to give you an update on Dad's condition." Sherry's voice diminished as her energy waned.

"Don't sound so enthusiastic about talking to me." Marla sighed. "All is well here. But how's Dad? I was hoping you'd get back to me last night when you brought him home from the ER."

"It was so late, and I was exhausted. I didn't have the energy to craft a text, let alone call. Turns out, Dad had a panic attack, which apparently isn't unheard of in older people. Anyway, he's home resting, and I'll be running the store until he's ready to return to work."

"But he's okay, right? Are the doctors sure that's what it was?"

"That was the diagnosis after a full array of tests."

"Thanks for taking such good care of him. Give him a big hug and kiss from me, please. Late last night I heard back from our dear brother over in Scotland. He'll call Dad later today. I don't think we'll be seeing him anytime soon. He's having a ball over there. With all the commotion, I didn't even get a chance to ask you how the cook-off went yesterday."

"Getting away to Scotland sounds nice." Sherry laid her head back on a cushion, lowered her eyelids halfway, and nestled in deeper. "I got lucky, and my appetizer won."

Marla must have put down the phone because all Sherry could hear was clapping and cheering.

Sherry waited for quiet. "Thanks. But I also have some bad news about the cook-off. There was a mishap right after, and the anchor at the host TV station is dead."

"What? That's awful."

"The poor girl was so young. There's talk of foul play, but I don't have all the details." Sherry pressed her arching shoulders level until they ached.

"What's with you and cook-offs recently? Are people taking competition to a whole new level? Meanwhile, keep me posted as always. Gotta run. Our cows don't head out of the barn without a good coaxing from yours truly, but thanks for calling. I'll ring you when I have more time to talk."

Sherry stared at her silent phone. *How does Marla always seem to turn the conversation back to her busy life out there on the ranch?*

"Guess she's not volunteering to help me out."

Sherry manipulated Chutney's folded ear between two fingers. The triangular fold of skin and cartilage reminded Sherry of a crepe, thin and pliable, with so many possibilities.

Sherry closed her eyes and let the quiet overtake her. When Chutney performed a full-body dog shake, her eyes popped open. She checked her text messages, but the one she was hoping to receive wasn't there. She set the phone down, and her chest deflated. "Better get you outside, little buddy."

The morning air smacked Sherry in the face with a frosty backhand when she opened the front door. Her prior night's restless sleep left her usually dependable wardrobe-choice ability as weak as salsa without jalapenos. She exited the house in a T-shirt and shorts, and, as soon as the cold air blanketed her exposed skin, she regretted her choices, but Chutney wouldn't turn back.

"Good morning, Sherry. Summer's over. You should have a sweater on." Across the street, Eileen was wrapped in her signature cable sweater. The neighbor picked up her blue-bagged newspaper and waved it at Sherry.

"Good morning, Eileen. You're right. I hate to say good-bye to those warm morning temps. I'm in complete denial that winter's around the corner." Sherry's arm was yanked diagonally as Chutney zeroed in on his chosen patch of comfort.

Eileen trotted to the edge of her property. "Heard about the death of that lovely Carmell Gordy over at Channel Twelve. Reports say it happened during a blackout. Weren't you there at that exact time, dear?"

"Yes, I was, unfortunately. So scary." Sherry enhanced her words with pauses and syllable emphasis.

"There goes my theory that local TV is devoid of chaos. I might as well switch over to the national channels, where bad news punches you in the gut all day long."

"Don't give up hope. They'll find out what happened, and order will be restored." Sherry said the words, but there wasn't much beef behind them.

"Do you need me to let Chutney out today? I'm always happy to do it."

"No thanks. I'll bring him with me to the store. I have to be there all day, so it's easier if he tags along. Thanks so much for walking him yesterday. You're a lifesaver. We got home from the hospital so late I was dreading walking him. You're the best."

"When you texted me you'd taken your father to the hospital, I was so worried."

"He'll be okay. Some rest and relaxation for a few days, and he'll be like new." Sherry pulled a doggie waste bag from her pocket and proceeded with the pickup.

"You're a good neighbor to clean that up every time. I've seen plenty of dog owners let their pets do their business and promptly walk away, leaving the pile for others to step in." Eileen gave one more newspaper salute and walked back to her house.

"Well, who better to clean up messes than me?"

Back inside, Sherry poured herself some coffee. Fighting the urge to check back in with Erno, she proceeded to rifle through a stack of papers on her desk. She picked up the top sheet and ran her finger down the numbered list.

"'One. Pick up pickle jars from Dumont farm before Thursday.' I think I can squeeze that in on my way to the store this morning.

"'Two. Preparations for recipe-tasting party: shop for ingredients, drinks, and clean house.' I can put that off one more day.

"'Three. Plan a night out with someone special.' There's no chance of that, mostly because there's no one special.

"'Four. Make teeth-whitening appointment.' Now why would I bother with that if there's no chance for number three? You don't care if I prowl the streets as a toothless monster as long as I feed you, right, boy?" Sherry leaned down and ruffled her dog's neck scruff.

Sherry got up, raided her pen drawer, and returned to her desk.

5. Check on Dad
6. Put garden to bed for the winter
7. Pick up engraved trophy at News Twelve
8. Schedule Founder's Day volunteer hours
9. Collect and dry bean seeds for next year's crop

"I better stop there, or I'll make myself crazy. To-do lists should be called 'What I could get done if I lived in a vacuum' lists. Problem is, my 'to-do' list doesn't take into account how much I 'do' for so many others besides myself, including you, Mr. Chutney." Sherry set the list aside and picked up the next sheet in the stack.

"Ha, this will have to wait." In Sherry's hand was a paper with the bold type heading, "Bucket List."

"Couldn't even get to number one on this list any time in the near future."

1. Compile recipes by theme for a cookbook.
2. Market a homemade product.

"Forget it. Those'll have to wait. Much too frustrating to read any more. I have to concentrate on running Dad's store for a while and not making a shambles out of that."

Sherry flipped the paper over and set it back on the pile. She found her phone nestled on a couch pillow. One new voice mail was making itself known on the screen.

"I hope Dad isn't having a problem." Sherry's hand trembled as she listened to the soft voice deliver the message. Her mouth curled upward when the last word was spoken. "Amber, you're the best."

Chapter 5

"I hope it wasn't a difficult drive down from Boston." Sherry rushed Amber Sherman and broadsided her with a hug, knocking her askew. The slender woman in the white linen pants and mint-green polo shirt returned the embrace after she regained her balance.

"Not such a bad drive because I came from Hartford not Boston. I was at my parents' place. When I got your message about your father falling ill, I packed up and jumped in the car." Amber spun her head toward the back of the store as Chutney came trotting across the wooden floor. Her strawberry-blond hair danced in all directions. "Hi, Chutney."

"The last e-mail I got from you, about ten days ago I believe, said you were enjoying a new part-time writing assignment, but I didn't realize you weren't in Boston anymore."

"It's not easy keeping track of my whereabouts over the past year. Ten days ago I was in Boston. When you and I met at The OrgaNicks Cook-off, shortly after my divorce, I had just taken a leave of absence from the marriage and family-counseling practice in Boston and relocated to Maine. That move was short-lived. I left Maine and returned to Boston. Not surprisingly, the practice had replaced me. So began a halfhearted job search that proved unsuccessful. My parents suggested I come stay with them in Hartford for a while to get my bearings. I had no good reason to say no. Your call may have saved me from the consequences of a rash decision."

"I took a gamble you were somewhat between opportunities when I reached out. It was an excuse to have you come visit, but I do feel guilty that you're here to be put to work. Thanks for coming down so quickly."

"I'm glad we've stayed in touch since the cook-off. Considering all that went on there, we share an undeniable bond that will last a lifetime."

"You're telling me! Plus, meeting a nice person like you was one of the best results of the cook-off."

"Thanks, Sherry. Let me set something straight right from the get-go. I'm here to help out, and, since your text said your dad was advised to stay out of the Ruggery for a minimum of three weeks, I'll be looking for a weekly rental after I'm done here today."

"No, no. I insist you stay with me. My place is your place. You're doing me a big favor. Dad will have a hard time staying away from his store but if he knows I have help he's more likely to listen to the medical advice he was given. Where's your stuff? If you want to change, bring your suitcase in. Have you had any food? I have some homemade granola bars, an almond butter sandwich, and chocolate bars."

"Slow down, friend." Amber tamped down the air in front of her. "Most of my necessities are in the car. I don't need to change, unless what you see isn't appropriate attire. I wouldn't turn down one granola bar to top off the turkey club my mom packed for me. But, rule is, I'm here to help you while your dad's out sick, so I'm not a guest, I'm a coworker. The fact that my mom packed a lunch for her thirty-four-year-old daughter who holds a graduate degree only proves that I'm in desperate need of asserting my independence. But until I find a place I wouldn't turn down your kind offer to put me up."

"Amber, you're as sweet as a red velvet cupcake with cream cheese frosting. It's settled. Until you find a rental you'll stay with me. Now let's get going; time is money. By the way, if you don't mind my saying, you look like you've been working out."

Amber looked down at her svelte physique. "Since I had some extra time on my hands, I've taken up serious tennis. It's given me a few muscles."

"Just as soon as I find the time, maybe I'll join you if you can guarantee the same results." Sherry allowed herself a giggle before she erased the smile from her face. "It's been a quiet morning, so we hopefully will have time to go through the list of store procedures I made."

"Honestly, I wouldn't have volunteered to come down if I didn't have store management experience. While I was in graduate school, I was assistant manager at a small clothing boutique in Medford. Opened up, closed up, ran the register. I need a rundown of your merchandise, pricing, order recording procedures. Get me started on those, and I'm off to the races." Amber pumped her fist and took a hefty bite of the granola bar Sherry had pulled from the concealed shelf under the counter. "Yum." A crumb hit the floor, and Chutney emerged from under the counter to vacuum the crunchy baked oatmeal up. "Thanks, buddy. It's good to see you. Sherry, I love your new hairstyle. Longer, with dazzling highlights. Girl, you're rockin' your new life."

Sherry brought her fingertips up to her hair. "Thanks. Do you think this is the image I should portray at my age?"

"Last I checked, you were young, so go for it."

"For the record, my so-called new life hasn't really gotten under way. I'm still deep in the life chosen for me, not by me."

"You need a kick start. Have faith." Amber studied the four-legged floor cleaner. "Chutney didn't bark at me when I came in. Is that a good sign or a bad sign?"

"Funny, he seems to know that people coming into the store means potential business. Here, he's more of a greeter than a defender. At home, don't mess with him because he's the one who's all business."

"I remember my first encounter with him. I got a good gander at his protective side." Amber pointed out the hook by the door. "Is this a good place to hang my sweater?"

"Perfect place." Sherry tossed her hand in the general direction of an empty hook.

"That hat seems awfully familiar." Amber moved closer to the well-worn beige brain warmer and ran her finger across the brim.

Sherry reached across Amber, picked up the hat, and banged it on her thigh to remove any extraneous dust before rehanging it.

"Yep, Detective Ray Bease is back, investigating the murder that took place after the Channel Twelve cook-off I was just in. It's a long story I didn't want to bore you with when I reached out to you, but the short version is, the detective stopped by to ask Dad and me a few questions to see what we might or might not have witnessed. He had the audacity to suggest Dad was on the suspect list. That's when Dad fell ill. In the rush to get him to a doctor, the detective left his hat. I'll call him and arrange a pickup. Not sure he can function well with an exposed head." Sherry squared a small piece of paper up with the edge of the cash register and wrote: *Call Ray Bease.*

Amber hugged her arms tight across her midsection. "Cook-off, murder, suspects. Why am I getting a sudden sense of déjà vu?"

"Probably because the last time we were together all of those things happened, but, thanks in part to your help, the cook-off judge's murderer was caught and convicted."

"It was due to your sleuthing, my friend, and don't you forget it. Sounds like you're going to be called into action again, if your dad is a suspect."

"The investigation is in the capable hands of Detective Bease, who I have full faith in. He just needs to keep things moving in the right direction so Dad can relax. Come on. Let's get started." Sherry placed her hand on Amber's shoulder and steered her away from the register.

Amber shadowed Sherry for the next hour, moving from the stockroom to the register and on to the product demonstration area, where Amber got to try her hand at hooking a small section of a rug.

"Amazing." Amber chose a ball of yarn, the color of an orange Creamsicle, to thread through the hooking tool before attempting to pierce the canvas tacked to a frame. After a few minutes she put the tool down.

"This may not be my forte. I think I'll stick to refining my cooking skills as my primary hobby for now, but this must be fun for someone who is artistically inclined. Luckily I don't have to be good at making a rug to be good at selling it." Amber picked up the punch tool and thrust it through the canvas. "I can see this has uses for people with anger issues."

Sherry patted her new coworker on the back as the doorbell sounded. Two women dressed in identical floral day dresses, with the exception of their color schemes, entered the store carrying on an animated conversation.

"I would never have believed she's capable of that if I hadn't double-checked with her neighbors. Needless to say, they're not friends anymore. Frances, what do I always tell you?" The taller woman wagged her finger at her petite companion.

"This is what you say, Ruth. 'You can't burn both sides of an open drawbridge with only one match.' That's what you always say."

Sherry presented the women with a broad smile. "Mrs. Gadabee, that sounds like one of my father's wise adages." *And just as hard to decipher.*

"That's why he and I get along so well." Ruth Gadabee primped her short, graying hair with her manicured fingers. "We've got a favor to ask of you, dear." She presented Sherry with a foil-covered casserole dish. "And who do we have here?"

"Ruth Gadabee, Frances Dumont, I'd like you to meet Amber Sherman. She'll be working here while my father recuperates from a health scare." Sherry carried the casserole over to the counter and set it down. She peeked under the foil.

"Nice to meet you, dear." Before Amber could stand, Ruth reached down and shook her hand, as did Frances.

"The same Mrs. Dumont who inspired Sherry to become a pickle vendor at the farmer's market?" Amber asked.

Frances flashed a warm grin. "The opposite is true. This lady inspired me to retire because I knew I had found the right person to represent the best pickle in all the land. It took a bit of convincing to get her fully on board. You know, our girl Sherry can get herself worked up into quite an anxious state when presented with too many options, but she succumbed to my pressure."

When Sherry gave Amber a sideways glance, Sherry picked up on her friend's sly smile.

"Here, Chutney. Come here, boy." Ruth squatted down and greeted the panting pup after he jettisoned from his favorite sample rug. "Congratulations on your latest cook-off win, Sherry." With a hoist from Frances, Ruth rose to her feet and hugged Sherry with such vigor her arms were pinned to her sides. "Augustin is the luckiest town on Earth having such a homegrown talent as yourself. And the daughter of the town's, and possibly the county's, oldest business establishment owner, no less. Such an honor for both you and your dad." Ruth released Sherry, who caught herself before melting to the floor. "Speaking of the cook-off, you were still at the TV station when poor Carmell Gordy met her fate. Must have been awfully frightening."

"Dad and I were trying to leave. I was waiting for him to return from the men's room. A tremendous storm rolled in, and the building lost power. I hunkered down until the power was restored. When the lights came back on, the poor woman was slumped over at her desk. Shocking, to say the least." Sherry tucked her hair behind her ears. "I didn't witness the act, but I was in the same room. Hard to say where Dad was at that point."

"Speaking of your dad, he was as pale as white asparagus today. Has he had anxiety attacks in the past?" Frances asked.

"How did you know he had a panic attack? Wait, you saw him today?" Sherry's eyebrows did a jig. "He wouldn't even let me stop over this morning on my way here."

Amber stood and backed away from the conversation. She headed toward the supply room.

A stone-faced Ruth Gadabee adjusted her pearl necklace. "Frances and I stopped by as soon as he called." Ruth cocked her head at a slight angle. "Friends supporting friends." She straightened her head and winked.

An involuntary "huh" escaped from Sherry's throat.

"Before I forget, we brought over a casserole we'd like your expert opinion on. The ingredients are orzo, lemon, capers, shallots, and chicken, but we think the balance is off. Don't we, Frances?" Ruth paused until her friend nodded in agreement. "Would you mind trying a forkful?"

Sherry had been in this situation many times. Friends, neighbors, and even total strangers asking her opinion on topics ranging from recipe suggestions to cooking methods and anything in between that pertained to the culinary world. It entered tricky territory when the inquirers were relatives, close associates, or frequent customers. Sherry hesitated before taking the fork presented by Ruth.

"It's not as hot as it should be, dear, but you must be used to that from your various cook-offs. I mean, how in the world can the food stay at the perfect temperature after it leaves your hands and goes to the judges' mouths?" Ruth asked.

"Ruth, if you don't stop gabbing, the casserole will be ice-cold." Frances reached over and pushed Sherry's hand closer to the food. "Go ahead, dear."

Sherry shoveled the silverware's prongs into the creamy mound dotted with greens and browns and took a bite. Sherry swept her lips with her tongue. "Delicious. I think it's perfect the way it is."

"That's great news." Ruth clapped her hands. "We didn't invent the recipe, but we tried to follow the instructions to a T, except for the fact that chopped spinach was called for, which I didn't have. Erno isn't partial to spinach anyway, so if you don't miss it, I'm satisfied he won't either."

"This is for my dad? He'll be thrilled. I was going to drop a meal by his townhouse later, but I wasn't sure when I'd find the time to prepare it." Sherry set the fork down and replaced the foil on top of the dish, tucking the corners in as neat as on a tamale. "I didn't even know he wasn't a spinach lover, how did . . ."

"Dear, can we talk a moment about your father's situation? He mentioned a Detective Grease made him feel like he was under suspicion for that TV woman's murder." Ruth smoothed a wrinkle in the foil before taking a step closer to Frances.

Frances clicked her tongue against the roof of her

mouth. "No. Erno said the man's name rhymes with grease. His name was Breeze, I think."

"It's Bease, Detective Bease. Mrs. Gadabee, I would prefer not to discuss the investigation. It's early yet. Any information offered up by people who weren't at the scene is speculation or judgment, neither of which is helpful toward gathering the facts."

"I understand." Ruth eyed her casserole. "I was hoping that, if there's any way you could find out who the murderer was, it would be helpful. Your dad needs this weight off his shoulders. He's sprouted hundreds of gray hairs overnight. I'm so worried about him."

"Wait, how often do you see him?" Sherry's hands popped up from her sides. She waited for a reply with as much intensity as a baker waits for the oven timer to ring.

"We enjoy each other's company, dear." Ruth's tone was nonnegotiable. "I'm sure you understand even folks in the winter of their lives have need for companionship and whatnot. Let's put it this way: if my life is a five-course meal, I'm in the dessert portion, so I want the dish served sweet."

Sherry let out a melodic sigh. "I'll do my best, Mrs. Gadabee. I promised my father I would try to sort out the facts, but I've got so much on my plate. Now, what else can I help you with?"

Amber emerged from the back room with arms crossed. She shuffled over to Sherry's side. Ruth and her friend exchanged glances.

"There's another reason we came in," Frances said. "We are on the Augustin Founder's Day talent search committee, as you may be aware. Had we known about the can of worms that was about to be opened when we volunteered, we would never have signed up. I could've organized the day in my sleep, but turns out every detail, down to the font choice on the brochure, has to pass through a myriad of groups, which takes forever. The biggest roadblock of all may undermine the celebration entirely."

Amber flipped the ends of her shoulder-length hair with the back of her hand. "Sounds like a fun day. What's the roadblock?"

Ruth waved her index finger. "There's a claim being made of a second founder."

"How exciting."

Ruth extended one arm forward, palm facing the heavens. "More ridiculous than exciting. You see, on one hand, you have the Swedish explorer Andre August Dahlback. The notion's been widely accepted that he founded our idyllic town bordered to the south by the Long Island Sound and to the north and east by the meandering and aptly named Silty Pretzel River. The man's onions built fortunes for the small town and its citizens." Ruth raised her other palm as if catching a downpour of liquid gold. "On the other hand, there has recently been a grassroots movement by a prominent family, who doesn't even live in Augustin, may I add, to have their ancestor recognized as Augustin's founder. If these people could be easily ignored, they would be, but that's proving to be an impossible task. I'm afraid they're dampening the spirits of the participants. My job is to showcase the local talent that gives Augustin such appeal, and that's hard to do if the roots of the celebration are embedded in sand. Maybe even quicksand, one might say."

"But, we're not going to let that happen." Frances

pumped her fists before clutching her bicep. "Ouch, I'm getting so creaky."

"I'm sure the dust will settle and the day will go off without a hitch. I'm happy to do my small part on the organization committee, despite any so-called controversy." Sherry peeked at the clock on the wall. "Ladies, I'm going to give Amber a hand with pricing the yarn. Give a shout if you need me."

"I never got to my point." Ruth took a step toward Sherry.

"You really must speak less and say more, Ruth," Frances chided.

"Point taken. Before you go, Sherry, Larson Anderson, has sent me here to persuade you to make an appearance on the podium during the ceremony? I have a letter from him to you outlining the ceremony he's hoping you'll take part in." Frances handed Sherry an envelope. "We will have a few of our most esteemed citizens onstage, including your father, when I ask him, that is. You'll be in great company. We have a local published author whose book, *The Watersport Workout*, has reached the Hillsboro County best-sellers list. We also have an octogenarian Olympic athlete who competed in the tandem bicycle event. It's a discontinued event, but to have an Olympic athlete who chose our town to retire in is so exciting. If you would bring some of your apron collection, people would enjoy that."

Amber gave Sherry a wide smile and a nudge.

Sherry removed the letter from the envelope and scanned the short paragraph. "Yes, sure." Sherry dropped her head as she stuffed the letter and envelope in her pocket. "But only if Dad participates."

"I'll ask him when I deliver this casserole." Ruth collected the dish of food. "He never says no to me."

Frances poked Ruth with her elbow. "Ruth, behave in front of the youngsters."

Sherry squeezed her eyes shut to block any unwanted images from entering her brain. She wasn't successful. "And can you tell him to call me, please. I think he may have forgotten where his charger is because my calls jump to voice mail as if his phone was powered down. On second thought, he seems to be accepting frequent visitors, so maybe I'll stop by."

Her sarcasm didn't appear lost on Ruth, who drew up one side of her mouth and let loose a nasal "humph." Ruth handed the casserole dish to Frances and linked arms with her. "Of course, dear. And, nice meeting you, Amber."

The two women let themselves out, accompanied musically by the doorbell's song.

"What just happened? Those two ladies know more about my father than I do, especially Ruth Gadabee. I'm suspicious Dad sent them here to check up on me, too. He's so transparent. That casserole was a pawn in their game, I fear."

Amber linked arms with Sherry as their recent visitors had done. "I don't know those ladies from a hole in the wall, but I gather, from the brief time we spent together, one of them may be more than friends with Erno."

"I think you might be right. No wonder he doesn't need me."

"Oh, I think he needs you more now than he ever has in his life. Maybe not as a caretaker, but who better than you to help him out of the tough spot he's in. You're pretty good as an amateur detective, need I remind you."

"I guess. Enough of the pity party. Let's get back to work." Sherry pulled her arm away from Amber's.

"By the way, are either of those ladies hooked-rug hobbyists or do they buy completed rugs? Don't answer that; I'm going to check their customer history the way you taught me." Amber walked over to the register and spun the Rolodex filled with index cards. "Ever going to computerize this info? And I'm not necessarily volunteering."

"It wasn't too long ago Dad began taking credit cards. Do you think he's ready to make the leap to computers?"

"If it ain't broke, don't fix it." Amber flipped the cards over. "I'm having trouble finding Gadabee. The card should be right here between Gabriel and Gamble."

Sherry peered over Amber's shoulder. "Gadabee should be there. Dad's meticulous about noting each purchase and any customer preferences and particularities."

Amber lifted a card high. "Right here. It's such a clean card it was stuck to the ink that bled through the 'Gabriel' card in front. She has one purchase, and it was a botanical fireplace rug eight years ago. For preferences, your father listed: roast duck and Merlot. The *O* in Merlot is a heart. Aw, that's sweet."

Sherry clutched her head in her hands and groaned. She raised her head and pitched it to the side. "I could have sworn she used to hook rugs as a hobby. I wonder why her card is so empty. Oh well, thank goodness we have other customers who spend a little more money here."

Amber continued to study the card. "The bottom of the card has a notation in red saying 'see Paladin, Brett.'"

"Really?" Sherry pulled the card out of Amber's hand and scrutinized it. She gave the card back to Amber and shouldered her way closer to the Rolodex. With a spin of the handle, she found the *P*s. She wriggled a card free. "Brett Paladin, well, what do you know? Now that's a full card. The first purchase was recorded years ago. Lots of supplies and even a rectangular rug depicting the family Labrador retriever."

"Who's Brett Paladin?" Amber asked.

"He's our local TV channel's morning anchor. He co-anchored with Carmell Gordy, the woman murdered after my cook-off. But why is his card cross-referenced with Ruth Gadabee's card?" Sherry tapped Brett's frayed card on her forearm until fragments began to flake off. "Oops. This is fragile. Well, anyway, that's curious." Sherry replaced both cards and closed the Rolodex cover. She checked the clock on the wall. "It's almost four. What do you say we tidy up and call it a day?"

Chapter 6

"Your house is as gorgeous as ever." Amber rolled her suitcase through the front hall and parked it at the bottom of the stairs. "Thanks for putting me up tonight. I'm here to help, not to be a burden, so no special treatment required."

"You're doing me such a huge favor. Are you kidding me?" Sherry stepped over Amber's suitcase and climbed the first step. She paused and collected a strand of Chutney's white fur wedged in the stair frame.

Amber laughed. "Still the same Sherry. Please don't tidy up on my behalf. Your house is the neatest, cleanest house I've ever been in."

"To me that piece of fur might as well have been the size of a landfill. Ugh, you're right. I'll never change. Watch. This is what I'm working on." Sherry replaced the white follicle on the step and continued upstairs, peering back twice. "I'll put you in the blue room, same as last time. When you're ready, come on down and tell me all about moving to Hartford."

After Sherry changed her clothes, she crept downstairs. While Sherry was in the midst of tossing Chutney's stair fur in the garbage, Amber's footsteps announced her entry into the kitchen. Sherry slammed the garbage can lid shut with such force it sprang back open. She secured it closed with her foot, hoping Amber was none the wiser.

"That was quick." Sherry's words were delivered with an unintended sarcasm that assaulted her own eardrums. She led Amber over to the kitchen table, where a plate of cookies was waiting.

Amber helped herself to an oatmeal chocolate chip cookie. "Tell me about your next cook-off. We didn't have much time for chatting earlier, but you mentioned one was on the horizon."

Sherry shoved a napkin under Amber's cookie as a crumb tumbled off. "I made it to the finals of the New England Leaf Peepers recipe contest. It's in a few weeks. But the way my schedule's filling up, I don't know if I'll have time." Sherry traced a circle on the table with her finger. "Thursdays I'm committed to selling pickles at the farmer's market. I have Dad's store to monitor, with your help, as long as you're willing, not to mention keeping an eye on Dad's health. Although, I now realize I'm on the B team for that assignment. I'm not even taking into consideration my daily chores and errands. Why did I ever volunteer for Founder's Day?"

"No chance you're missing that cook-off." Amber bit off another chunk and chewed. "Can your sister or brother lend a hand?"

"They're busy. I'm pretty sure I'll pull it all off. My hopes and dreams will have to wait."

"You're being heroic, but as a semiretired therapist, I suggest accepting help where you can get it and maybe even asking for some. That'll ease your stress. You might be surprised who offers. But that's enough shoptalk. These cookies are too good. Take them away." Amber pushed the plate closer to Sherry.

"Let's concentrate on you. So, you relocated back to Boston before your move to Hartford. What happened to your escape to Maine?"

"I tried to make my life work up there, but I felt compelled to go back to Boston and tie up loose ends. I decided not to return to my family therapy practice or rather my practice decided not to invite me back. Now I write an online column. Kind of a modern-day *Dear Ann Landers*, if you've ever heard of her. People write in with family and relationship issue questions, and I offer advice. The benefit is the job's as portable as my laptop. I'm required to submit twice a week, so I have plenty of time to work here as long as you need me." Amber cleared her throat. "Can I help myself to a glass of water?"

Sherry leapt out of her chair. "I appreciate your help so much." She opened a cabinet door and pulled out a bar glass. "Filtered or sparkling?" The logo on the glass depicted a four-leaf clover and a brand of Irish beer.

"Filtered is great. Love the glass."

"Thanks. I collect them from various places I've been. Sometimes I need a visual reminder that I leave Augustin every now and again." Sherry handed Amber a full glass of water. "If a glass catches my eye, I often ask the waiter or bartender if I can buy it. I loved the good luck symbol on this one. I want to mention that I have a taste-testing get-together about once a month, kind of my version of a book group, where I cook up some new recipes and get feedback from the guests. Helps me in future contesting while filling tummies. This month's get-together has crept up on me fast. Only three days away. Hopefully you'll still be here. I'm not sure how many dishes I'll have time to make, but at least two."

"Of course. Sounds like a lot of fun."

"Great." Sherry got up, found her purse, and fished out her phone. "I'm giving Dad a call. If you want to relax in the living room, please, go right ahead. I shouldn't be too long."

"I'm jumping right on my laptop to find a weekly rental apartment." Amber left the room.

"Remember, you're welcome here for as long as you want," Sherry called out.

"Thanks, I appreciate it," Amber replied.

"Hi, Sherry. So happy you're checking in. I just finished a wonderful casserole I heard received your blessing this afternoon."

"Hi, Dad." Sherry left the kitchen and walked over to the stairs. She took a seat on the second step so she could pet Chutney while she talked. "Yes. Your lady friends seemed excited to be taking care of you while you took some time off. You're a lucky guy."

"I'm lucky to have you too, sweetie."

"Thanks, Dad. I wasn't sure you needed me since you have so many others watching out for you. I admit I feel responsible for your being at my cook-off in the first place, and I want to make sure you make a full recovery. Speaking of recovery, Amber did a great job today, so no need to rush back to work. She's noting her hours, so we need to set that money aside to pay her. She says she can stay as long as you need to be out, so that's a relief. No worries." The word "worries" stuck on her tongue like a spoonful of peanut butter. Chutney shook his head, flinging Sherry's hand off his fur.

"I'm a little worried." Erno cleared his throat. "When Ruth and Frances were here today, Frances mentioned her grandson had been complaining about mismanagement at Channel Twelve. He's a good kid, fresh out of college. Not making any money, but the experience should pad his résumé." Erno's voice was weak.

"Well, that information should take some heat off of you, wouldn't you think?" Sherry fixed her gaze on her relaxed dog. "Once the investigation focuses on the station's volatile work environment, you'll be off the suspect list faster than a slow-cooked short rib falls off the bone. When you say you're worried, what specifically are you worried about?"

"Once they start heavy-duty snooping around, someone's going to find out I'm not completely innocent, Sherry. Do you think you can help?" Erno emitted a soft rumble. "I have to go. I'm so tired."

"Dad, you shouldn't say things like that. I mean about not being innocent. Are you there?" Sherry studied her phone, but saw no sign the call was live. Erno wasn't himself. He hadn't served up even one paternal passage of perception.

"You look like you've just seen a ghost." Amber hovered over Sherry's slumped shoulders.

"I think I feel a headache coming on. Maybe an early glass of wine will help. Are you in?"

* * *

The next morning, Sherry, Amber, and Chutney got to the store an hour before opening. They used the extra time to sort through and familiarize themselves with the month's orders. Sherry unlocked the front door to customers at 10:00 a.m.

"Tomorrow you're on your own because it's farmer's market day. We'll use today to think of any questions you might have, so tomorrow isn't trial by fire. You can rearrange the rugs, put out your favorites, whatever makes you happy. Oh, I almost forgot to mention, no dogs are permitted at the farmer's market, so you can either keep Chutney here for company or I can leave him at home and have my neighbor Eileen walk him once or twice. Your choice. No pressure."

Amber turned her head toward Chutney, who had settled down in a prime spot by the front window to sunbathe in the light streaming in. "He stays with me."

"Great. There's a patch of grass in the back parking area where he can do his business. Just put the 'Back in Five Minutes' sign on the front door. Regular customers know exactly where I am when that sign goes up. I'll drop the dog off when I unlock the place for you. I haven't had a chance to get a spare key made, so opening and closing are on me. Are you sure you don't want to spend one more night at my house?"

"Not necessary. The rental starts today. Isn't the Internet the best? Seek and ye shall find. It's furnished and move-in ready."

"I'm kind of sad you won't be staying with me

longer. That had to have been the world's shortest apartment search."

"Internet, e-mail, your scanner for the contract printing and signing. That's all that was required to secure a weekly rental."

"Darn technology. Sometimes it's too speedy for its own good." Sherry smiled.

The doorbell's fervor stole their attention. In strolled Ruth and Frances, in near-matching pastel sweaters and beige ankle pants, arms linked. Sherry deferred to Amber for the greeting.

"Mrs. Gadabee, Mrs. Dumont, how nice to see you again. What can I do for you this morning?" Amber set down the bottle of environmentally friendly spray cleaner Sherry had supplied her with and tucked the cleaning cloth in her pants pocket.

"You have the most beautiful hair, Amber," Frances Dumont cooed. "If strawberries and honey had a baby, the result would be that warm color.

"What a nice compliment. Thank you." Amber bowed her head.

"She's right, dear." Ruth presented a travel coffee mug embellished with an elaborate logo. "This is Erno's mug. We, I mean he, acquired it in his travels. We have this routine most mornings. Frances drives me to get coffee, and we drop it off here in one mug, and I bring the other one home to clean for the next day. The system works like a well-oiled machine. I know you, Sherry, don't usually come in until early afternoon, so we like to make sure he's caffeinated." Both women giggled until they had to pull out tissues from their purses to dab their weeping noses.

Sherry took the mug and clutched it with both

hands. She eyeballed the hotel logo before rotating the mug with a quick gyration away from her line of sight. She walked the mug over to the register and set the cup down.

"We're here for another reason." Frances followed Sherry. "We think there's some information concerning the murder at Channel Twelve you ought to know."

"Mrs. Dumont, I told my father I would do some sniffing around, but I'm hesitant to go all in. Detective Bease is the lead investigator, and I'm sure he could make better use of your information than I can."

"Don't be silly, dear. That detective will move at a snail's pace. Why should he care how much your father's suffering? We need to get this done quickly, and you're the one for the job. It's not a secret you've solved a murder in the past." Frances put her hand under Sherry's chin and lifted until their gazes met. "Hear me out."

The doorbell sweetened the air with a melodic note. In walked a man and a woman. They stood inside the door, taking in the surroundings.

"I'll get this." Amber, sporting a welcoming smile, made her way over to the couple.

"Your father needs help; we all agree." Frances offered. "There are two tidbits of information you need to know. My grandson Steele feels the owner of Channel Twelve, a man named Damien Castle, has mismanaged funds that were to be used to keep the small station on the air and serving the community. Granted, a fair bit of that money was his initial investment after buying the station, but it's becoming a bleak scenario over there. Steele said paychecks are often late, with the exception of Carmell Gordy's, who made a show of getting hers on time. Steele guesses there was a clause in her contract about always getting paid on time or"—Frances paused—"or there would be some sort of consequence. Pretty clever of her."

"I did meet Damien Castle the morning of the cook-off. He seemed like a nice man." Sherry shifted her weight from one foot to the other. She rubbed her palms together. They were as clammy as New England's signature chowder. "I hate to ask, but how would an unpaid intern be so privy to all this inside payroll information?"

Ruth nudged her friend. "You knew you'd have to tell her."

Frances continued, "Steele and Ms. Gordy were an item, as the young folks say. She was quite forthcoming with him, airing the station's dirty laundry."

Sherry's knees softened. She tensed her thighs to compensate. "I'm so sorry for his loss. I had no idea."

"It was a relatively brief affair, as these things go, that ended a few months ago," Frances said. "But she still saw him as an ally, so to speak. Certainly sounds as if she needed one. Steele told me the relationship put him in quite a tight squeeze, balancing loyalty to both sides, pro-Carmell and anti-Carmell."

"I've lost count. Have you told me both items you wanted to share?"

"I'll take it from here," Ruth said. "You also should know that Brett Paladin is my stepson. I was married to his father for many years after his mother passed away. My late husband, George Gadabee, Brett's father, died in a horrendous car crash."

"Yesterday, Amber and I were sorting through

Dad's customer cards, and on your card was noted 'see Brett Paladin.' We followed the trail to your stepson's card, though we didn't know he was your stepson at the time. Of course, we were curious what the connection between you two was. Now it's beginning to make sense, kind of. Seems he was an active customer for a time."

"Brett was extremely helpful in the period after his father's death. I suffered a minor breakdown and couldn't leave the house, so he picked up my rug-hooking supplies for me. Thank goodness for the hobby that got me through a dark phase. Couldn't have been much fun for a young single man to take care of his stepmother, but he was a good sport about it. When I began to feel better and was able to leave the house, Brett was kind enough to bring me to the store because I'd lost my nerve to drive. In time, it became more about the shared love of a hobby with Erno. Not as much about the actual rug hooking. When I felt strong enough Brett moved out and we grew apart. We weren't blood relatives so the connection between us grew weaker over time. When Brett pursued his career in broadcasting he took his late mother's maiden name because Gadabee didn't roll off the tongue like Paladin, he said. Personally, I think people give too much credit to names and how they represent the person, but to each his own." Ruth leaned in to Frances's hand that had landed on her shoulder. "Frances is now my chauffeur, and, sadly, I can't remember the last time I spoke to Brett."

"Seems like Brett was very helpful when you needed him most. That can't be said of all stepsons." Sherry's head bobbed forward and back with acknowledgment.

"I'm telling you all this because Brett might be able to provide some insight in your investigation," Ruth added.

"It's not my investigation. I may do some, well, for lack of a better phrase, independent investigating, but I haven't figured out where to begin." Sherry's words came out with a little more heft than she intended. "Also, I don't know when I'll ever get a chance to talk to Brett." Sherry paused and tapped her fingernails on the counter. "I do have to stop by the station and pick up my engraved trophy at some point. I haven't gotten the call that it's ready yet."

"I've got the perfect excuse for you to ask for a moment with him when you pick up your trophy." Ruth reached in her pocket. She pulled out a suede pouch. She loosened the drawstring on the pouch and, with two fingers, fished out a gold piece of jewelry. "This is his father's money clip that he loved so much. I want Brett to have it. Right here are his father's initials, *GAG*, George Alexander Gadabee. Would you mind bringing it to Brett when you go? That should hopefully gain you entry into a conversation with him." Ruth dropped the clip inside the pouch and handed the bundle to Sherry.

"I can do that for you." Sherry walked the pouch to her purse and secured it in a side pocket. When she lifted her head, Amber waved to get her attention. "Pardon me for a moment; I need to go give Amber a hand."

"Of course. We're going to browse in the meantime. We'll be on our way soon." Frances gathered Ruth by the elbow. "We haven't said hi to Chutney yet."

With Ruth in tow, Frances led the way to the lattice-frame display.

"If you see anything you like, let us know." Sherry knew the words were an empty formality. The real object of their interest was resting himself at his townhouse.

Sherry made her way over to Amber, who was ringing up a purchase.

"I have a couple here who would like to be introduced to you." Amber fluttered her open hand toward Sherry as if she were introducing a game show contestant to his or her prize options.

"Hi, I'm Sherry Oliveri." Sherry extended her hand to the couple before swapping bug eyes with Amber.

"We're the Bornsteads. We saw you on TV in our hotel room. You won a cook-off. How exciting." The woman clapped her hands. "We're doing a driving tour of New England, and this store was recommended as a must-see." She rummaged around in her purse. "Have you seen this? It was in our hotel lobby. Oh, it's not in my purse. Do you have that flyer, dear?"

The man yanked a small paper from his rear pants pocket. He proceeded to unfold it before handing the sheet to Sherry.

"This is a flyer about your town's upcoming Founder's Day, and there's a spotlight on you and your father. Isn't that fantastic?" The woman poked her finger at the paper.

Sherry scrutinized the flyer and laughed before returning it to the woman. "Either this flyer was printed overnight, or I was asked to take part in a ceremony I had already been unknowingly part of. I don't deserve any recognition, but I'm flattered. I like recipe contests and have had some success in them." Sherry handed the flyer back. "But thank you for showing me. I hope you have a nice trip."

"You're so humble," Mrs. Bornstead commented.

"Does the flyer mention some people are trying to undermine the festivities by claiming their relative was the actual founder of Augustin?" Frances broke through the gathering around the register. "Hi, I'm Frances Dumont, and this is Ruth Gadabee."

"I didn't see what you're referring to." Mrs. Bornstead backed away from Frances. "There's mention of a Swedish onion farmer, who I believe had the middle name August."

"It won't be long until the other side of the so-called controversy hits the airwaves with their version of who founded our town, so buckle up. They're a force to be reckoned with," Frances said.

"We have to excuse ourselves. We're trying to get to Boston before rush hour." Mr. Bornstead collected his purchase, put his arm around his wife and guided her out the door.

"You scared them off, Frances. Some people shy away from conflict, unlike you." Ruth's laugh was as sweet as port wine and equally as full-bodied. "Let's make like a tree and leave, too."

"That joke never gets old," Frances giggled, "unlike us." She hooked her friend's arm in hers, and they promenaded out the door.

"I want to be them when I grow up." Amber pulled out a clean index card from under the counter and began recording the Bornsteads' purchase information. "I think I hear your phone ringing."

Sherry circled the counter and found her phone in her purse. "Missed it. It says 'unknown caller.'" She played the voice mail message. "My trophy's ready. What do you say we close up at lunchtime and pay News Twelve a visit?"

Chapter 7

"Sorry about the mess in here."

"That's a joke, right?" Amber ran her finger across the door panel. Her digit came up spotless. "I've never seen a car this clean, except in the dealer showroom."

"That's nice of you to say." Sherry slowed the car to merge onto the parkway. "I can hardly keep my eyes off the gorgeous fall colors on the trees." Sherry pressed harder on the gas pedal. "I could've used a second pair of eyes when I was driving yesterday. I was so distracted by the gorgeous fall leaves on the trees, I almost missed my exit."

"Do you need help now?" Amber gripped her armrest.

"No. Don't worry. My full attention is on the road." Sherry's peripheral vision caught Amber bracing herself. "I can't help but notice that ever since yesterday there are so many more reds on the trees. That's my favorite fall color." Sherry saw her opportunity to slide between two cars and gunned the accelerator. "Hold on!"

"Would you ever like to be on one of those competitive cooking shows on TV? I don't mean a mild-mannered cook-off. I'm talking about the high stress, fast-paced shows where they systematically eliminate cooks round by round. You're so good at keeping your ducks in a row, I bet you'd win."

Sherry laughed. "I tried out for one once. I was interviewed to be a contestant on the show *Double Boiler*, but they didn't choose me. Those shows aren't just about cooking skills. For entertainment value, they want a good backstory for each contestant. That makes good TV. I'm plain boring, too orderly, I guess." Sherry squirted the windshield with wiper fluid to remove some bug sashimi.

"I'd think they'd like you to be a bit devious, too. It's not too late to change your nice ways, Sherry Oliveri. You could drop your sweet persona like you dropped your husband's last name, hot-potato style." Amber belted out an evil snicker.

"I'll give that consideration."

"That's got to be it. Telltale huge tower and satellite dishes." Amber pointed her finger across Sherry's line of vision.

"That's it. And there's the *Doppler Ten Thousand Weather On The Go* truck. They advertise it's the most accurate forecasting tool around besides the acorn."

"Did you say acorn?" Amber asked.

"Local lore says that variables, like the acorn's size, the amount the trees produce, their shape, when they fall from the trees, and the quantity the animals forage, are the best predictors of what the New England weather will deliver."

"And a lot cheaper than the cost of that truck with the catchy name, I'm guessing." Amber laughed so hard Chutney uncurled, stood up on wobbly legs, and popped his head through the center console.

The car turned into the driveway, where Sherry located a large parking lot by the sprawling one-story building. As they neared the front entrance, Sherry kept her eye out for a convenient short-term parking spot. She crept the car past a gray sedan sadly in need of a wash. "I wonder if Detective Bease is here."

"I think we should proceed with caution if he is," Amber said.

"We're here to pick up my trophy and to deliver his father's money clip to Brett. If we happen to get a few questions answered along the way, that's frosting on the cake."

"Can you park there?" Amber pointed to an empty spot within steps of the building's entrance. "Wait, we can't. Sign says 'Reserved for Carmell Gordy.' I guess that's why the spot's empty."

"I see one. 'Thirty-Minute Parking.'" Sherry guided the car into the parking spot. "You stay in the car, boy. We won't be long." Sherry and Amber grabbed their purses and unloaded. Sherry locked the car.

"Someone grabbed Carmell's spot." Amber pointed in the direction of what had been the vacant slot, now filled by a blue sports car.

The car door was wide-open, and someone in the driver's seat was pulling off a long-sleeved garment. After the figure emerged from the front seat, she leaned down and retrieved a small item from outside the car. She gathered her long locks in one hand and twirled them into a sphere. She secured the hairdo with whatever item she had picked up off the ground.

"Wait a minute. I thought the driver was a female, but now I think that's Steele Dumont. The hair fooled me." Sherry mumbled the information behind a shielding hand. "Interesting that he would park there."

Sherry watched Steele slam the car door shut and sprint the short distance to the building. She and Amber crossed the parking lot before stopping at the sports car.

"Have you ever seen someone do this before? Charlie used to put his ceramic mug on top of the car while he loaded in his briefcase and computer. He was good about not forgetting it, though." Sherry wrapped her hand around the pearl-white travel mug perched on the car's soft convertible top. The beverage container was adorned with a detailed design.

Sherry studied the circular drawing on the mug. "Let's return the mug to its rightful owner."

They reached the News Twelve building and made their way to the metal detector, feet from the receptionist's desk. The woman next to the hulking security guard took her eyes off her computer screen and scanned Sherry.

"May I help you?" The woman removed her reading glasses. "Oh, I know you. You were at our cook-off, and you won. You don't have to pass through the detector. We're expecting you."

The man in uniform moved a step closer to the receptionist, never taking his hand off a bulge at his waist. "Please state your name."

"Sherry Frazzelle." Sherry felt a sharp elbow in her side. "I mean, Sherry Oliveri. And this is Amber Sherman."

"These ladies are invited guests." The receptionist pushed the visitor sign-in book toward the women. Sherry doodled her name and handed the pen to Amber.

"I wanted to say how sorry I was about the death of Carmell Gordy. That was so awful. I can't imagine returning to a sense of normalcy any time soon." Sherry's tongue felt as dry as an overcooked chicken breast. She swallowed hard to drum up some saliva.

"I got a call saying my cook-off trophy had been engraved and that I could come pick it up. I think they said it was in Damien Castle's office."

"Of course. I'll call for our intern to accompany you to Mr. Castle's office." The receptionist put her glasses back on and typed on her keyboard. She stared at the screen as if she were a hungry diner reading a four-star menu. She looked up. "He'll be right over. Please have a seat. Oh, and please power down all cell phones. We can't have them ringing or even lighting up during production."

Sherry and Amber retrieved their phones from their purses and shut them off.

"Who's Damien Castle?" Amber whispered.

"I guess you didn't hear when Dad's lady friends were describing the situation over here at the station, as reported by Frances Dumont's grandson. He works as an intern here. Long story short, Damien Castle is the owner of the station, its majority investor. But there might be trouble simmering between him and the employees. Frances mentioned there are some hard feelings about the star-status treatment Carmell Gordy had been receiving. Seems Damien's not been seeing the forest for the trees."

Before Sherry was able to continue, Steele Dumont walked up to the seated women. "Hi, I'm Steele Dumont. We met at the appetizer cook-off." Steele took Sherry's hand as she stood and shook vigorously. "And you are Amber Sherman, I'm told." He shook Amber's hand. "Let me take you to Mr. Castle's office where he's holding your trophy."

Sherry sidled up to Steele and motioned Amber in tight. Amber put her hand over her mouth to steer a comment Sherry's way. Sherry dropped back and leaned her ear in close.

"Isn't he the guy we saw taking the best parking spot? He's an intern. How does he finagle that privilege?"

Sherry put her finger to her lips. She picked up her pace and caught up to Steele. "Is this, by any chance, yours?" Sherry lifted the white travel mug up to Steele's face. "We noticed it resting on the roof of the car you got out of."

Steele accepted the mug and brought it down to his side. "Thank you. Bad habit I need to break. One day I'm going to drive away with a full cup of coffee up there."

"Nice car, too, if you don't mind my saying." Amber crossed her arms, hugging her purse in tight to her chest.

"Fun to drive, but it's not mine." Steele turned and resumed his walk

"Not his car," Sherry muttered.

Sherry and Amber made their way through a set of

double doors after Steele waved his badge across a sensor. They entered a windowless hallway.

"Steele, I run into your grandmother quite often. Just this morning, as a matter of fact. Sure is a small world."

"Where was that?" Steele peered back over his shoulder at Sherry.

"She came into my father's store, the Oliveri Ruggery."

"I'm guessing she was with her partner in crime, Ruth Gadabee?" Steele let out a laugh. "Talk about small worlds. They're best friends, and now I work with Mrs. Gadabee's stepson, Brett. Let that be a lesson. You can't get away with a thing in this town. Too many eyes and ears monitoring your every move."

Sherry felt a tug from behind. She checked back and received a return wink from Amber. "In passing, your grandma mentioned you dated Carmell Gordy. I'm so sorry for your loss."

A moment later, he turned to face Sherry. At the same time, Amber bumped into her friend when she abruptly came to a stop. Sherry noted Steele's expression was as serious as sriracha sauce.

"Carmell and I dated for a while, but it was never heading anywhere. She had much bigger aspirations than to be Augustin's local News Twelve anchor, and I was a brief stopover on her journey." He studied the floor. "She wasn't making many friends here, which is too bad. But the question is, who would murder her? I can't say the thought didn't cross my mind when her last to-do list for me was more about picking up dry cleaning and dog food than work-related. She had a way of making me feel stepped on, like a doormat." Steele stomped his boot on the floor with a dull thud.

Sherry took a step back. "I can't imagine how shocked you were when you found out. You wouldn't wish that on anyone."

"Were you in the studio when the mur . . . the mur . . . her death happened?" Amber asked.

"I was probably in the supply closet sorting out her wardrobe. That room's like my second home, I spend so much time in there. At least I don't have that fun task hanging over my head anymore." He spun on his heels and took off. "Keep your voices down. They're rehearsing." Steele opened the thick metal door to the studio. After Sherry and Amber passed through, Sherry watched him shut it with noiseless precision.

When Steele reached one of the camera operators, he slowed his pace. "Hey, Lucky, thanks for the sweater loan. I owe you one. I'll bring it by later," he whispered.

Lucky removed his face from the camera viewfinder and lifted his thumb high in the air. The circular collection of hair on top of his head wriggled in unison with his hand gesture.

"You two could be twins," Amber remarked in a hushed tone. "I can't be the first to say that."

"We get that all the time. He's a good dude." Steele put his thumb up and waggled it. "Stole my flavor, though."

"Flavor?" Sherry asked.

"You know, my style, my look," Steele answered.

"Imitation is a form of flattery," Amber added softly.

"Wonder if I can ever find my flavor," Sherry considered.

From her vantage point at the back of the room,

Sherry could make out Brett in front of a green screen. When she closed in on a monitor, Sherry could see, from the enhanced shot, Brett was pointing out a weather situation in Connecticut. She took a step closer to Steele and leaned toward his ear. "Is Brett a weatherman too?" She watched Brett's arms sweep across his body, simulating the movement of a passing cold front.

Steele cupped his hands around his mouth. "Budget cuts. Our meteorologist, Blitz Gale, got the axe last week, and Brett got the assignment. He tapes the weather twice a day, and the station loops the segment throughout a twenty-four-hour period. If he directed people to look out the window, they'd get a more accurate report."

"Or if they studied the local acorn population," Amber whispered as she reached her hand over her shoulder and patted herself on the back.

Steele led the ladies through the studio exit. He knocked on the next door they came to. The plaque secured to the door read "Damien Castle." Steele turned the knob and pushed. He wedged his head into the sliver of an opening. He mumbled some words before shutting the door. "He needs a minute."

Sherry positioned her body to face Steele. "Do you enjoy working for Mr. Castle? Do you think he's a good leader?"

Steele glanced at Damien's office door and lowered his voice to a near whisper. "This place is hanging on by a thread. A really weak thread. Mr. Castle was under so much pressure to serve Carmell a fat paycheck on a silver platter, he left his longstanding employees starving. Granted, I don't make a dime here, but if I were a paid employee, there would be another reason to be enraged with the girl. To me, Mr. Castle gives off a shady vibe. He seems to have his own agenda, with total disregard for the big picture. Doesn't seem to be a team player. Best guess is someone is constantly in his ear, like a puppet master. Even when you're talking to him, he doesn't seem engaged with what you're saying. Like he's waiting for confirmation from another source that whatever point you're trying to make is valid. Middleman would best describe him, even though he's supposed to be the head honcho."

The door opened and out stepped Detective Bease. Damien Castle was behind him with his hand on the doorknob. Sherry caught a gasp as it attempted to escape her chest. Only a mousey squeak left her lips.

"Ms. Frazz . . ." Ray whacked his palm on his forehead. "Forgive me. I mean Ms. Oliveri and Ms. Sherman, so nice to see you here. This is quite a surprise."

Sherry detected a note of contempt in the detective's words.

"Ray, I mean, Detective Bease, I assume you're on official business, as are we." Sherry wasn't sure she delivered her words with authority, so once they left her lips, she longed for a second try. "We're picking up my cook-off trophy."

"Ah, very good." Ray shimmied to the side to let Sherry, Amber, and Steele pass. "Sherry, I'll be contacting you shortly about a certain matter, if that's convenient. And do you still have my hat?"

"That would be fine, and, yes, your chapeau is safe and waiting to be picked up at your convenience."

"Right this way, ladies." Damien pointed toward his

office. "Dumont, give us five minutes before you escort these ladies back to the lobby." He waved Sherry and Amber through and shut the door, leaving Steele in the hall with Ray.

"Have a seat, Ms. Oliveri." Damien's vision lingered on Amber. He smiled and pulled out his phone.

The ladies took seats facing Damien's desk. Damien sat in a leather captain's chair at the head of the desk. He typed on the phone's tiny keypad before revisiting Amber. "I'm sorry, have we met?"

"This is my friend, Amber Sherman. She's helping me at my father's store while he recuperates from a health scare." Sherry scanned the room and located her spatula trophy perched on a box in the corner. "Is that mine?"

"Yes." Damien collected the trophy and handed it to Sherry. His gaze darted to Amber. "I wish I had one for you, too." He tugged at his shirt collar.

Amber shifted in her chair.

Sherry sighed. She turned the trophy over to check the engraving. Her name without the Frazzelle surname sent a ripple of imbalance through her core. Sherry had begun cooking contesting on a whim soon after she married Charlie Frazzelle, the man she had tutored in organizational skills through his law school days and fallen in love with. Competitive cooking was a hobby she excelled at, and her ex-husband was always so supportive of her culinary experiments, for better or worse. She considered his stamp of approval her good luck charm when it came to her recipes. The trophy she held was the first she'd won under her maiden name. Considering her aversion to change, the sight was going to take some getting used to.

"I hope your father's doing okay. I heard he was under the weather. I did get a quick word with him the day of the cook-off. He seemed healthy at the time. I was telling the detective, coincidentally, that I thought Carmell had upset your father that morning because I saw them having an animated discussion. The girl can be fierce, you know. Or she used to be, I should say."

Sherry's temple began to pound in unison with the quickened beat of her heart. "I'm sure it was a misunderstanding. Dad's delivery can come off harsh, but he's a sweetheart." Sherry wasn't sure Damien heard her reply because he was thumb typing on his phone again. She hoped her words hadn't registered with him after she reconsidered how they could be misinterpreted. "Such a tragic loss. Carmell Gordy was a rising star."

"There are lots of people who might disagree with you, maybe even your father, but I tried to make her stay with us memorable, not knowing the time would be so short. Her budding career was going places, I believe. We're small potatoes here at News Twelve, but I take our viewership seriously, and I want to provide the audience with the best on-air talent. Signing Carmell was quite a coup, if I do say so myself." With a sudden jerk of his hand, Damien put his phone on the desk and gave it a shove so it slid across the table, just beyond his reach. He curled his hands into balls. His knuckles turned white.

"I'm surprised there weren't any eyewitnesses to Carmell's murder. But the place was pitch-black." Sherry's scalp prickled. "In the corner, where the camerawoman, Kirin, I think her name was, and I were, it was impossible to see a thing. But when the lights came up, I remember Kirin was horrified at what she saw through her camera viewfinder. I'm curious. Did you see or hear anything? Were you in the room at the time of the blackout?"

Damien massaged the back of his neck with both hands.

"I left the building on a personal emergency. I didn't even have time to sign out. The storm was so bad, I had to make a mad dash for the parking lot. Unfortunately, when I got to my car, I realized I had left the top down on my convertible. What a mess the storm made of my car's interior. Would have been nice if Brett's forecast had been a little more precise." Damien's phone began to vibrate. "Please don't be strangers." He reached in his wallet and pulled out a business card. He slid it across the desk toward Amber, who picked up the card.

Sherry gave Amber a sideways glance before standing. "I was asked to deliver this while I'm here." Sherry pulled the jewelry pouch from her purse. "This is for Brett Paladin from his stepmother, Ruth Gadabee."

The color drained from Damien's face. "Now there's a name from the past." Damien shook his head, and the color returned.

"You know her?" Amber asked.

"Her husband owned the station before me. George Gadabee, I think was his name. When he died, the family was in the process of attracting investors, and I stepped in."

"Makes sense you would know the Gadabee family then. So interesting Brett is the son of the station's previous owner." Sherry swiveled her head from

Damien to Amber and back again. "Is that how he got his job here?"

"Yes and no. He worked here part-time, off-camera, behind the scenes, before his father died. Shortly after, he applied for a permanent job here. When I read the application, I didn't know it was the same young man. He was using the surname Paladin instead of Gadabee by that time. I liked his résumé. He was interviewed, impressed everyone, and got the job. Fair and square. You're full of questions, Ms. Oliveri. I'd think your interest would lie in finding out why the murder weapon used originated in your father's store."

Sherry wiped her brow with her knuckles. "That's the detective's job."

Damien inflated his cheeks.

Sherry held up the jewelry pouch. "Ruth Gadabee would like me to personally see that Brett gets this. Would that be possible?"

There was a knock on the door. Steele stepped inside. "All set?"

"Steele, these ladies need one minute of Brett's time." Damien eyeballed his phone. "He should be done with rehearsal. Would you mind escorting them to see him? He's usually in the kitchen on his break about now." Damien walked to the door.

"No problem." After a forceful exhale, Steele took off down the hallway, followed by Sherry and Amber scrambling to keep up.

It wasn't long before they stopped in front of another door. At eye level on the front panel there was an off-color rectangle and two holes where something clearly had been removed.

"I'm sorry. I need to check inside before we find Brett." Steele turned the doorknob. When the door was halfway open, he squatted on his haunches. There he encountered a yapping ball of fur that scampered over to investigate the intruders. "Hey, Bean, you doing okay?"

"Is he yours?" Sherry pushed in through the doorway and knelt next to the wriggling creature, beckoning him closer with her fingers. "He's so cute. I'm partial to Jack Russells. I have one myself."

"Bean is, was, Carmell's dog." Steele explained.

"Is that the dog I heard barking behind closed doors the day of the cook-off?" Sherry asked.

"That's right. Carmell has no family in town, so I'm taking him in until I figure out what to do with him. He basically hates me and everyone else besides Carmell. Strange, I once had a theoretical conversation with her about what would happen to the dog if she wasn't able to care for him, being as busy as she was, and, like an idiot, I said of course I'd take him. So, here I am with a new dog but same old tricks. Guilty conscience, I guess."

"I think he's sweet." Amber lowered herself down beside Sherry and made kissing noises. "He doesn't know who he belongs to anymore."

"I need to fill his water bowl. Give me a minute." Steele scooped up the empty bowl in the corner and hustled out of the room.

Sherry stood and flexed her knees. She walked over to the one stick of furniture in the room, a tiny metal desk, and sat on the edge. "Hard to bend that low anymore. I better get back to yoga, if I ever have any free time. That was quite a significant detail Ruth

Gadabee left out about her husband's owning News Twelve before he died, don't you think?"

Amber nodded and let out a soft laugh. "This town is getting smaller by the minute."

Sherry scooted her bottom back across the desk surface and, in the process, knocked a paper to the floor. She retrieved it and examined the typewritten sheet before remarking, "Definitely Leila's handiwork."

"Leila?"

"Augustin's finest meter maid. This is a parking ticket. Dated the day of the cook-off and . . . oh my God." Sherry fumbled in her purse for her phone. With shaky hands, she squared up the parking ticket to the edge of the desk and tapped the camera icon. She grazed the shutter button and heard a satisfying click. She leapt up when the door opened, bulldozing the paper behind her.

Bean began barking.

"Here you go, Bean. Don't be so ungrateful." Steele clanged the bowl on the hard floor as he set it down.

Bean retreated under the desk.

"He's fine, so let's keep moving."

"Bye, Bean," Sherry sang out as Bean peeked out from his hiding place.

"Bye, cutie," Amber called out.

Steele closed the door behind them, and they proceeded to the kitchen. They entered the modest-sized room, furnished with a rectangular table and wooden chairs and outfitted with all the necessary kitchen appliances. Toward the back of the room, Brett and Truman were engaged in a conversation.

"Sorry to interrupt, but these ladies need a quick word with Brett," Steele said.

Truman backed up and leaned against the microwave, crossing one ankle over the other.

"Sherry, you must be here picking up your trophy. I saw it in Damien's office." Brett thrust his hand forward.

Sherry rocked back on her heels.

"While you're here, can I get you to taste this? When last we spoke, you had a few suggestions, and I took them to heart. I think this breakfast cookie is new and improved and ready for mass market. Your friend can try a bite, too."

Sherry broke the cookie in half and handed a share to Amber.

"Is this what your taste-testing parties are like?" Amber nudged Sherry.

"Taste-testing party?" Brett and Truman said in unison.

Brett's eyes widened.

Sherry studied the cookie half. She bit off a chunk, moved it around in her mouth, and then swallowed. "I host a dinner once in a while to get recipe feedback from friends. I make a few of my newest recipes and serve them up for suggestions and constructive criticism. I give each guest a ballot so he or she can vote on his or her favorite recipe. It brings out the inner cook-off judge in my guests, and they seem to have fun." She tipped her head toward Amber. "This is Amber Sherman. Amber, this is Brett Paladin, and, I'm sorry, your name escapes me."

"Truman Fletcher." The man in the gray suit put

his hands on his hips. He rubbed the flat surface of hair at the top of his head.

"First, I wanted to tell you again how saddened we were when we learned of Ms. Gordy's passing." Sherry paused, half expecting a response, but none was forthcoming.

Brett's vision was locked on the remaining cookie portion in Sherry's hand. He raised his eyebrows and opened his mouth, but stayed mute. Truman tapped his toe to a slow, deliberate beat.

"And second, I ran into your stepmother, and she entrusted this to me to pass along to you when she found out I was on my way here." Sherry presented the pouch.

Brett's face bloomed a reddish hue Sherry hadn't seen the likes of since her last attempt at making borscht. "This is my dad's." He opened the tiny sack and peered inside. An extended, low hum resonated from his nose. "Thought she'd never give this up. Thank you."

"Ruth is a friend of my father. They spend a lot of time together, I'm learning." Sherry smiled. The smile was not returned. "Seems as if you know my father. I saw you talking to him the day of the cook-off. As a matter of fact, Dad seemed to know Carmell, too."

"Turns out that might not be such a good thing." Truman rubbed his palms together, creating a chafing sound that gave Sherry goose bumps.

Sherry recoiled at the caustic noise. "Why's that?"

"A detective was here for the second time asking lots of questions about your father and who he knew here at the station. If I was presented with the facts, I would be a little curious as to why the murder weapon was from the Oliveri Ruggery. If you put two and two together, the potential outcome of the investigation reads like a poorly written mystery lacking even an ounce of suspense." Truman walked to the table and picked up a clipboard.

"You're not reading good enough mysteries then, Mr. Fletcher, because while it may appear my dad left a trail of evidence, looks can be deceiving. Detective Bease is hard at work getting to the truth. No one should jump to conclusions. The facts are definitely not all in, rest assured."

"Time will tell." Truman gave a royal wave and left the room.

"I'm on my way out too." Brett shoved the pouch in his blazer pocket. "Thanks for the delivery. If you see Ruth, will you send her my best?"

"You wouldn't want to thank her yourself?" Sherry winced when Brett shot a harsh glare her way.

"She knows how I feel." Brett left the room.

Sherry twisted her mouth to steer her words in Amber's direction. "I wish I got the chance to ask Brett where he was during the murder, but I couldn't think of a natural segue." She flipped what was left of the cookie around in her hand. "I'm glad he forgot to ask my opinion of his cookie." Sherry grimaced and surveyed the room for the trash can.

"Is this what you're looking for?" Steele pressed the pedal of the flip-top garbage can.

"I'll join you." Amber brought her cookie remains over with Sherry.

Brett charged through the kitchen door. "Ms. Oliveri, I forgot to get your opinion."

Sherry retracted her hovering hand so fast from

the garbage receptacle grazed Amber's arm, causing cookie bits to take flight.

"Let's see." Sherry took a second bite. "This batch is moister than the last, but not necessarily in the most desirable way. The texture is more on the gummy side now. You might have over-mixed the flour. That causes the glutens to get pretty rubbery. At the same time, I think you used too much liquid sweetener, I'm guessing maple syrup, and you may have overbaked them in an attempt to firm them up. Did they spread out too much on the baking sheet? I'm guessing you reformed them halfway through the baking time because the edges are so ragged and the top is very uneven."

Brett rubbed a red patch on his cheek. "You know what? This wasn't a good batch. I had a sinus headache yesterday when I made them." He pivoted and left the room.

"It's gonna be a long day for me now." Steele frowned. "Brett takes constructive criticism about as well as I take a loss by the Patriots. The effects could last a long time, or at least until he gets back in his kitchen to make a new batch."

"Sorry about that. I had no idea." Sherry tossed the cookie in the trash. She checked the time on her phone. "I think all our business here is complete. Time to get back to the store."

They followed Steele's lead out of the kitchen.

"I'm running into a bit of a time crunch." Steele waved his arms at a figure down near the studio entrance. A young man dressed in blue jeans and a white T-shirt sprinted over. "Lucky, would you mind showing these ladies back to the front lobby? I have to run."

"No problem. Ladies, you're in good hands. They don't call me Lucky because I'm cursed," the young man said.

"Wow, you two really could be twins," Amber noted. "You and Steele share an amazing resemblance."

"I'm certainly a better dresser." Steele punched Lucky in the arm.

"Thanks to the addition of my sweater," Lucky added. "Are you ever planning on returning it?"

Steele shrugged and pivoted toward the women. "Have a great day and keep watching News Twelve. We need every viewer we can muster."

Sherry stuck out her hand. Steele hustled over to reciprocate, during which time Sherry leaned in and whispered in his ear.

Chapter 8

"What have we gotten ourselves into?" Sherry used a backward heel kick to shut the door behind her. She freed the wriggling dog clutched in her arms. Chutney dashed to Bean's side. "We're in deep now."

The sides of Amber's mouth curled up. "Can you keep him at your house for the night, while I have a chat with my rental agent? I'm sure she and I can work out an arrangement, and I'll be able to keep him. I'll have to pay for extra cleaning service visits, but that doesn't bother me. I have the advantage because she let it slip that she and her husband are newly separated. She may be in need of some free family therapy, so I think we can strike up a deal."

"You may get some content for your advice column, too."

"All side benefits, plus Bean gets a new home." Amber performed a short victory dance. "A win-win. Bean wasn't Mr. Popularity at the station. I'm afraid he was heading for the pound. Steele seemed more than a bit stressed and not at all in the position to have more responsibility dumped in his lap."

The two terriers disappeared under the hooking demonstration table.

"I didn't trust anyone there had Bean's best interests at heart," Amber commented.

"Because they didn't. Steele literally squealed with delight when I asked if we could adopt Bean. I'm sure it's a load off his shoulders. Did you see the mock salute Brett gave Bean when we left? 'Good riddance' was written all over it." Sherry hung the two leashes on a hook by the door. "We'll alternate dog-walking duty. Except, of course, on farmer's market day. You're on your own that day. We've got this covered." Sherry offered Amber a high five, and the ensuing clap enticed the dogs to bring their roughhousing out from under cover.

"I'm going to the back room to finish matching canvases to yarn bundles. Give a shout if you need me." Amber dragged a wooden Shaker-style stool inside the small storeroom. Her dangling legs were visible kicking in time as she hummed a tune Sherry couldn't identify.

Sherry took a seat behind the sales counter. "Hey, Amber. What did you think of the characters at News Twelve? Are any of them capable of murdering their colleague?"

Amber leaned through the doorway, holding balls of yarn over her ears.

"Sorry, I didn't mean to yell so loud. I didn't know if you could hear me. Was that overkill? Oops, *overkill* is not the right word."

"I'm pretty sure the whole block heard your question." Amber laughed.

Sherry lowered her voice. "Is this better?"

"Perfect." Amber leaned back out of sight, with the

exception of her bouncing legs. "Do you have anyone in particular in mind?"

"Let's start with Brett Paladin. Seems a bit uptight, but there's heavy pressure on the anchors to represent the station in every capacity, I'm sure. When the cameras stop rolling, that's when his persona as a trustworthy and unbiased community reporter can turn off, but I think that's really who he is. Not much of a sense of humor that I could detect, but understandable as the news he reports these days can be pretty dismal. Plus he has such a strong connection to the station's history. Honestly, if Brett wanted to murder anyone, it would be me."

"You?" Amber exclaimed.

Sherry let out a puff of air. "He didn't take kindly to my comments about his cookie recipe, but if he didn't want the truth, he shouldn't have asked me for advice, twice. I'm not going to sugarcoat what I know best in order to make friends. Ask me about another topic and I'll give you a fluff answer to keep the peace, but, with any cooking concerns, I shoot straight from the hip. I have a reputation to uphold."

Amber purred in agreement.

"It's hard to assess what Brett's relationship with his morning show co-anchor was like. He seemed to genuinely care for Carmell. I only saw them together briefly, and the rest of what I know is hearsay. I did notice the name of their morning show is written one way on the cook-off apron they gave me and another way on the show's credits. Before Carmell joined News Twelve, the morning show was all Brett's. The name of the show was *Sunny Side Up with Brett.* Fast-forward and Carmell is on board. The name of the show becomes *Sunny Side Up with Carmell and Brett.* The apron I wore at the cook-off read *Sunny Side Up with Brett and Carmell,* so obviously there was a short phase when Brett got top billing. That name change ping-pong game is more confusing than the idea behind Baked Alaska. I mean, think about it. You bake ice cream topped with whipped egg whites until they're browned, and somehow that's reminiscent of our forty-ninth state?"

Amber called out from the other room, "Where does someone even begin to dream up that recipe?"

Sherry shook her head. "Anyway, my gut feeling is Brett Paladin showed less animosity toward Carmell than some of the others. And he had some right to be angry, if indeed he got booted from top billing. He did blurt out that the police should have arrested Steele on the spot that morning, but I'm chalking that up to the chaos of the moment. The two of them seemed on fine terms when I picked up my trophy."

Amber leaned forward and presented a ball of green yarn through the doorway opening. "This is gorgeous."

"I know. Romaine-lettuce green. What was your impression of Damien Castle?"

Amber's legs uncrossed, waggled around, and crossed again. A ball of yarn came tumbling off Amber's lap, and Bean took off to retrieve the rolling sheep fibers.

"Well, what do you know? Maybe Bean can teach old Chutney new tricks." Sherry followed the perky pup across the room. When Bean sat, she coaxed him to release the yarn from his jaws, with the aid of her best imitation of an enabling mother. "Good boy!"

"Damien seemed nice." Amber cocked her head to the side. Her eyes widened. "Striking hair, strong jawline, commanding build."

"Glad you think he's cute, but I mean any suspicions about his involvement in the murder?" Sherry clicked her tongue on the roof of her mouth. "He came on a bit strong, wouldn't you say?"

"I didn't get that impression." The lilt in Amber's voice lingered.

"Steele Dumont's not a fan of Damien. He all but blamed the instability at the station on him and the special privileges granted to Carmell. If there was enough pressure on Damien to coddle the star of the show while not getting any return on his investment, that could be a definite motive."

Amber let out a short hum that dipped in scale. "I don't think so."

"Damien didn't have much of an alibi. He didn't provide the name of anyone who saw him outside of the studio. He claims there was a personal emergency he had to attend to and that there was no record of his exit from the building that morning. There's no real proof he was or wasn't in proximity to the murder."

Amber leaned back out of sight. "I think you're getting ahead of yourself, Sherry. Speculating isn't concrete evidence." Amber stepped back into sight and set down the canvas she was working with. "I have to use the bathroom." Amber marched off and shut herself in the bathroom with a slam of the door.

"Did I put my foot in my mouth? I have to stop doing that." Sherry eyed Chutney, who was sniffing the drawer that held his treats. "Here you go." She handed each dog a mini dog biscuit.

A few minutes later, the bathroom door clicked, and Amber's soft-soled shoes squeaked as they padded across the floor.

"I was thinking," Amber said. "What do you make of Steele Dumont's possible motives? Seems to me, he's the one who was pushed around hardest by Carmell, maybe to his breaking point. People are like animals. They can lash out when they're boxed into a corner."

"But his grandmother is one of my favorite people." Sherry frowned.

Bean began barking.

"This is why I could never be a detective. Too much empathy for my fellow man. But you're right. Steele has multiple reasons to have wanted Carmell gone."

A phone rang from under the checkout counter. "Hold that thought."

The barking became incessant.

"What's the matter, Bean?" Sherry dove for her phone before the call was diverted to voice mail. "I hope it's Dad."

"Hello. May I come in?"

"You didn't have to call if you're right outside the door. This is a place of business. If the 'Open' sign is out, come on in." Sherry ended the call.

Bean's bark morphed into a guttural grumble.

"Seems like Bean sensed someone was lurking outside. And that someone is on his way in." Sherry smiled.

"Doesn't that ringing drive you crazy?" Detective Bease stared up at the reverberating metal bell.

"We need to know when our customers have arrived." Sherry took a step toward the man in khakis with a brown tweed blazer and a baby blue oxford shirt peeking out at the collar and cuffs. "There's your hat." She pointed at the row of hooks. "Have you ever considered how cliché a hat like that is for someone in your profession?"

Bean scampered over to the visitor and sniffed his pants so sorely in need of ironing.

"Who's this?" Ray extended a hand toward the dog.

Bean took off in the opposite direction.

"Our newest family member, Bean. We rescued him, you could say. He was Carmell Gordy's dog, and his prospects for a smooth transition to a new owner were bleak. He's getting along peachy with Chutney. Amber's going to see if she can keep him, depending on her temporary housing situation."

"That's thoughtful of you two." Ray's gaze made a slow survey of the store. "Nice stuff. Reminds me, my place could use a little color."

Sherry let her gaze roam the length of the detective's body. She crossed her arms. "Let me guess, it's all beige?"

Amber emerged from the back room. "May I show you a particular rug?" She moved over to the display area. "Rich, real-world colors are what make these rugs beautiful. The head of romaine lettuce hooked on this rug was matched exactly to the leafy green's color."

"Next time. Today I'm here for a follow-up interview, if all parties are willing." The detective glared at Sherry. "When I spoke to your father on the phone this morning, in hopes of finishing our interrupted conversation from the other day, he mentioned that he knew both Carmell Gordy and Brett Paladin before the cook-off. Were you aware of that?"

Sherry smoothed out a fold in her cotton shirtsleeve. "People know people. No crime in that." She recoiled at her word choice before beginning a search for another area of fabric to straighten.

"Okay. Had *you* met them prior to the cook-off?" Ray's tone was light, as if he were cajoling a child through a crying spell.

"Carmell Gordy isn't from Augustin, otherwise I might have had ample chance to run into her in town. The cook-off was our first introduction. Brett's from Augustin. He's a bit older than me, so we wouldn't have been in school at the same time. He did come to my high school English class to speak once, many, many years ago, but I wouldn't call that a personal meeting. By the time I met Ruth Gadabee, Brett was using Paladin as his last name professionally, so I never made the stepson-stepmother connection." Sherry cocked her head toward her shoulder. "Do you think TV personalities come down for breakfast every morning and announce to their family, 'Good morning, thank you for joining me today. Stayed tuned and we will eat after this brief commercial break.' I mean, when do they turn themselves off?"

Ray cleared his throat and swept his shoe back and forth along the floor. "You're getting a little sidetracked."

"Sorry. There's a lot to think about."

"To be clear, what you're confirming is that *you* hadn't met Mr. Paladin up to the time of the cook-off?" the detective asked.

"That's right. Been in a classroom with him, but can't say we actually were introduced. I've known of Ruth Gadabee since I started helping out at the store and I familiarized myself with the customer list although when we might have first been introduced, I don't recall. Does any of that matter?"

Ray stayed silent for a moment. He bounced his gaze from the elaborate cornice above the window to Sherry. "When I took initial statements from those who were in the TV studio at the time of the murder, more than one person noted that Carmell Gordy and Brett Paladin had heated words with your father right after the conclusion of the cook-off. Anyone can have a spontaneous argument, set off by who knows what, but witnesses say both Carmell and Brett sought out your father, asking for his whereabouts, as if to pursue an ongoing issue. So, makes sense to ask his daughter whether she had any knowledge of past history with these people, whether it be yours or your father's." Ray rested his hand inside his blazer.

Sherry gave Ray ample time to continue, but there was only the sound of dog paws on the wide plank oak floors. "I don't have any more to add to what you're saying or implying."

The detective removed his hand from his blazer. "Okay."

"My father is close to Brett's mother and apparently has been for quite some time. I'm trying to wrap my head around their closeness, as a matter of fact. He doesn't seem to need me outside of work, like he used to, and I'm guessing her presence is the reason why. With respect to any disagreements between Dad and Brett Paladin, I would think Brett would be thrilled to have my father court his stepmother. Why should Brett even care, frankly? It doesn't sound as if the Paladins and the Gadabees spend holidays together, let alone any other time."

Sherry bent over and picked up a leaf that had hitchhiked a ride inside the store on Ray's shoe. As soon as Sherry lowered her hand to the floor, Chutney and Bean circled around their leashes.

"I have no idea what any alleged argument could have been about, if it was even an argument," Sherry added. "As for Carmell Gordy, it shouldn't surprise you to learn I've done some legwork on my own, and, what I've discovered is she is, or was, the center of the universe over at News Twelve. When someone gets used to the star treatment, good isn't good enough. Her demands might have been approaching diva status. But I don't see how that involves my father." Sherry visually checked her fingernails one by one before plunging her hands in her pockets.

"Yes, people at the station mentioned they saw Carmell talking to my father that morning. And yes, maybe the conversation was a bit animated. And yes, the murder weapon was from this store, but there's a sensible explanation for all that because he didn't commit a crime. Erno Oliveri has never broken a law in his life, as far as I know. The single black eye on his record is an unpaid parking ticket, which he claims is his way of paying homage to Leila. The ticket was issued the day Leila went to witness her grandchild's birth and the town had a temp do her job. Dad loves the fact that Leila would never put a ticket on his twelve-year-old Subaru if it was parked in front of the store. So, he's not going to pay the fine until one or the other of them retires. That's what he claims."

"Leila?"

"Augustin's traffic enforcement officer."

"I see." Ray turned his back to Sherry, took two steps, and turned to face her. "If you're not communicating as much as you used to with your father, isn't your knowledge of his guilt or innocence mere speculation?"

Sherry squinted as if vinegar had been splashed in her eyes. Her temples pulsed. "You don't get it. Dad shouldn't be bothered right now. He's a bit fragile. You need to leave him alone."

Amber faced Ray. "Detective Bease, Sherry's dad is the kindest gentleman I have met in a long time. You're wasting your time if you think he's involved in any way with a murder, other than being at the wrong place at the wrong time." She shot a fast glance at Sherry. Amber raised her chin high. "Steele Dumont should be the one you're investigating, not Erno Oliveri."

Ray, again, placed his hand inside his blazer. He pulled out a pen and began flipping it between his thumb and his middle finger. Each time the pen did a somersault, an image on the barrel shell came to life.

"What's that?" Sherry grabbed the detective's wrist, and the pen froze.

"A buffalo stampede. From the great state of Wyoming," he said.

"How many more states until your collection is complete?"

"Thirteen."

Amber tapped the tip of her shoe on the floor. "I'll be in the back room if you need me."

"No, stay." Sherry's tone was urgent.

"Back to business." Ray cupped the pen between his hands and rolled it back and forth. "Steele Dumont. That's interesting because he's the grandson of your father's girlfriend's best friend."

Sherry's knees gave way like a meringue that had been prepared by stirring, not folding. "No one said anything about her being my dad's girlfriend."

"When I spoke to your father, he was saying goodbye to a Frances Dumont and a Ruth Gadabee, who were paying him a visit at his home." Ray removed a pressed paper from inside his coat. He unfolded and studied the sheet. "Your father used the term 'sweetheart' for one woman and the name 'Frances' for the other." I heard the women say, 'see you tomorrow.' Your father replied, 'thank goodness tomorrow is a new day and I haven't made a mess of it yet.' I transcribed it word for word as he spoke."

"I'm not surprised he felt that way," Sherry huffed. "He's had a rough couple of days, starting with his trip to the emergency room day before yesterday."

Amber checked the clock. "Some could argue you were the reason why he had to go."

"Amber, are you proposing Steele Dumont should be a person of interest?" The detective's voice was as warm and inviting as a fresh buttered roll.

"Steele Dumont may be a scorned lover." Amber crossed her arms. "He told us he dated Carmell but their relationship, up until her death, became more about catering to her needs than being a partner. That can be a bitter pill to swallow for a man, or anyone, for that matter. I counseled many couples in my practice where one partner had become the other's live-in workhorse. By the time the couple decides the imbalance needs adjusting, it's often too late. Steele wasn't getting paid. The poor guy was dog sitting during his workday, along with running Carmell's personal errands, instead of gaining the valuable work experience in television he signed up for. That's all pretty demeaning." Amber uncrossed her arms and stepped toward the front door without meeting Sherry's gaze. "I'm going to walk these guys. I'll be right back." Amber hooked the dogs up to their leashes and closed the door behind her.

"She had a bit of a tone." Ray tapped his pen on the palm of his hand until ink freckles appeared.

"She doesn't like my suggestion that the owner of News Twelve had reasons to want to see Carmell gone." Sherry handed Ray an antibacterial towelette from a dispenser by the register.

"Damien Castle? I'm thinking out loud here, but why would he take the life of the person who's the face of his franchise?" Ray tossed the ink-stained wipe in the trash can. He pointed the pen tip at Sherry. "If Castle's station was leaking money, the way his colleagues suggest, why did he even hire an expensive personality who he must have known he couldn't control?" Ray tapped the pen on his forehead.

Sherry passed him another towelette with her gaze on the new ink stains.

"But why would any of that bother Amber?" The detective asked.

"She and Damien kind of clicked on their first meeting. You know how that goes."

Ray's eyebrows rose.

The jingle announced the return of Amber and the two terriers. "All canine bladders are empty." She leaned down to unhook the leashes and was knocked down when the front door swung open.

"I'm so sorry." Leila set her pad of paper down on the floor as she offered Amber a hand up. "Might not be the best place to do your dog grooming."

"No problem. Here you go." Amber retrieved Leila's pad of tickets and handed it to her. "I hope you don't give me a citation for parking myself in a loading zone."

"Good one." Leila adjusted her cap, which had shifted askew when she stood upright. "No tickets this morning. I want to know if the gray sedan outside belongs to anyone in Mr. Oliveri's store. The meter has expired."

The detective peered out the front window. He raised his hand above his head. "Guilty."

"Only a soft warning, sir. I would never penalize you for spending your money at the Ruggery. Want you to be aware of the violation."

"Thank you, um . . ." Ray moved toward Leila and zeroed in on the name tag on her headgear. ". . . Leila. I was winding things up here."

"No problem, sir. Have a great day." Leila let herself out.

"So, that's the infamous Leila. Your father's got a lot of people campaigning for his best interests. Lucky guy." Ray shuffled toward the door, passing the tool collection set out on the counter. He picked up a shiny metal punch tool with the sharp pointed end and the wooden handle.

"Can I get a quick demonstration of how this works? Doctor says hobbies can lower blood pressure, and that would mean fewer office visits."

Sherry rolled her eyes.

"I'd be happy to show him, Sherry." Amber spoke as if Sherry needed convincing. "I could use the practice explaining the process."

Sherry pushed her hair behind her ears. Without lowering her hand, she then flicked her hair back to its original arrangement. "Of course. I would never turn down the chance to enlighten a potential customer." Sherry eyed the tool in the detective's grasp. "You don't need that. All the supplies are already over there at the table. You can leave that right where you found it." She directed her open palm toward him. He took his time handing over the tool. Sherry closed her grip and watched as the pair settled in at the demonstration table.

After a few minutes, Amber and the detective rejoined Sherry at the front counter.

"Are you hooked?" Sherry's pun collided with Amber's cringe. "Trade joke."

"I think I'll pass for now, but I can sure see how that tool could leave a serious puncture wound." Ray held out his finger painted with a drop of blood. "You have to be careful handling it." He favored the wounded finger as he collected his hat. He adjusted the brim over his forehead. "Thank you, ladies."

"Ray?"

"Yes, Ms. Oliveri."

"I'm asking you the following, and I'm not addressing Detective Ray Bease, but rather a person I have reached a certain level of familiarity with who hopefully cares about the well-being of one of my family members. May I have your word you'll not approach my father with questions that will upset him and that you'll contact me first, if need be?"

"I have a job to perform, and I'll do it with the utmost professionalism. I don't make deals." Detective Bease pulled the door open and slipped out of the store.

"I should've had lunch with him when he asked me months ago." Sherry leaned her elbows on the checkout counter and cradled her head in her hands.

By late afternoon, store traffic subsided. Sherry savored a moment of inactivity. "Amber, I'm going to give Dad a quick call. And I'll give these pups their afternoon meal." Sherry clapped her hands and whistled. Chutney and Bean scampered over. Before heading to the back room, Sherry pulled out the Rolodex of customer cards.

"Oh, and while we were out, Beverly Van Ardan left a message that she might stop by before closing time, so if you wouldn't mind reading her purchase history, I think the knowledge would be valuable in guiding her. She has a tendency to get carried away with her projects, while at the same time losing sight of the big decorating picture. She's tried to return gorgeous custom rugs because she chose the wrong green or brown, and we can't do that. The important tip to remember about her is her motto: 'always give me colors that can be found on the food pyramid.' Dad had to bring in a cantaloupe, a mango, a steak, rare not medium, and lobster shells to match her color choices to our yarn dye. She does keep us on our toes.

She's one of our best customers, so she requires the velvet-glove treatment."

"I look forward to meeting her. She sounds intriguing. I'll tap into my best therapy etiquette, firm and soft at the same time." Amber laughed.

"Think hard-boiled egg. Firm touch, soft delivery."

"Being around you makes me so hungry, for some reason. Has anyone ever mentioned that?" Amber made her way to the index card collection and began sifting through.

Sherry carried her phone to the back room, where she prepared two bowls of dry food for the dogs. Each canine attacked his nuggets with vigorous conviction when she set down the bowls. A symphony of crunches filled the air. Sherry took a seat at the small table.

"Hi, Dad. Are you taking it easy today?" Sherry watched the dogs lick their bowls spotless. "Hope you're not going stir-crazy."

"Hi, Sher. I thought I would enjoy the rest, but, yes, I'm getting a bit antsy. You know what I always say, 'taking a seat at the table doesn't mean you'll enjoy the meal.'"

Sherry reached down and tickled Bean's neck. "I've never heard you say that, but I'll give your words full consideration." She scooted forward on the stark wooden chair. "Detective Bease was here earlier." She paused when a low grumble came through the phone. Sherry arched her aching back, causing her to nearly slide off the edge of the seat. "He said he spoke to you again. Dad, if you could pinpoint where you were at the exact time Carmell Gordy was murdered and identify someone who can confirm what you say, that will help your cause. We need to figure out how the

Ruggery's hook tool found its way into Carmell's neck. Wouldn't hurt to offer an explanation of why you seemed to be having words with Carmell and Brett, which was witnessed by a number of people." Sherry's tongue caught on the roof of her mouth as she forced the last words out.

"I was in the men's room. When I left you, that's exactly where I went, although I did open a few doors that weren't the bathroom before I found the right one. There was no one else with me. I passed no one, and the men's room was empty. What's the chance the one time you would ever want someone listening to your business in the lavatory, not a soul? I passed Steele Dumont as I was leaving the men's room, now that I think about it. He was moving at breakneck speed, which is probably not the best choice of words, and nearly knocked me over when we met head on. I bet he won't remember that. He was fiercely in pursuit of something. His eyes were cloudy with distraction."

Sherry stood, causing a canine tsunami of excitement. The dogs pranced around Sherry's feet. "Do you think Steele was involved with the murder? There's plenty of concrete evidence that Carmell and he had a contentious relationship. I don't suppose Frances Dumont has ever mentioned her grandson's personal life, has she?"

"Steele has a loyalty to the station, she has often commented. Yes, he was involved with Carmell Gordy for a time, but his internship was more important to him. He's not an angry young fellow, like a lot of kids today. He's a hard worker, who may suffer from an overeagerness to please. He's the light of Frances's life. You can't suspect my friend's grandson. You can't."

Sherry put her phone on speaker and clicked the photo library icon. She scrolled through her recent photos and found the one she had taken at the television station. "One more question about Steele."

"I don't know him beyond the picture Frances paints of his genuine character. I met him one time when he drove my gals over to the store to bring me some coffee. Frances usually does the driving, but had cut her hand splitting a bagel. The boy didn't even come through the front door. He said 'hi' as he held the door open for the ladies. He waited for them in the car."

Sherry swiped the phone screen. She clicked the photo library icon and scrolled to the picture of the parking ticket. With a swipe of her fingers, she zeroed in on the ticket date. "The morning of the cook-off, did you go out at all before I picked you up?"

Erno let out a hum. "I stopped by the store that morning. That's when I picked up the punch tool. I know that fact sounds incriminating, but that's the truth."

"Why did you bother to bring a punch tool with you?"

"I was going to show you my new brainchild. I had the greatest idea of using the tool to carve a canyon down the length of your pickles so you can stuff them. Don't you love stuffed olives? But how in the world do they get the tiny stuffing in the tiny hole? Well, I've got the answer. I think it's an idea whose time has come." Erno sighed. "I'm beginning to get a headache. Do you mind if I cut this conversation short and go lie down?"

"Of course. Take care and love you." Sherry put down the phone and stared at the dogs that were transfixed on her. “Amber?” She sidestepped the small mascots and found Amber working with index cards. “Any sign of Mrs. Van Ardan?”

“Judging by your description of the woman, I definitely would know if she was in the store, even without ever having met her. But no. No sign of her.” Amber squared up the index cards. “Good news. I got a text from my rental agent, and she has convinced the landlord to allow Bean to stay with me. So, I can take him home after work tomorrow hopefully. My bank wired an amended security deposit to cover the extra cleaning, and, when I get the go-ahead, Bean comes with me. But it’s worth every extra penny. I’m so excited.”

A young woman entered the store, holding a toddler’s hand. Bean scooted under the table, leaving Chutney as official greeter.

“What a sweet dog.” The customer picked up her child. “Are you Sherry Frazzelle, or, I’m sorry, Oliveri? I’ve seen the name listed both ways in our committee notes.”

Sherry waved her hand. “I am, both, I mean. But more of the latter. No, only the latter. What can I do for you?”

“I’m on the Augustin Founder’s Day oversight committee, and I understand you accepted our invitation to stand on the podium along with other town dignitaries.”

“I’m not a dignitary of any sort, Mrs. . . .”

“Kristi Cornell, and this is my daughter, Kayla. You’re our home cook extraordinaire. I’m here in hopes of persuading you to bring your signature dish for the local talent display table.” The woman lifted her little girl and tipped the youngster toward

Sherry, as if offering up a pitcher of margaritas. The toddler reached out her gherkin-size fingers and rubbed Sherry's arm.

Sherry's skin tingled under the toddler's gentle touch. "Sure."

"Perfect," Kristi cooed. "Mission accomplished."

Heads turned as the singular note of the bell pierced the air. Beverly Van Ardan in an all-white pantsuit sauntered through the door. She tightened the knot in her peach and green scarf and adjusted the cuffs of her white gloves. "Hello, Kristi. Your daughter is as adorable as ever. Hello, Sherry." Beverly turned to face Amber. "Who do we have here?"

Sherry nudged closer to Amber. "Mrs. Van Ardan, glad you could make it. This is Amber Sherman. She's working here until my father feels up to returning."

"Nice to meet you, dear." Beverly reached out and cradled Amber's hand.

Sherry rolled down her shirtsleeves to warm her chilled arms. "I'm finishing up with Kristi, but Amber is free to assist you, Mrs. Van Ardan."

Beverly dropped Amber's hand and transferred her gaze to Kristi. "How are preparations going for Founder's Day? And, more important, are you giving all who wish to have a say equal opportunity to be heard?"

"When you say 'all who wish,' I presume you mean your family? In the spirit of Andre August Dahlback, who was open to all opinions when he laid down the plans for our great town, our committee has decided to give a representative from your family a reasonable amount of time to present his or her findings during the opening ceremonies. We will be contacting you shortly with details. Have a good day." Kristi Cornell cradled her little girl's head, turned, and left the store. "Thank you again, Sherry."

"Finally, someone with a grasp on reality," Beverly huffed. "Now, let's map out my rug design, shall we?"

Chapter 9

Sherry led the dog parade through the patio doors. In one hand she held shriveled string bean pods that contained the seeds for next year's crop. In the other were four jalapeno peppers. She released her grip and let the contents cascade onto the kitchen counter. Sherry tore off sheets of paper towels, lined a spot on the counter with them, and began removing the beans from their shells. The wrinkled, chipped, or otherwise unusable seeds were tossed out. The remaining beans were laid in a single layer on the paper. Sherry found a clear storage bag that would hold the beans when they were dry. She labeled the bag with the day's date and "string beans" and placed it beside the paper towel. She washed her hands, found her to-do list, and sat down at the kitchen table.

Sherry showed the list to her four-legged shadows. "I can cross off 'put garden to bed for the winter.' One more season come and gone. 'Collect and dry bean seeds'—done and done." Sherry dropped the list. She examined the jalapenos. "I'm going to see if I can make myself a pest spray with these peppers, a little soap, mint oil, and vinegar. Who knows, maybe I have the makings of the next great garden-critter repellent right here in my kitchen."

Sherry checked the time on the wall clock. The minutes were ticking by faster than she hoped. The morning sun had risen with the sluggishness of the looming autumn season, and she had lost the inspiration to get out to her garden early. The ripple effect of procrastination left her short of time prior to dropping the dogs with Amber and continuing on to the farmer's market.

Sherry rummaged for a blank sheet of paper and pen and took them to the refrigerator. She surveyed the chilly contents of the door shelves. The momentum of the door opening must have spun a jar around because the label wasn't facing her as she had left it. The offender that dared to be different was easily spotted among the conformers. She repositioned the condiment and nodded in satisfaction that all was in order. As she pulled her hand away from the mustard jar, her phone rang. In an effort to catch the call, she jettisoned the door shut with such force that glass rattled inside. Her shoulders arched up with the clatter.

The phone on the counter sat in silence. She moved over to her desk and lifted the lid of her laptop. She accepted the incoming video call. "Hi, Marla. You got my text. Thanks for getting back to me so soon. You're just the person I need to talk to." Sherry carried her computer to the living room sofa and settled in. Seated in front of the window, she caught sight of Eileen picking up her paper across the street.

"I hope you don't mind, but I need to finish my breakfast while we chat. I wasn't going to call until later because I thought today was your day at the farmer's market. Usually you're out early at the Dumont farm picking up your jars to sell. It's unlike you to be running late. What's up?"

Sherry shifted on the soft seat cushion. She sank her fingers into a tangle in her hair that her image in the upper right of the computer screen reflected. "There's so much going on I thought I'd pick up the pickles last night to save time. They're all in my car ready to go. I'm glad I did because I'm already running behind schedule." Sherry adjusted the laptop lid until she got the desired lighting. She inclined her head, in hopes of reducing the shadows under her eyes. "I need more sleep."

"Speak up. I didn't hear that." Marla leaned into her computer screen. "Stop fussing with yourself."

"Guess what? I've got a new mouth to feed, but not for too much longer." Sherry tipped her laptop camera toward the floor. "Say hi to Amber's new dog."

"He's precious," Marla cooed. "I was thinking about you last night when I was watching *Pressure Cooker* on the Oven Lovin' Network. That show cracks me up. The host makes the cooks do the craziest tasks for the sake of a new blender. It's not even about being a skilled cook. Made me think that it must be about time for your next taste-test party."

Sherry laughed as she reframed herself on the computer's camera. "You know me too well. It's tomorrow night."

"Any cute guys invited?" Marla winked.

Sherry hurled a glance to the ceiling. "My neighbor Eileen's husband is pretty cute. He'll most likely be here."

"What am I going to do with you, my dear sister? I meant eligible men." Marla clicked her tongue against the roof of her mouth and shook her head. "What's the theme of the party, besides 'help Sherry get her social life together'?"

"I don't have time for a social life. This is as good as it gets." Sherry watched Marla take a bite of a pancake oozing with syrup. "The theme is Judge'n Curry. I'm making my Peanut Butter Chicken Curry and Spinach Lentil Curry. The winning dish voted on by my guests gets submitted to the Hurry Up, Curry Sup recipe contest that's run by *Modern Renaissance* magazine."

"Sounds like you can pull the evening off. Cool as a cucumber as usual, everything under control." Marla didn't bother swallowing her bite before she spoke.

"To be honest with you, I'm thinking of canceling the evening because Dad is in a tough spot, and that's deflating my already weak party spirit." Sherry's attention drifted to the window, where she spotted Eileen at the bottom of the driveway waving her newspaper in an effort to get Sherry's attention. Sherry waggled her fingers toward her neighbor.

"Are you there?" Marla thrust her face toward the computer, distorting her image as she closed in on the camera.

"Sorry, Eileen's performing her morning happy dance outside my window." Sherry turned her attention back to the window. "Dad's not doing much to get himself out of Detective Bease's crosshairs. And the detective isn't happy I've begun sniffing around his territory. If by under control you mean total fiasco, you've hit the nail on the head."

"Forget about Dad's aiding in his own defense. You've got to step in. No hesitation. The correct outcome's in your hands because you were at the cook-off together; you invited Dad to accompany you in the first place." Marla pumped her fist. "You have no choice."

Sherry squeezed a gravelly groan out of the top of her throat.

"Do you have any notion of who might have killed Carmell Gordy?" Marla asked.

"If I didn't know any better, I'd join the crowd and be on board with Dad's being the prime suspect. Beyond the evidence left at the scene, I'm having trouble piecing missing segments of time together. Dad doesn't have much of an alibi." Sherry rested her chin in her hand. "The problem is the cast of characters there is as complex as a cioppino. To make matters worse, the person I suspect might have committed the murder is closely related to Mrs. Dumont, the pickle lady and a close friend of Dad's. The runner-up on my suspect list is someone who has put a twinkle in Amber's eye, and she's not happy I'm considering him. How can I even think of having a party when no one is in a festive mood? I feel like crawling back in bed and pulling the covers over my head."

Marla put down her fork with a sharp clank. "I'll take a stab in the dark and assume you recorded the cook-off?"

Sherry gasped. "Marla, don't say stab in the dark."

"Poor choice of words, but you know what I mean. If you taped it, you have to watch it. Maybe there's a detail you missed in real time that could provide a clue. Could be worthwhile to pinpoint Carmell's mood that day. Did she have fear in her eyes? Was she projecting anger as she read her lines? Did she act anxious and twitchy on camera? Body language is a real science. Maybe you should read up on that."

"I did tape the show. I haven't had the inclination to watch it yet. Besides, Carmell wasn't even involved in the cook-off. The other anchor, Brett Paladin, introduced us, interviewed us while we cooked, and gave out the winning trophy. Carmell made an appearance at the end to do a short promo for the next segment, but didn't even try a bite of anyone's food. She couldn't get off the set fast enough. She said the lights were too hot and her makeup was beginning to run. The reason the room was hot was because it was a small set and we were roasting our appetizers at high heat in portable mini ovens to save time. There wasn't any ventilation in there either. Must have been a fire hazard, come to think of it. But that's beside the point." Sherry paused and wiped the back of her hand across her chin. "I did set the recording for eight that morning because we weren't given an exact time of the cook-off, only a ballpark estimate. I might have caught Carmell before and even after the cook-off. So, tell me, what would I be looking for if I watched the tape?"

"Think about it this way." Marla picked up her fork and waggled the silverware in unison with her words. Bits of pancake sprayed in all directions. "When you're initially writing a recipe for a contest, what's the first step?"

Sherry shut her eyes and envisioned an empty kitchen counter. "I begin with the theme of the contest. Let's say, quick appetizer or best use of phyllo dough. That notion helps steer my direction right away. I go through my recipe collection to see if I have any recipes fitting the theme."

Marla thumped her fork on the table. "Exactly."

Sherry's eyes popped open. "Exactly what?"

"When you have to narrow down your choices, you do so according to the contest theme. You know how you take a tried and true recipe, come up with a magical spin on a classic, and suddenly it's a Sherry original." Marla skewered another bite of pancake.

"Yes, but what does that have to do with the tape of the cook-off? I'm getting confused."

"I'll leave you with this nugget. Tackle your investigation like you would a recipe contest. The motive of the murder is the theme, the recipe you have to create is made up of the clues you uncover, those are the ingredients, and the prize isn't a trophy or a check; it's much, much bigger. Clearing Dad's name is the payoff. The recording you made might be able to help you put the Sherry spin on how things went down that morning. I've got to get moving, Sher. But I believe in you. Talk soon." The last Sherry saw of her sister was her finger reaching for the keyboard.

"Sometimes my family is harder to figure out than how to make mashed potatoes without lumps." Sherry shut her laptop and faced her kitchen. "Let me see if I have all the ingredients for my curry recipes."

Sherry walked to her spice rack and pulled out the cumin, coriander, chili flakes, turmeric, and black pepper bottles for her curry blend. She set a new container of peanut butter, two sweet potatoes, and a large onion on the counter. She found the bag of bulk lentils in the cupboard, along with a jar of chutney, some olive oil, and the chicken stock. She broke the ingredients into groups, according to each recipe and length of time for preparation.

"I'm set. All the other ingredients are in the refrigerator. I'll start cooking after work." Sherry reached down and stroked each dog on the head. "Thanks for being such a good audience, guys." Sherry backed away from the kitchen counter and ran her eyes down her organized ingredients. "Okay, Marla, these are my recipe ingredients. Now if only I could be as clear when recognizing clues."

Chapter 10

"Dad, I'm short on time. I can't talk long. I have to unload the pickles." Sherry peered over her shoulder at the boxes of brined cucumbers lining her car's back seat. Outside her parked car other farmer's market vendors were unloading their wares from their vehicles. She clicked the phone's speaker setting and set the device on the dashboard. She retrieved her purse from the front passenger seat. "I'm running a bit late because I dropped the dogs off with Amber. Actually, I've been running late all morning."

"I called because Marla said she spoke to you. She hinted that you felt you weren't getting much help from me where the investigation is concerned, but I don't know what else I can offer. She also said you have a strong suspicion about someone in particular being the guilty party, but refused to spill the beans. I think I know who you suspect, though. Please prove yourself wrong, Sherry."

Sherry heard her father exhale a windstorm into the phone. As she waited for the squall to subside, she reached in her purse for her cashbox key. Erno wasn't going to like what she had to say, but Sherry had to get the looming weight off her chest. She squeezed her eyes shut and opened her mouth. "I'm convinced Steele Dumont's guilty, but I'm having as hard a time wrapping my head around the idea of Frances Dumont's grandson being a murderer as you are."

"I can't believe it. I won't believe it." Erno's voice was no louder than a whisper. "Ruth and Frances were here this morning with my coffee and a breakfast burrito they made for me. It'll break their hearts if what you're saying is true. I'd rather the authorities arrest me and spare the ladies any pain."

"You don't mean that. So many signs indicate Steele reached a breaking point after one too many personal requests from Carmell Gordy. His relationship with her ended on a sour note, her dog hates him, and I took a picture of a parking ticket on a desk in the room where Steele was keeping Bean down at the station. The ticket was dated the day of the murder."

"People get parking tickets. What's the big deal?" The conviction in Erno's voice came across as diluted as skim milk.

"The location noted on the ticket was in front of your store, time stamped exactly when you would have been there before the cook-off. Seeming like the perfect opportunity for him to get in the store and help himself to a punch tool. I could send you the photo of the ticket with all that information if you want to see for yourself."

"I don't want to see it. Besides, the murderer somehow got his hands on the punch tool when I misplaced the darn thing inside the station. If Steele did it, and he didn't, he needn't have made a special trip to the Ruggery. Seems I was amenable enough to bring the murder weapon right to the scene."

"Dad, you have to tell me if Steele was in your store that day."

"I told you. Prior to the cook-off, I met the young man one time when he drove Frances and Ruth over with my morning coffee. He was doing them a special favor. Yes, I admit I saw him again the morning of the cook-off through the window, by Wine One One, but he didn't see me. He seemed to be waiting for someone. His arms were crossed, and he was leaning against the side of a snazzy sports car." Erno paused.

"You're making that noise, Dad." Sherry screwed up her brow. "I know that tongue-snapping habit you have when you have something you're trying to say, but you can't get the words out."

Erno sighed. "Maybe he was in my store for a minute that morning."

"Dad!"

"Steele must have seen the lights on, even though the 'Closed' sign was on the door. He asked if he could use the restroom. I'm not running one of those hoity-toity establishments that turns people away if nature calls at an inopportune time. That's uncivilized."

"So you must have seen him come and go, right? Was he carrying anything out when he left? Was his hand in his pocket?" Sherry's voice took on more urgency than she had felt the time she had one minute left on the contest clock to plate four stuffed chicken breasts for the judges and she couldn't find her spatula.

Erno's tongue castanet began again in earnest.

"Dad?"

"I didn't want to be late for you, so I locked the door from the inside and asked Steele to close up when he was done with the restroom. Even if he had access to any number of punch tools while he was in the store, what does that prove?"

Sherry gripped the dashboard with both hands, dropping the cashbox key in the process. She banged her forehead on the steering wheel when she leaned forward to find it. She wedged her finger in the back of the brake pedal to retrieve the small key and stuffed the metal piece in her pocket. "Did you just hear yourself ask that question? What would your answer be? By the way, you don't just have one punch tool marked 'do not remove from O.R.,' do you? Amber and I have found at least two others in the last few days. Do you know how many you had on the day of the murder?"

Erno hummed a descending scale of notes. "Definitely more than two, but less than eight. Or nine. Hard to say because even though I mark them 'do not remove,' if a customer who misplaced his or her tool comes in in an emergency situation, I lend them a store model. Like I always say, 'If I have two of something, you have won. That's won with a *w*."

"Right." Sherry closed her eyes and smiled. Her smile morphed to a frown as her eyes popped open. "They all must have your fingerprints on them. But that's not proof of much, because the tools are from the Ruggery, so, of course, you've touched them. Realistically, if Steele committed the crime, he could have used the tool you brought to the station, which somehow found its way out of my cook-off supply bag. Or, he might have brought in his own that he picked up at the store sometime. If he wanted someone else blamed for his dirty deed, he might have seen you as an easy fit. Maybe he has a vendetta against you, Dad. Does that make sense?"

"Why would he have a vendetta against me? You're making me feel guilty for being considerate." Erno cleared his throat. "I don't know what Steele was doing parked outside the store that morning. I think I need to use the restroom, sweetie. Didn't you say you have to get to work?"

Sherry set the phone down on the dashboard and removed her sunglasses. The rising autumn sun streaming in through the windshield stung her eyes. She dabbed the trail of a tear from her cheek.

"Dad, I'm going to have a chat with Detective Bease later, so if you think of any more information to add, please call me." Sherry heard a mumble, but didn't attempt to interpret the meaning.

Her phone was silent. Erno was gone.

Sherry made four trips between her car and her vendor table, carrying the boxes of pickles. The "Dumont Farm Perfect Storm Pickle" banner was the final detail she wrestled with. The giant pickle sign hung behind her pickle-paraphernalia-laden table to entice people to purchase the briny spears and chips. She draped the cloth along the makeshift partition that defined one side of her space.

Sherry filled her cashbox with twenty-five dollars' worth of small bills and coins for making change. She organized the money by denomination, turning all the bills presidential face side up and squaring the edges in a stack as neat as the layers of a buttercream-filled Napoleon.

A voice startled her as she closed the cashbox. "Sherry Oliveri? Would you permit me to interview you after we go on-air?"

She raised her head.

"We're doing a live feed, so I want to make sure we don't surprise you." Brett Paladin approached with a microphone in one hand and his cell phone in the other. "We're doing a remote from the market this morning to celebrate the fall harvest." Brett turned around and called out to a group of three individuals huddled together behind him. "Hey, guys, could we get the camera over here?"

"Sure. I'm here all day, so anytime, as long as I'm not involved with a customer. I love to talk about our product. Our pickles are the best in . . ." Sherry's words drifted to silence as Brett turned and walked away.

He joined Damien Castle, Truman Fletcher, and Kirin, the camera operator.

Sherry surveyed the increasing number of potential shoppers trickling in.

A little girl yanked her mother's arm, directing her closer to Sherry's table. "Mommy, over here. Pickles. My favorite."

"How much salt is in your pickles?" a woman in a fuzzy black fleece asked. "I get puffy if I so much as sniff a granule of sodium." Her mini-me daughter dropped her mother's hand and reached for a Perfect Storm jar. Sherry held her breath until the tiny exploring hand retreated.

"We reduced the sea salt used in our secret recipe a smidge this year." Sherry saw Salt Restrictive Woman's mouth twist into a judgmental pucker. "The result is the bold brininess we are famous for, with a nod to customer preferences. Our pickles are so packed with perfectly balanced acidic fortitude that a spear or two is all that's needed to perfectly complement whatever you're serving. I recommend restricting the addition of salt on the rest of the meal, and let our pickle partner with your food and, not unlike a good marriage, the result will be a strong bond that brings out the best in both sides."

The woman's mouth relaxed. "I'll take two jars."

As the woman and child backed away from Sherry's table with their purchases, a man with a telltale hat took their place. "That was quite a sales pitch. Pickles and marriage share a close bond. Who knew?"

"Detective Bease. I'm a little surprised to see you here." Sherry picked up a pickle jar and held it label-side out toward Ray. "This season's batch is exceptional. You can't leave without a jar." The word "can't" was punctuated by the jar's being thrust toward the detective.

"How can I resist if it also comes with the guarantee of a good marriage?" Ray's lip curled upward enough to expose a dimple. He accepted the jar from Sherry's hand. "Can you explain the pickling process to me?"

Sherry inclined her head. "Are you serious?"

"More serious than a bowl of my grandmother's hand-churned espresso ice cream."

Before Sherry could begin her tutorial, a man as bald as an Ugli fruit and a woman with hair the color of champagne approached the Perfect Storm table. "We would also love to hear how your pickles are made, if you don't mind." The man picked up a tiny plastic fork and jabbed a sample pickle off a paper plate. "You're right. These are fantastic."

"Happy to share." Sherry sucked in a breath. "The magic starts at the Dumont farm located right here in Augustin, which is certified organic. Pickling cucumbers grow in raised beds there. From midsummer until early fall we harvest the little critters. The farm has a certified kitchen where this year it was up to me to sterilize hundreds of jars and lids. I mixed up huge amounts of hot brine using water, white vinegar, dill, dill seed, garlic, sea salt, and a pinch or two of red pepper flakes. Again, all organic."

"Do you do all that work solo or do you have a partner?" The hair-challenged man picked up a jar.

"Anyone significant?" Ray asked.

Sherry let her gaze fall to the table. She blinked hard before making eye contact again with Ray. "Mrs. Dumont occasionally pitches in because the operation is still in her name. I guess you could call her my significant other. But I'm really her intern."

"Sounds like the brine recipe is a secret," the woman added.

"When those thumb-size babies get in the hot water blend, it transforms them into flavor machines." The man laughed from deep within his belly.

"Getting into hot water." The detective jutted his chin forward. "That can also happen to people, but more often than not it doesn't end on a positive note." Ray put the jar down in front of Sherry. "I'll take this one, please."

"And we'll take two, please." The woman pushed two jars beside the one Ray had chosen.

"You go right ahead. I'm in no hurry." Ray picked up his jar and hugged it to his chest.

Sherry rang up the two jars and collected the money. "Thank you so much. Enjoy." Sherry reached her hand toward Ray's potential purchase. "Are you ready for me to write that up now?"

The detective fingered the brim of his hat. "Yes,

thanks." He slid the jar toward Sherry, along with a ten-dollar bill.

Sherry counted out the change, but, instead of passing the money along, she curled her fingers tight. "Did you know Steele Dumont drives Damien Castle's car to run errands?"

"I was not aware of that."

"I realize Steele's not a paid employee, but isn't it unusual he would drive the boss's car? That seems like a pretty nice perk." Sherry checked the man's expression.

He was stone-faced.

"Have you checked into what Steele's daily duties are over at News Twelve? Maybe he wasn't doing as many personal errands for Carmell Gordy as he said he was. Could it be that Steele had transferred his loyalty from team Carmell to team Damien? If Carmell wasn't happy about that, she might have been punishing Steele. Another reason he was pushed to his limit."

"I've been to the station a number of times. I had an informative meeting with Damien Castle. I can't go into details, you know that, but I can tell you Steele's duties are in line with an intern's. The job description is left extremely vague for a reason," Ray said.

"I think he's the one all signs point to. Steele, that is. Maybe Damien Castle isn't an innocent bystander, either. His kid-glove treatment of Carmell might have contributed to her diva behavior. I couldn't help but notice the only reserved spot in the parking lot was for Carmell Gordy. Not even one for Damien or co-anchor Brett Paladin."

Sherry put the coins in Ray's hand. "It might be time to act."

"I appreciate your insight, as always, but acting in haste fueled by sentiment is not a chapter in *The Effective Detective.* I can hear my fledgling ex-partner flipping through the pages of that textbook that served him so well, this very moment in search of a directive. But what's not in the detective training manual is the role intuition plays in the investigative process. That's what makes a veteran a veteran. Detective Ray Bease is a gut instinct–driven bloodhound from the mean streets."

Sherry raised her nose high in the air and, in doing so, misdirected some of the coins she was depositing in Ray's hand. One rolled off the table and disappeared in the trampled grass.

"Have you spoken to your father today?" Ray plunged his change in his pocket.

Sherry's gaze drifted to Ray's pants. "A coin pouch would make organizing your change a snap."

"So would being able to use a credit card. Imagine that. I wouldn't need any cash at all." He stared at the "Cash Only" sign next to the register.

"The credit card processing fees are prohibitive for an operation our size. Anyway, yes, I spoke to Dad, and I don't wish to say any more about that."

The detective exhaled with heft.

"Excuse me, Sherry. In two minutes the broadcast will be live. Oh, hey, Detective. Bease was it?" Brett Paladin hustled over to the edge of Sherry's table and held the microphone up to his lips. "Testing, testing."

"I guess I'm almost on." Sherry adjusted two jars of pickles that were out of alignment with the others. She angled her head toward the detective as he stepped aside. Ray greeted Damien Castle and gave lengthy admiration to the handheld camera Kirin was balancing on her shoulder.

Brett sidled up next to Sherry, and the light on the camera glowed red. "Brett Paladin here at the Augustin Farmer's Market. We have flown south from Chessie's Chick-Inn Custom Birdhouses and joined Sherry and her Dumont Farm Perfect Storm Pickles. Guess you could say everyone's in good spear-its here today." Brett tilted his head toward Sherry, who in turn recoiled. "Our faithful viewers may remember Sherry recently won News Twelve's Appetizer Roast. It's dill-iteful to see you, Sherry."

Sherry put her hand on the stem of the mic. "Appetizer cook-off. It was a cook-off not roast."

"My mistake. Sherry is Augustin's top home cook and possibly top pickler, too. She's a busy lady." Brett uncurled his fingers and dropped his hand to his side, leaving Sherry the sole bearer of the microphone.

"I'm helping out a friend who's considering retirement from the pickle business. I do jar my own pickles at home, but here at the farmer's market, we sell the Dumont family's heirloom organic pickle. Would you like a sample?" Sherry used the butt of the microphone to point out the paper plate showcasing the pickle spears.

Brett helped himself to one. He studied the dark green vegetable while flipping the briny cucumber from front to back. He snapped it in half, and the force of the crisp break sent up a shower of tart juice. He took a few bites, chewing with such enthusiasm his jaw muscles bulged. "This very well may be the perfect pickle, as the name suggests. Folks, you've got to come down and buy a jar. Any cooking competitions in your future, or is that a secret?"

Sherry let a robust laugh escape that she immediately wanted to recapture. "There's one coming up, yes."

"And how do you get your culinary muscles primed for the big day, Sherry?" Brett's voice took on a voluminous quality. A small crowd was beginning to form behind the camerawoman.

"After I've chosen a couple of recipes I'd consider entering, I host a tasting party. My guests provide the feedback to help me narrow down the choices. I think my track record of wins proves the idea behind the party's been a success. I'm having one tomorrow night, as a matter of fact." Sherry's gaze followed a young family as they bypassed her table. "I better get back to work." She placed the mic in Brett's hand.

"Well, folks, there you have it. The secret to a cook-off champion's success. After the commercial break we'll be visiting the Norman family, whose farm, aptly named Berried Alive, supplies the market with the freshest berries around. We'll return in two minutes." Brett lowered the mic. "Thanks, Sherry. Have a good day." Brett backed up a few steps, where Damien Castle joined him.

They exchanged words before Damien moved forward.

The man, who was a head taller than Sherry, thrust his hand out. "Ms. Oliveri, nice to see you again."

"We'll see you at the berry stand, boss." Brett left with Kirin.

Sherry grimaced as another potential customer circumvented her pickle display. "Of course, good to see you again. Would you be interested in a jar of pickles? They make a great hostess gift for your next night out." Sherry's words were cushioned in a pillow of breathy urgency.

"I'm interested in giving your friend Amber a call to see if maybe she might join me for a bite to eat sometime soon. I would ask you for her number, but I don't want to put you on the spot, so I'd be grateful if you would pass along my business card with the invitation to give me a call." Damien located the wallet in his pants pocket from which he produced a business card. He set the small rectangle of information on the table. "Thank you so much. Good to see you." Damien stowed away his wallet and checked his phone that was embedded in his other hand. He scanned the card on the table before trailing his colleagues on to the next location site.

"He could have at least bought a jar as a token of appreciation." Sherry sighed.

Sherry spent the warmer side of the morning and sun-kissed afternoon answering pickle inquiries, managing inventory, and keeping her confined area tidy and inviting. With thirty minutes until closing, and the barrage of people thinning to a sparse few, she squashed a developing yawn before her growing weariness was publicly advertised. Piercing the sleepy fog that was beginning to build in Sherry's brain, a voice jarred Sherry's half-opened mouth shut.

"Long day?"

Shifting her gaze left, Sherry met the gaze of a woman in a beige barn coat and navy slacks. She was carrying a notepad and a recording device. "Patti Mellitt. Nice to see you again."

"Equally nice to see you, Sherry. You spread yourself thin, don't you? Cook-offs, working at your father's store, pickle purveyor. How do you find the time?" Patti set down her ever-present notepad on Sherry's table, spun a jar of pickles around to the non-label side, and studied the contents through the clear thermal glass.

"Good question. I feel like I don't get most things accomplished to the degree I'm satisfied with. More quantity than quality. I'm on autopilot, trying to chip away at the minimum daily requirements of all the day's activities."

Patti picked up the glass jar. "You must be doing something right. Looks like you had a lucrative day. Three jars left? Make that two; I'd like this one, please."

"The Dumonts had a lucrative day. I don't make a cent because, if I did, I couldn't enter any more amateur cooking competitions. I can't earn money from any food-related entity or I'm considered a professional. But that's all right. I'm dipping my toe into entrepreneurship to see if I like it." Sherry took Patti's money. At the same time, she eyeballed Patti's notepad. "Were you covering a story here?"

"Yes. The pre-winter pop-up table, Holly Daze, began today. The holiday-themed knickknacks like peppermint soaps and decorated pinecones are selling like hot cakes. I don't usually write non-food-related articles, but I made an exception this time because it's my cousin Bella's operation. That's what makes Augustin such a special place. The small town sensibility of protecting your friends and relatives has deep roots here."

"Mrs. Dumont," Sherry whispered.

"I'm sorry?" Patti leaned in. "What did you say?"

"Just mumbling." Sherry cast her gaze on her hands.

"I was thinking about a friend who may be going through a tough time soon."

Patti lowered her voice. "Sounded like you said 'Mrs. Dumont.' So, you must have heard the news. Another characteristic of a small town: word gets around in supersonic speed."

"News?"

"I heard it from the News Twelve crew as they were rushing out of here. Their intern, Steele Dumont, was found dead."

Chapter 11

Sherry covered one of the baking dishes with foil and pushed it back from the edge of the counter. She let the scent of the curry spices lull her into the dreamy state of contentment over a recipe well constructed. In the other baking dish was a luscious, peanut-buttery chicken curry boasting toasted spices and a touch of mango chutney for a sweet note that married well with the West African inspired flavors. She tore off a second piece of foil and covered the dish. The casseroles would be put in the oven when the first of the guests arrived. The food was ready for the party.

In an attempt to accommodate her somber mood, Sherry had scaled down the routinely larger number of guests to the smaller core group she could count on to understand her muted enthusiasm about the night's task. She would ply them with wine and whet their appetites with a layered goat cheese dip and toasted pita chips before the taste-testing began, but after that she couldn't guarantee maintaining a light atmosphere.

Sherry wiped her hands on her blue apron. She

balled the cloth up before carrying it upstairs to the laundry room. She tossed her version of a superhero cape in the washing machine. Her stomach dropped as her favorite garment left her sight and fell to the bottom of the drum. She sighed and made her way to her bedroom. She opened the door to her closet. Green. She felt like dusty green was the color of one of her curry dishes. Her eyes shifted over to the grays and browns, where they lingered until she willed them back to the brighter colors. She caught sight of a green linen shirt. She didn't want to influence her guests' votes, though, because she herself was unsure which dish she preferred. A burnt orange scarf tied loosely around her neck would serve as a nod to the chutney that rounded out the chicken dish.

Sherry gathered the pieces for her outfit and tossed them on her bed. She checked her wall clock for the time. When she saw the hour, her legs collapsed, planting her backside on the edge of the bed. She could change into her party clothes at leisure on this occasion because Amber had both dogs at her apartment, so no last-minute dog walk was necessary. The canines were invited to the party, just not the pre-party prep. Time was, for once, on Sherry's side.

As she removed her shirt and took aim to slip on another, her phone reverberated from the kitchen. She speared her arms through the shirt sleeves and sprinted down the steps. In a feat worthy of the senior Olympics, she skidded across the floor on her stocking feet and snagged the cell phone with a swing of her arm.

"Hello?" Sherry's voice was dripping with a blend of curiosity and exasperation at the fact that the caller identification read "Blocked." If it was a sales call, her gymnastic move had been for naught.

"Detective Ray Bease here." The man's voice was hard-hitting. "The murder investigation of Carmell Gordy has taken a turn. We're now linking a second murder at the News Twelve station to Ms. Gordy's."

"I was wondering if that would be the case." Sherry pinched the phone between her ear and her shoulder as she worked on buttoning up the shirt. "I'm conflicted because I was so relieved when Dad told me the body found in the station's storage closet wasn't Steele Dumont, but I'm still sad for that young man, Lucky. I don't know if Frances Dumont would have survived news of her grandson's death. But, of course, my deepest sympathy goes out to the family of the deceased."

"Be that as it may, I'm abiding by your wishes and asking you a question regarding your father, rather than asking him directly."

Sherry shuddered. "This is ridiculous. Dad had nothing to do with Carmell's murder. He certainly had nothing to do with Lucky's."

"Who said your father was involved with the second murder? I certainly didn't, and I advise you not to put words in my mouth."

Sherry lowered the phone and tilted her head left and right. The neck kink that was developing dispersed with a resounding click. She raised the phone back to her ear. "Can you tell me why one murder may be linked to the other?"

"I believe I was asking the questions," Ray said.

Sherry heaved a sigh.

"If I may continue."

"Please do."

"It's evident the shelf in the storage room that

toppled onto Lucky Pannell's head had all but one supportive screw loosened. Not the typical loosening that occurs over time. The shelf that hung over the equipment Lucky was in there to gather was secured with heavy-duty three-inch screws that wouldn't have come undone to the degree they did unless they were tampered with. They were dangling by mere threads. That can only be achieved deliberately with the use of a screwdriver. Only took a tap on the shelf, and its heavy load came crashing down. Lucky was found holding the camera battery he had gone in to get."

"How awful." Sherry squeezed her eyes shut, but the image of Lucky's tragic ending lingered.

"I'm obligated to ask where your father was yesterday."

The words Sherry's father had used to praise the versatility of the punch tool flooded Sherry's brain. Erno had extolled the virtues of the tool for every function from unclogging a drain to unscrewing a screw. Unscrewing a screw. Come to think of it, he hadn't actually specified that particular function, but Sherry imagined it was one of the punch tool's many attributes.

"Dad was home. I talked to him as I was arriving at the farmer's market. I didn't ask him how he planned to spend the day, but I can assure you, loosening storage shelves wasn't on his to-do list. What about Damien Castle? He and Truman Fletcher should have been on top of the situation over there. Wouldn't they know who comes and goes to that closet?"

"Those I interviewed at the station corroborated that the storage closet was entered by Lucky, in the early morning," Ray said. "He went in to collect supplies for the shoot at the farmer's market. Damien

Castle is the only person, besides Steele Dumont, who has the key, and the closet is always kept locked. The second key, which is usually in Steele Dumont's possession, was in the door keyhole when the body was discovered by the security guard, on his rounds."

"I have to ask, where was Steele Dumont yesterday morning, and why wasn't he in possession of his key? He wasn't at the farmer's market shoot, as far I saw. Only Brett Paladin, Castle, Fletcher, and Kirin, the camerawoman, were there."

"Lucky was doing Steele a favor by covering for him because Steele was running an early morning errand outside the station," Ray said. "Steele said he passed the key on to Lucky so he could get in and asked for the key to be returned as soon as Steele returned from his errand. When he did return, he couldn't find Lucky anywhere in the building. Steele eventually confessed to the security guard that he needed help locating Lucky. Steele didn't want anyone to know he'd lent out the storage room key because that's strictly prohibited. Steele admitted he had Lucky wear his sweater so if he was spotted from a distance, or from behind, Lucky would be mistaken for Steele. That's why, when the body was discovered, the word quickly circulated it was Steele's because the sweater was all that was visible. It took so long to excavate the body from under the debris that, for a full hour, Steele was the presumed victim." The detective paused.

"Poor Lucky." Sherry's tone softened. "Can't the deduction be made that Damien Castle saw Steele Dumont as a Carmell ally? And possibly that Steele knew too much about Damien's growing animosity toward his anchorwoman? As the holder of the only other copy of the key, couldn't Damien have made an earlier visit to the closet to loosen the shelf? On the other hand, why would Steele Dumont be the intended target when he's the one who had every reason to have committed Carmell Gordy's murder?"

"Points taken, though you may be overthinking this. I do want to share a disturbing piece of information. At the scene, a note on the back of the storage room door read, 'Why is a hooked rug like an intern? Because they're both so fun to wipe my feet on.' Sounds certain to me Steele was the target."

"In the time you've spent with my father, have you ever known him to make such a bad joke? Never. Why is someone trying to pin Dad as the murderer? Twice now. That note might have been left to pile on the evidence against Dad, but it's not valid because Dad doesn't make bad jokes. He makes good Erno-isms."

"I have to continue to gather the facts, Sherry. You're saying your father's whereabouts that morning are documented on your cell phone?"

"When I spoke to Dad on the phone, he had finished his morning coffee get-together with Ruth and Frances, and they had left. The ladies will happily attest to keeping him occupied around the time. Lucky got unlucky in the worst way." Sherry powered on. "Were there no security cameras trained on that area of the building that would show whomever it was who fiddled with the shelving?"

"The station canceled their video security contract two months ago, according to their financial documents," Ray said. "Cost-cutting measures."

"Or part of the plan." Sherry checked the clock on the upper right of her phone. The tiny numbers blurred as a thought crossed her mind. She wrestled with the idea in silence before blurting out, "I need to get moving, but I'm having a very casual taste-testing dinner this evening, in about sixty minutes actually. If you'd like to stop by, you can get an idea as to how I choose which recipe to enter into my next recipe contest. No business allowed, though, except when it comes to judging my food."

Sherry thought she heard tapping as if the detective were drumming a pen on a desk. The noise stopped. "I'll check my schedule. Thank you for the invitation." The phone called ended.

"What's the expression? 'Keep your friends close and your enemies closer.'" Sherry double-checked her phone to ensure the phone call had indeed ended. A shiver of embarrassment traveled through her core at the possibility that Detective Bease might have overheard her musing.

Sherry carried the phone upstairs and returned to her bedroom. She couldn't resist leaning back against her favorite pillow and letting the familiar cushiness caress her head.

Sherry's eyes were jarred open by a noise. She patted the comforter in hopes of locating her phone. "You're kidding me. How could I have fallen asleep?" As she raced down the stairs, her bulging shirt collar scratched the underside of her chin and she realized something was amiss with her buttons. She peered out the front entry sidelights and saw three familiar faces. She had no choice but to open the door rather than keep them waiting.

"Hi. The gang has returned," Amber said as Chutney and Bean scooted inside. "Did I catch you at a bad time?" Amber pointed to the misaligned buttons on Sherry's shirt.

Sherry pulled the corners of her mouth up. "I'm not sure what you're implying, but, hardly. You caught me changing for dinner. It was my second attempt. I thought I had plenty of time to get ready, and now I'm running late. How does that keep happening to me?" Sherry eyed Amber's shirtdress. "Do you think my pants are dressy enough?"

"Remember, it's your party. You're in charge." Amber extended a broad smile as Sherry rebuttoned her shirt. "Do you mind if I give these two some water? I can fill the bowls in the kitchen while you finish getting ready."

"That would be great. I'll only be five minutes. I desperately need to brush my hair." Taking two steps at a time, Sherry bounded upstairs.

When Sherry returned to the kitchen, Amber was seated at the table reading the newspaper. She stood and met Sherry at the counter. Amber picked up a small card next to Sherry's grocery list.

"Damien Castle's business card. I'm curious why you have two copies." Amber pointed to the identical card remaining on the counter.

"I saw him at the farmer's market yesterday. News Twelve was doing a story there, and he was with the crew." Sherry paused. "He asked if I would pass his number along to you. He didn't want to seem too forward, so he went the indirect route through me. He's interested in having dinner with you sometime. I meant to give the card to you at the store earlier, but I have so much on my mind."

Amber's forehead pinched tight. "I guess it's good I noticed it, or I might never have had the option to call him." Her gaze lingered on Sherry until Sherry blinked. "Sherry?"

"Amber, Damien Castle is way up high on my suspect list. Both he and Steele Dumont have the most blatant reasons for animosity toward Carmell. Steele has dropped down a notch on my list because someone tried to kill him at the station yesterday morning. In all likelihood, the same person who killed Carmell struck again, and, in both instances, evidence left at the scene implicated my father. How can I not be concerned that Damien wants to socialize with you? How am I supposed to know whether he's a nice person or truly dangerous? It gives me shudders to think he might have sabotaged the closet shelving, then proceeded on to the farmer's market to film a segment as if all were right with the world."

Amber put the card in the pocket of her shirtdress. "I know you're coming from a good place, but I'll be fine. You have plenty on your mind. Don't give my social life another thought. I promise, if I do see him, I'll make sure to be in a very public and safe place."

"Asking me not to worry is like asking an avocado not to turn brown twenty minutes after you slice it open. Can't be done. Be that as it may, you're an adult and welcome to hang out with whomever you see fit."

Sherry went to the cabinet, removed her white dinner plates, and set them next to the casseroles. She swatted at the hair dangling across her forehead with the back of her hand. "I need one more spritz of styling mouse to hold this rebel in place. If you want to get place settings of utensils out of the drawer, that would be so helpful. I'll be down in a minute or two."

"Of course," said Amber.

Sherry scurried out of the kitchen and up the stairs

to her bathroom. She squirted mousse into her hand and stroked the white foam through her hair. "Not bad," she said as she saw her reflection smile back at her.

When Sherry reentered the kitchen, she caught sight of Amber stuffing her phone back inside her purse. With only steps to go before she reached the counter, Sherry caught her foot on the edge of the area rug. She regained her balance by clutching the wall she collided with.

"That was quite an entrance." Amber laughed. She pushed her purse to the side and turned to the flatware drawer. "You didn't give me much time to get my job done."

Sherry's gaze drifted from Amber's purse to the cutlery drawer. "We'll knock this job off together. Otherwise all that's left is to put out cocktail glasses and the paper and pens for the voting ballots. We can get to that in a bit. There's one thing I'd like to do before the party starts. I'd say we have thirty minutes before Eileen and her husband appear. Follow me." Sherry led the way to the living room.

"By the way, how do you know your neighbors will be arriving in exactly thirty minutes?"

"They're always at the door exactly on the nose of the stated start time, and they're also the first to leave. Standard operating procedure. I'd be a wreck if they weren't the first here after all these years. Bad karma." Sherry grinned, but her dry lip stuck on her teeth. "I could use some water, but this is more pressing."

"What are we doing in here?" Amber asked as she took a seat.

"We're going to review the cook-off video I recorded. I haven't had a chance to view it yet, and, with you watching too, we can double the chance of spotting what might be a red flag. We don't have much time, but let's see what we can come up with. It's Marla's idea, and I think it's a good one. I don't feel confident about my ability to recognize any unusual behavior Carmell, or anyone else for that matter, might have exhibited. She wasn't involved in the cook-off, so she'll only be on in the moments prior, and, hopefully, some after, until the station's power loss."

Her friend's cheerful expression turned dour.

"It's worth a try to see if we can tell if she was fearful, irritated, or anxious. My sister said that might be valuable, although I'm hoping it won't drum up more questions than answers."

Sherry punched the buttons on the DVR and took a seat next to the recliner Amber was seated in. The television burst to life with the musical introduction of the News Twelve morning program, *Sunny Side Up with Carmell and Brett.* Sherry and Amber sat in silence as the program moved through traffic reports, school announcements, weather, and local police blotter activity. The anchors were calm in their demeanor and polished in their delivery. Sherry pinched her lips shut to stifle an impending yawn.

"I don't see any red flags. Maybe I'll speed through the boating news unless you see any reason not to. We're running out of time." Sherry put her finger on the fast-forward arrow on the remote control.

"Hold up one second. I have one observation." Amber pointed to the television.

"You do? What is it?"

"Not about the anchors themselves, but why does the producer let them keep so many knickknacks on the desk. Makes for a cluttered scene."

"In all the years I've been a viewer of the morning

show, I've never noticed that detail." Sherry sat up a little straighter. "You're right. Cell phones, laptops, papers, eyeglasses, drinks. So messy. I'm off my game if that didn't bother me." Sherry let out a clipped chuckle. "See on the side of the anchor desk? That travel mug has a familiar logo. Where have I seen that before?" Rather than fast-forwarding, Sherry rewound the playback slowly until she found the best frame of Carmell's tall beverage mug. "When I was in the studio, she had a green smoothie in a clear container on the desk during her segment on Founder's Day, but that mug's different." Sherry clicked the *pause* button. "The sports car roof!"

"What does that mean?" Amber asked.

"That's where I saw the same logo as is on the mug right there." Sherry walked up to the TV and put her finger on the screen. "Remember Steele left his mug on the car's roof, and we returned it to him when we went inside the building?"

"That one. I do remember. I never zeroed in on what was on the mug. You're very perceptive," Amber said. "Do you think that's important?"

"Provides a connection between the two, I guess. Maybe Steele and Carmell bought them together. Or maybe they share a mug, which would be both cute and unsanitary at the same time. Let's see if I can make out what's written across it." Sherry leaned in so close to her TV her statically charged hair rushed forward and clung to the screen. "Says MediaPie. Anything with the word *pie* as one of the syllables is all right by me. Let's take a break and revisit this later. We only have a few minutes before the guests arrive, and I need to preheat the oven."

As Sherry was turning off the TV, Chutney began barking. She peeked at the little clock on her DVR. Six o'clock on the nose. "Why am I not surprised? Would you mind turning on the oven?"

"What temperature?" Amber asked.

"Three fifty. Thanks." Sherry headed to the front door, stopping first to check herself in the hall mirror. "I forgot earrings. Too late now." She fluffed her hair until her under-accessorized earlobes were fully covered. She shushed the dogs and yanked open the door.

"Welcome, welcome. Hope the traffic wasn't horrendous." Sherry craned her neck forward and surveyed the street up and down. "That joke never gets old. Come in, Eileen. J. Foster, I haven't seen you out and about in days. Thanks for coming."

Eileen's husband, J. Foster, bowed his head. His black glasses slipped down the bridge of his nose. He used the knuckle of his index finger to guide them back in place. "Good evening, Sherry. I've been feeling a bit under the weather, but I wouldn't miss this evening for anything." He unwrapped a cough drop and popped the lozenge on his tongue. "I don't think I'm contagious, but I won't give you a kiss as a precaution."

"He's a hypochondriac, dear. He always gets a tickle in his throat when the seasons turn over." Eileen unbuttoned the top two heart-shaped buttons on her black cardigan sweater. "We're so excited to taste your latest creations. We do have such a hard time voting for a favorite, though. It's like picking a favorite child. All your recipes are delightful and worthy of entering in a contest."

"That's why we're here, Eileen, to help her whittle down her choices. She can't enter every single recipe. We haven't let her down yet." J. Foster laid his hand on his wife's back and gave her a gentle push forward. "I personally have no problem making up my mind."

"My friend Amber will pour you a drink if you wouldn't mind finding her in the kitchen. I see a car pulling up, so I'll stay put." Sherry shut the door behind the couple, but kept her grasp firmly on the knob. A moment later she opened the door for Erno, Ruth Gadabee, and Frances Dumont.

"Come in. Come in," Sherry sang. She gave her father a hug.

Ruth edged over and gave Sherry an air kiss. Frances blew Sherry a kiss from behind Erno. A fourth person emerged from the shadows. Larson Anderson, a man Sherry imagined used an immeasurable amount of sunblock every summer, extended a nod in Sherry's direction. He was as fair-skinned as a white peach. His squinting sapphire-blue eyes were in a losing struggle with the setting sun's glare as it peeked from under the porch overhang.

Larson's hand was on the small of Frances's back as the group passed Sherry on their way into the house.

Once inside, Frances turned back toward Sherry. "Sherry, I believe you know Larson. He said he met you at the Ruggery. Since his wife passed away last year, he hasn't had the occasion to pop back in. Hooking rugs was *her* hobby, of course, and she was the reason he spent time at your father's store, but he mentioned how lovely your family was to her during her illness. He's been successful with the honorable task of recruiting you and your father for the Founder's Day ceremony, right?"

"Thank you for that introduction, Frances," Larson said.

"Yes, that's right. So nice to see you again, Larson." Sherry glanced side-eyed at her father. "Dad didn't mention you were the date Frances was bringing tonight. I'm so happy to have you. Let's have a drink on the patio while the sun sets, that is, as long as we're warm enough. It's a small group tonight. I couldn't get my act together to accommodate a larger crowd. Follow me."

As Sherry reached the kitchen, Chutney began another round of barking in harmony with Bean's higher pitched yap.

"Who could that be? Everyone, this is Amber Sherman. She's helping us out at the store until Dad returns to work. I'll be right back. Let me see who's here. Amber, would you mind pouring a few more glasses?" Amber welcomed the newcomers with glasses of wine as Sherry reached across the counter and helped herself to a glass of pinot grigio before making her way back to the front door. She stopped at the door's sidelight with her hand in mid-reach for the knob. When she saw the silhouette outside the window, her other hand jerked upward, spilling wine on her welcome mat.

Sherry sucked in a breath, turned the knob, and opened the door. "Damien Castle. What a surprise."

Amber walked up beside Sherry. "I hope it's okay. I invited Damien."

"Come in. Welcome." As Sherry backed away from the door to let him enter, the heel of one foot caught the toe of the other, and she lost her balance. The result was a collision with the doorframe. The remainder of her wine jettisoned from her glass and saturated the already moistened welcome mat. "I need to get back to yoga. My balance is way off these days."

Damien extended his hand, in which he held a small bouquet of chrysanthemums. "Thank you, Sherry. I was sure surprised when I got the call from Amber inviting me to come over. Surprised in a pleasant way, of course. Hopefully you, too." Damien tipped his head to Amber, who delivered a half-smile back. "Thanks for giving her my card."

"The more the merrier." Sherry heard the trite comment bubble out of her mouth and grimaced at her lack of originality. She accepted the flowers and put them up to her nose for a sniff. The musty smell of the mums made her eyes water. Fall flowers never boasted the sweet perfume of summer blossoms, but they offered the promise of a last gasp of summer.

"I'll put these in water. Amber will show you where to get a drink, and I'll mop up this mess before the front hall smells like a frat party. I'd better pop the casseroles in the oven first, though."

"Already done," Amber said.

"Lifesaver." Sherry carried the flowers to the kitchen, but not before taking one more peek outside the front window. She found a glass vase in a cabinet, filled it with water, and set the flowers inside. "Pretty dusty-rose color," Sherry said as she spun the vase around to inspect the bunch from all angles. "If I didn't know any better, I'd say he was buttering me up. But for what?" Rather than set the flowers out on a more visible table, she left them on the kitchen counter. She collected a sponge and a spray bottle of homemade white vinegar cleaning solution from under the kitchen sink and attacked the wine spill in the front hall.

When Sherry was satisfied her front hall smelled less like a winery and more like salad dressing, she peeked out the sidelights. She shrugged. "Guess he decided not to come."

Sherry scooped up a new glass of wine and headed out to the patio. She was dismayed at how crisp the air had become and how the sky had emptied itself of sunlight. Before joining the conversation, Sherry assessed the party's dynamics and decided on joining the trio of Erno, Frances, and Larson, who were huddled around the hors d'oeuvre tray.

Frances put her hand on Larson Anderson's shoulder and leaned in. "Sherry, you're finally out here. We were discussing Larson's role as committee chairman of this year's inaugural Trivselbit presentations. We unofficially decided he has such a strong Swedish connection, he must be related to Andre August Dahlback and was the obvious choice for the position."

"That may be overstating the truth, Frances, but I did settle in Augustin because the local history spoke to my family's Swedish heritage. I admit I was inspired by that connection to lend the term *trivselbit* to the ceremony," Larson said.

"What does *trivselbit* mean, and why is the term part of Founder's Day?" Amber asked as she and Damien approached the group.

"Good question." Larson wriggled away from Frances's arm and turned to face Sherry. "You'll appreciate this, Sherry. Our Trivselbit presentation ceremony will commemorate accomplished citizens who we feel best represent the town's spirit of attaining goals by exercising the highest level of excellence. That's what Augustinites are best known for. The Swedish word *trivselbit* refers to the last piece of cake or pastry left on a serving tray. It's meant to remain on the tray, as a symbol of comfort and security, and leaving that last morsel is a sacred rule of Swedish table manners. The symbolism of that last piece is the essence of our Founder's Day celebration. What's left when the last disappears? Where's the continuity? The legacy? Nothing. Protecting our town's values, striving for the good of everyone without compromise, and never letting the well of community spirit run dry is what we're all about."

"You've got to love that philosophy," Erno said. "As I always say, you need only taste a crumb to know whether it's a great recipe."

"Dad, I don't think I've ever heard you say—" Sherry began.

"Erno, your words are as precious as caviar," Ruth said, interrupting Sherry.

"The point is," Larson continued, "I wanted my committee to choose Augustin citizens who represented the variety of what this town has to offer. Sherry and Erno are two of the finest examples. You two would leave the last piece of cake on the tray. You two care about Augustin's staying the same Connecticut town that helped mold you into the successful citizens you are. Your success didn't come at a cost to the town's integrity."

"Larson, you're lecturing." Erno's shoulders dipped.

"I'm hoping nothing changes, even if the grass is greener on the other side," Larson said.

Erno backed away from the group and reached for the lone pita chip on the tray. He picked up the crispy triangle and drew it to his lips. He set it back down on the tray.

"My goal is to have the day go off without a hitch, with the culmination being the Trivselbit presentations, but the Van Ardans aren't making that easy. Right, Erno?" Larson reached around and gave his longtime friend a pat on the back.

Erno plunged his hands in his pockets. "The success of the day isn't up to me, thank goodness."

"That's not what Beverly has been spreading around town. She's told anyone who'll listen that Erno Oliveri is onboard with her family's ancestor, Knut Eklind, being recognized as the true founder of Augustin," Larson said. "Though, their claim that the 'spirits' he brought with him in the late seventeen hundreds laid the foundation for future riches for a settlement barely eking out a meager existence is somewhat farfetched. First of all, the fact that the Van Ardans don't even live in Augustin themselves speaks volumes. Second, the spirits I'm referring to aren't the ghostly, floating vapor variety or even the rah-rah cheering kind. Rather, it's the eighty-proof liquid that can paralyze a community as fast as its citizens can become inebriated. Third, nowhere is the legacy of Swedish distilleries less evident than in Augustin. I dare anyone to find me an artifact from Eklind's heyday. They can't because there aren't any. It wasn't a period the town wishes to relive or, heaven forbid, celebrate. And finally, even if the scenario were fact, who would want to live in a town named Knutville or Knutport?"

"What prompted the Van Ardans to come forward with their claim, I wonder?" Sherry took a step sideways toward her father. Erno tucked his chin to his chest.

"All in the name of the almighty dollar, I'm afraid," Frances said. "Let's not cloud the evening with negative talk. I, for one, am counting my blessings that my grandson is alive and healthy after a terrible scare. So, let's give a toast to that."

As everyone raised his or her glass, J. Foster called out from inside the patio door. "Sherry, your timer's buzzing. Good thing I went in to use the men's room, or your recipes might have been ruined and everyone left hungry and desperate. Your dinner party could have turned into the Donner Party."

Chapter 12

"Someone call nine-one-one. Sherry killed it with the Peanut Butter Chicken Curry." Erno licked his fork clean before letting the silverware clank down on his plate.

Sherry gasped. "Dad, that's not funny. By the way, my other dish, Spinach Lentil Curry, was one of my best efforts, so this could be a tight race."

"You're not supposed to advertise which dish you're voting for, Erno," Ruth scolded. "It's called a secret ballot for a reason. There aren't supposed to be any undue influences."

Sherry glanced across the table at Damien. He'd been quiet throughout dinner. "Damien, is there one dish you prefer over the other? A simple yes or no is fine. You can expound on your reasons on the written ballot."

"Yes," Damien said.

Sherry held a steady gaze on the man. Damien put his fork down on his empty plate and folded his hands in his lap. The man's unwavering stare wrestled with Sherry's until she blinked.

"If everyone is done eating, I'm going to hand out the ballots. Dessert and voting, the perfect combination. And remember, there are no wrong answers." Sherry stood and began gathering plates. When she saw Larson pick up his plate, she added, "I've got those. Keep your seat and relax. You're all doing me such a big favor. I'm so appreciative."

Back in the kitchen, Sherry gathered the notepad sheets and a handful of pens to distribute to her guests. As she walked the collection back to the table, Amber met her halfway.

"That was such a good dinner, Sherry." Amber shifted her stance. "I hope I didn't put you in an awkward position, inviting Damien at the very last minute, but I thought it was a safe environment for a meeting. I don't know if he's having much fun, though. He's barely said two words."

"Imagine my shock at seeing him at the door. You know I've got some conflicting thoughts about him. On one hand, there are reasons to suspect him of foul play and, on the other, I don't want to sour relations between you and me. So, to be quite honest, I'm biting my tongue and behaving my best when what I really want to do is shine a bright light in his eyes and question him until he confesses so my father can find some peace."

"Let me finish the date, if it really can be classified as such, and if you still feel the same way tomorrow, I'll keep my distance from him until the dust settles. Agreed?"

"Agreed. But promise me you won't find yourself alone with him at any point."

Amber let out a sigh. "With all due respect, I repeat,

I'm a big girl. I can take care of myself." Amber relieved Sherry of the pens and paper and left the kitchen.

Sherry cut the apple cake she'd been thawing throughout the day. She scooped vanilla bean ice cream on the side of each dessert plate before arranging them on a tray. With the finesse of a veteran waitress, she transported the dessert to the living room without so much as a displacement of an apple chunk. As she entered the room, her guests rushed to curl their hands across their ballots to conceal their votes. Sherry circled the table and placed a dessert in front of each guest. They in turn placed their ballots on the tray.

"While you were dishing out dessert, our new friend Amber was dishing on the advice column she writes for an online publication," Ruth said.

Amber cleared her throat. "Your father was simply asking for an example of the sort of issues I touch on, so I gave one I'm working on for this week. I won't give away my response. You'll have to pay full price for that."

Frances placed her elbows on the table and rested her chin down in her open hands. "Fascinating."

"Can I get a recap?" Sherry sat and spun her dessert plate around so the cut of cake was square to the edge of the table.

Amber poked a small piece of cake and dipped it in the thawing ice cream until the confection was fully coated with the melting goodness. She took a moment to savor the bite while everyone waited. Her tongue lapped up a rogue drop of ice cream from her lower lip. "A woman e-mailed explaining she was suspicious of the behavior of her fiancé, who she was concerned was hiding a secret life. The reason her suspicions were growing was because he was so protective of his phone. He wouldn't allow her to touch the device in any way, shape, or form. She felt that was a major red flag, and now she can't move forward with their future plans. She wanted my advice on the situation. She signed her e-mail 'Disconnected.'" Amber tipped her head to the side and scooped up another piece of cake.

Next to her, Damien kept his eyes on his final course.

"So, that'll be in your column?" Frances asked. "No hints whatsoever?"

"If she told you, she'd have to kill you." Erno laughed.

"Dad! Now I know where Marla gets her knack for inappropriate comments." Sherry clicked her tongue on the roof of her mouth. "But, I admit I'm dying of curiosity. That can't give the poor girl much feeling of reassurance, if the man she may be spending the rest of her life with is hiding parts of his life from her. Hope he hasn't committed a crime he doesn't want her to find out about."

"Sherry, you haven't collected my ballot," Damien said. "I wouldn't want to miss out on being included in the process." He handed Sherry a piece of paper. "I want to apologize ahead of time. When you read my ballot, even though supposedly you don't know who wrote what, you'll see that I only named my choice. I don't like to give my opinion about situations I don't fully understand." Damien lowered his eyelids, strengthening the impact of his serious expression.

The skin on the back of Sherry's neck tingled.

"I think I'm speaking for all of us when I say your two dishes didn't disappoint," J. Foster announced.

His wife, Eileen, nodded. The rest of the table clapped.

Sherry touched her heated cheek with the back of her hand as she pulled her chair up under her. "Thanks, guys. I can't think of a nicer group to cook for."

Larson erupted in a chuckle. "Except, we have no giant game-show check to present you for your winning efforts." He pulled a folded pamphlet out of his back pocket. "While we're enjoying dessert, I wanted to pass around the final mock-up of the Founder's Day leaflet. You'll notice a blank section waiting for one of Sherry's recipes. There's a blurb about Sherry and Erno that hopefully will be acceptable. The paper outlines the timetable for the day's scheduled events, all leading to the stunning climax at the Trivselbit presentation on the green at the town square."

"I'll e-mail you the recipe by tonight, I promise. If it's too late to include it I'll personally make copies and tape one to each leaflet. May I take a look?" Sherry extended her hand. She unfolded the papers and let out a melodic coo when she saw the cover. An onion superimposed over a map of Hillsboro County, with a "You Are Here" flag indicating where Augustin was located, entertained her eyes. At the bottom of the cover, in a bold but sassy font, were the words "Peel back the layers and see what Augustin's made of." She flipped over the front page. Her eyes bulged when she came face-to-face with a startling illustration.

Larson waved his fork at Sherry, apple cake speared on the prongs. "No problem. The printer's on standby, ready to finish the job when I provide your recipe.

Your scrunchy face tells me I shouldn't have put that advertisement on the inside cover. I initially wanted a portrait rendering of Andre August Dahlback. I have to tell you, the amount of money the committee received for that ad placement from MediaPie Corp, made 'no thanks' impossible. The sum was enough to pay for the deluxe-size podium and stage upgrade with the full trim package, and that sealed the deal."

Sherry swore she heard "hypocrite" uttered from the direction of Erno's seat.

"No, no, it's fine. This is the second or third time I've seen this logo recently. What's the MediaPie Corporation's interest in Augustin's Founder's Day, I wonder?" Sherry squinted as she visualized the mug on Carmell Gordy's desk brandishing the same image. Her father shifted his body to the edge of his chair. In the process, he grazed his dessert plate and knocked his fork to the floor. He retrieved the pronged poker before Chutney secured it in his snout. Erno waved off Sherry's attempt to hand him a clean fork.

Frances raised her voice to an urgent shout. "I'll tell you what their interest is." Crumbs flew from her mouth. "MediaPie is a media conglomerate owned by the Van Ardans. Obtaining a stronghold on radio and television stations in the northeast is their main objective. The same family who wishes to undermine Founder's Day. By placing that ad strategically inside the front cover, they're sending the strong message that Augustin can be bought. Don't you all agree?"

"You said we wouldn't discuss this tonight," Larson said with a note of desperation in his voice.

"Frances, you're being dramatic." Erno straightened his posture.

"Erno, you're the one who's starring in a drama, since you and Beverly have grown very close." Ruth peppered her words with a number of huffs. She turned her attention to Sherry. "That woman even gave your father flowers when he wasn't feeling well. That certainly was going above and beyond, I'd say. For the amount of money she probably spent, she should have known they were city flowers. I could tell. If she had purchased them locally, they would have been hydrangeas or chrysanthemums; they're fall bloomers. She gave him delphinium and larkspur, obviously not locally grown at this time of the year. Only a city dweller would be oblivious to the art of proper flower bestowal. I suppose it's the thought that counts, even if the action is ill conceived."

Erno raised his chin and opened his mouth. He blew out a noisy burst of air before he snapped his jaw shut.

Sherry set down her fork. "Damien, I checked out the recording I made of the News Twelve cook-off. There was a moment on the tape when I noticed a mug on the anchor desk brandishing that same MediaPie logo. Does MediaPie have connections with News Twelve? I thought the station was a shareholder enterprise, but I'm no expert on media entities." Sherry's peripheral field of vision was singed by Amber's searing glare.

"It's getting late, and talking business is so tiring. Would you all please excuse me? I have a full day ahead tomorrow." Damien removed his napkin from his lap and set the linen on his place mat. He stood and extended a parting wave. "Thank you so much for the glorious meal. I hope Amber will let me know the voting results."

"I'll bet the winner's the Peanut Butter Chicken Curry," Erno added.

Damien took a misstep and hit the chair leg with his shin. He winced and uttered unintelligible words under his breath.

"I'll walk you out." Amber pushed back her chair.

"Sherry, that was a bold move," Larson said. "There have been a lot of questions about the future of News Twelve. Makes sense to think Damien Castle is the one who knows the answers."

"Don't try to deflect attention from your questionable actions, Larson," Ruth said. "You were swayed by the dollar bills that family waved in your face. So for you to pass judgment on Mr. Castle seems petty. If management over at News Twelve has intentions to join up the Van Ardans, that's one more facet to MediaPie's emerging empire. Losing Augustin's local channel would hurt the town. MediaPie would surely remove all the local programming along with the charm and character of our special town we all tune in for. You and Erno need to decide which side your bread is buttered on."

"I appreciate what you're saying, but I shouldn't have put Damien on the spot like that. The words came flying out. I couldn't help myself. He was Amber's, he was Amber's . . ." Sherry rose from her seat. ". . . Amber's date, so I should have been a more gracious host." She set her napkin on her place mat. "Can I offer anyone some coffee, tea, or another piece of apple cake?"

"I couldn't."

"I've got to get to bed."

"I'm stuffed."

"Can we help you with the dishes, Sherry?" Frances asked.

"No, no. Thanks for the offer, Frances. I enjoy the process of cleaning up. It's very relaxing."

"In that case, we'll take off." Erno slid his chair back and stood.

One by one, Sherry's guests gathered their belongings and headed to the door. Sherry followed after her guests. There, through the window, she caught sight of Amber and Damien presumably saying good night at the end of her driveway. As much as she was tempted to keep vigil, she turned her head away. Sherry hugged each of her guests as he or she left her house. As she closed the door behind her father, who was the last to leave, an arm thrust through the small opening.

"Don't lock me out." Amber's voice was as cool as the evening air. "That was a very nice evening. Let me help you clean up."

"You've been so much help already. I couldn't accept any more."

"You have to accept my offer. Gives us an opportunity to talk." Amber led the way to the kitchen sink, where a stack of dishes awaited.

The two women washed, dried, and put away the dinner dishes with assembly-line efficiency. Chutney and Bean provided occasional distractions when they got under foot, but warnings directed at the dogs were the only words spoken until the task was complete.

"Now that that's done, I have a few things to say," Amber began.

Sherry wiped her hands on the dish towel. She drew in her breath and hugged her arms across her midsection. "Uh-oh."

"You were right," Amber said. "Damien's covering up. He shared it with me outside."

"Did he confess to Carmell's murder? Oh my God, Amber. Did he threaten you? I told you not to get yourself in a situation where you were alone with him. I'll call the police."

"No, No. Don't call the police. I took the opportunity to test the waters by fudging that e-mail from the woman concerned about her fiancé's behavior," Amber said. "I might have gotten a somewhat similar question from a reader, but tonight I put a personal touch on it by saying the man in question was overly attached to his phone, the way Damien seems to be."

"Really? I was thinking of eating my words because I didn't see him check his phone one time all evening." Sherry searched Amber's eyes for evidence of where this conversation was leading.

Amber rubbed her temple with the back of her hand. "A beehive doesn't buzz as much as his phone. He's very good at concealing it in his napkin, but being seated right next to him, I couldn't miss his checking and texting, checking and texting, time after time. I wanted to ask if there was a problem like an emergency at the station, but I let his silence dictate our time together. If I have to do all the initiating in the conversation, that's a deal breaker. But, by the end of the evening, I'd given up. I didn't even want to know who he was texting with."

"What did he tell you outside, if I may ask?" Sherry

put down the used dish towel and opened a drawer to remove a clean replacement.

"I now have to eat my words," Amber said. "Seems he's battling a gambling addiction. He apparently needs to get constant texts from his support sponsor to get him through the day. He said someone here, possibly your father, used the word 'bet,' and Damien immediately broke out in a rash. Damien's therapy is in its infancy, and he's coping as best he can. His goal is to get a grip on his destructive habit."

Sherry's eyes widened. "Do you think that could be where News Twelve's cash is bleeding out to? I mean Damien does have access to the funds as the majority shareholder."

"Does add up, but no. He said he told Detective Bease that he never gambled with the station's funds. Would Damien commit murder to rid himself of an employee or two who it might have been a mistake to hire in the first place? It's anyone's guess at this point. Unless you know more than you're letting on."

Sherry shook her head.

"Honestly, Sherry, my gut feeling is Damien didn't kill Carmell. He explained that he had thought some gambling might be a fast way to double or triple his personal cash reserves, but that didn't work out."

"You're not convincing me. Maybe Damien tried his best to fix a deteriorating situation one way; but when that plan failed, maybe he became so desperate to eliminate his biggest mistake he killed the star he hired." Sherry's voice quivered as her words painted a gruesome scene. "Steele was always driving Damien Castle's car. Do you have any idea why?"

"Yes. Damien said that car was won on a bet, but

was a bad reminder of how his habit escalated. He doesn't have the heart to trade it in quite yet. Letting Steele drive the car was Damien's way of compensating Steele for the time he spent running errands for Carmell. Steele also took Damien to his early morning Gamblers Anonymous meetings."

Sherry's gaze drifted to the ceiling and back down to Amber. "Were those meetings, by any chance, in town by the Ruggery? That has to be it. Makes sense why Steele has been seen over there, waiting with the car. I'm going to check and see if a Gamblers Anonymous group meets in that location."

"We touched on the fact that Damien knows he's on the suspect list for the murders at the station. But, he has a solid alibi. The traffic ticket you photographed, proves he had gone to an early morning Gamblers Anon meeting. When Damien arrived, he was told the meeting was canceled and rescheduled for later in the morning because the leader of the group had fallen ill. Damien returned to the station, later went back to the rescheduled meeting, during the time the murder took place, and was promptly called out of that second meeting to return to the station to attend to the crisis. His attendance was documented. He's had to tell the News Twelve employees about his personal struggles because the details would be going public, in a matter of time, during the investigation. He's surprised at the positive effect on morale the disclosure has made over there, he said."

"A small silver lining to all the workplace unrest." Sherry lowered her gaze. "Rehabilitating his destructive habits may be too little too late if funds are drying up, though."

"At least he's cleared of any suspicion involving the murder. He's not a bad guy. His heart is breaking for the employees, he said, but there is a way out. We didn't get into what that would be, though. There's also a glimmer of a decent date potential in the future if I can get him to put down that darn cell device. By the way, which recipe won tonight?"

Chapter 13

"A tie, a dead heat. Four votes for the Peanut Butter Chicken Curry and four votes for the Spinach Lentil Curry." Sherry kicked a pebble toward the river.

"I guess I would have been the deciding vote." Ray tugged at his hat as the sun emerged from behind a cloud. He pulled his sunglasses from his blazer's breast pocket.

Sherry and the detective continued down the woodchip trail that ran beside the Silty Pretzel River. The half-mile path had been worn down to the topsoil in spots from years of hosting bikers, joggers, and dog walkers. Tall ornamental grasses bordering the banks of the river served as a dynamic golden barrier between the trail and the gently flowing water. The breezes picked up the dried fronds and tossed them about at will. Giant swans and mallard ducks cohabited the stretch of water and dry land between Augustin's library and the town center. The waterfowl's graceful majesty provided a shock of white on the sparkling dark blue water.

When a foraging bird caught Chutney's eye, the

dog strained at the leash, but Sherry was content to keep her distance. The swans had been known to take offense to nosy canines that got too close to their goslings, so she took no chances.

"Actually, I decided to count my own vote. Yes, my opinion counts, so there was a five to four majority, but I'm keeping the results hush-hush." Sherry kicked another pebble. The pebble took flight and landed in the water. The splash alarmed the swan, whose long neck was buried deep in the grasses. Big Bird whipped his head in the direction of the disturbed water before taking flight. Chutney sank down on his haunches and refused to move forward until Sherry coaxed him with the promise of a treat.

"That bird could do some damage with those massive wings," Ray said. "Good thing your dog has the sense to stay away from trouble like that."

"Why didn't you stop by last night?" Sherry kept her eyes on Chutney, who had resumed his determined terrier pace.

"When I'm on a case, I have no shut-off valve. I eat, sleep, and breathe the investigation. I had to make a trip back to News Twelve for a follow-up."

"The visit couldn't have waited until this morning?" Sherry shot Ray a fleeting side eye.

"You, of all people, should be fully invested in my working overtime to hasten the outcome. Besides, you don't think there would have been the slightest degree of awkwardness with my being included on the guest list with your father and Damien Castle in attendance?"

Sherry ignored the question. She pulled her phone out of her back pocket to check the time. "We've gotten off track, and I have to get back to the store. I haven't even eaten lunch yet. What did you want to talk to me about?"

"Your father called me this morning," Ray said in a near whisper.

Sherry stopped and jerked her body to face the detective. "What did he say? You didn't upset him, did you? He's doing so well; I don't want any setbacks."

"He said he received a threat."

"What do you mean a threat?" Sherry choked on the word "threat." "He didn't mention a threat."

"He said he got up early this morning and checked his e-mail. He says it's a habit every day to see when his coffee is going to be delivered, whatever that means. I wish I had a morning coffee delivery system." Ray raised his eyebrows and turned up the edges of his mouth. "Anyway, he read the e-mail without his glasses because he said he has set his phone to display in an enlarged font. Well, the single new e-mail he had received had the word *contest* in the subject line, so he assumed the message was from you. Problem was, the e-mail came through in a smaller font, and he strained to make out the words. When he couldn't decipher the content, he replied, asking 'cooking?', thinking he was corresponding with you. He received an immediate reply to his reply. By this time he'd found his reading glasses and could make out the word *confess* not *contest* in the subject line. The body of the return e-mail simply read 'Confess or you'll be next.'"

Sherry tightened her grip on Chutney's leash. The dog coughed when his collar pinched his neck too tightly.

"Sorry, boy." She loosened the tension. "Is Dad okay? Can an e-mail be traced easily?"

"I had him forward it, and our techies are working on it. As a matter of fact, my old partner Cody Diamond is working on identifying the e-mail's origin. This sort of thing is right up his alley. In the meantime, your father has been advised to be alert, lock his doors, and double-check every detail of his surroundings. Your father knows I'm meeting with you, and he asked me to tell you he's fine."

"One more reason to get this crime unraveled. Some lunatic is having his or her way, and my Dad is taking the brunt of it. What aren't we seeing?" Sherry slapped her thigh with her free hand.

"There's no 'we' in this scenario. This is a murder investigation being conducted by the proper authorities," Ray said. "This was news I wanted to deliver in person because I respect your integrity, not for any other reason. Outside interference is not beneficial. Do I make myself clear? This case will be solved in due time, I assure you."

"I'm not feeling at all assured, I assure you." Sherry spiced the word "you" with extra zing. "I've got to get going." She turned back toward the town center. "I appreciate your contacting me, Ray. Tell Detective Diamond to hurry, will you?" Sherry trotted off with Chutney in tow.

"Wait. I'm really curious which recipe you're going with."

Sherry heard the question, but chose not to respond. If all her questions weren't answered, his needn't be either.

When she reached the Ruggery, Sherry was breathing hard, and her empty stomach was churning. She wiped a drip of perspiration from her forehead before it reached her brow. "Whew. I'm out of shape. I need to get back to yoga or maybe tennis."

"Hey, Sherry. You returned in the nick of time." Amber held the door open.

"What's going on?" Sherry scanned the surroundings, but saw no one else in the store. "You wouldn't happen to have any leftover lunch, would you? I never got a chance to stop at the deli. My meeting with the detective went a bit long."

"I have half a turkey avocado wrap, as a matter of fact. I'll get it for you. First, let me explain those mugs on the counter."

Sherry peered over her shoulder at three lidded travel cups lined up next to the cash register. A step closer and she got a perfect view of the unmistakable logo on the cups. "Were the Van Ardans in by any chance?"

Amber opened her mouth to respond, but all Sherry heard was the angriest clang she had ever heard the doorbell make, followed by a dull clink. The door had swung completely open, hitting the fallen brass bell so hard the instrument catapulted across the room, only coming to a rest after hitting the demonstration table. The dogs were left cowering in the corner.

"I'm so sorry. The Ruggery is better off without that ding-dong devil anyway. But I'll have the charming bell repaired if you'd like." Beverly Van Ardan closed the door with an exaggerated slow motion.

"Dad is pretty attached to that bell. He says 'an entrance without music is no entrance at all.'"

"It'll be back to its old self soon enough. Your father needn't know anything's changed. I know how set in his ways he is. Seems to be a strong trait in this town."

Beverly collected the disabled ringer off the floor. “Sherry, the reason I rushed in was we were pulling away when I saw you come in, and I had to make sure you got the message I left with lovely Amber.”

Sherry’s gaze rolled in the direction of Amber. “Amber gives me all messages, have no doubt about that.”

Amber’s pinched faced smoothed out.

“So, do you agree?” Beverly asked.

Sherry inspected her shoe, which was garnished with some grass and mud from the walk along the river. “Actually, she hasn’t had a chance to give me any messages I got while I was out.”

“I dropped off these travel mugs, and I was hoping you’d keep them by the checkout counter. It was something Erno and I had discussed before his illness.” Beverly put air quotes around the word “illness.”

“And he agreed to that? We have a policy against solicitations and outside advertisers. We want clean and simple inside the store. I’m very surprised he would okay displaying a company’s logo that has no bearing on his product.” Sherry tiptoed over to the door and took off her soiled shoe. She opened the door and tapped the shoe on the side of the building until the casual leather flat was spotless. “Clean and simple, that’s what we’re all about. I think I’ll double-check with Dad when we talk later.”

“Whatever you say, dear. You’re in charge while he’s out.” Beverly smoothed out a fold on her skirt.

The door opened in silence, and in walked a man with a blue blazer slung over his arm. His distinctive flattop hairstyle complemented the serious expression he wore. Sherry’s usual customer greeting stuck in her throat.

"Ms. Oliveri, nice to see you again." In one hand the man held a shopping bag. He presented his empty hand. "Truman Fletcher. And Mrs. Van Ardan, this is a surprise to see you."

"A not too unpleasant one, I hope," Beverly said.

Sherry shook Truman's hand. "You remember Amber Sherman?"

Truman nodded in Amber's direction. "Of course, hello."

"You two know each other?" Sherry pointed from Beverly to Truman.

"Beverly works tirelessly promoting her husband's MediaPie venture. I met her when she and Erik came to the station for a pitch meeting with Damien, Carmell, and myself. I guess nothing ever came of it because Damien still owns the station and, of course, Carmell no longer has any input. I was there as a third set of ears. Isn't that accurate, Beverly?" Truman ran his hand from the neck upward through his hair, providing a pronounced lift. He tamped down the flat top to ensure a level plane.

"I'm curious." Sherry hurled a glance from Amber to Truman. "I was watching a replay of the appetizer cook-off, and there was some footage of Carmell and Brett at their anchor desk as the morning show opened. There was a MediaPie mug exactly like those." Sherry pointed to the three tall, cream-colored beverage holders with the globe imprint on the counter. "Seems odd that what amounts to another media company's advertisement can be seen during the broadcast. That would be like me showing up at the National Chicken Cooking Contest with a beef stir-fry recipe. I find it hard to believe management was okay with that."

"You have a good eye for details, Sherry. Maybe that's why you do so well in competition," Truman said. "You would always see that mug on set when Carmell was on camera. Steele had the bright idea one day soon after the mugs arrived at the studio to conceal her tubes of lipstick in them. The deal was, though, the logo must always face away from the camera. I'm surprised that mistake was made."

"Maybe *mistake* is the wrong word," Amber said.

"That mistake was our good fortune," Beverly sang out. "It's only a matter of time until it won't matter which way the cup faces. Interesting use of the mug, may I add, to hold lipstick. To each his or her own, I suppose." Beverly grabbed Sherry's arm. "Watch out, dear. You're about to be hit." She guided Sherry away from the door as it flung open. "I guess that's why you need that warning bell contraption."

"My goodness. What a crowd." Leila, in a royal blue blazer and skirt, wedged herself between Sherry and Mrs. Van Ardan in order to get the door shut properly. "The fancy limousine outside is now sporting a ticket I'm hoping doesn't belong to anyone in here. It's parked over the line. New York plates."

Leila closed her ticket pad and curled up the side of her mouth. Sherry sent her a wink that Leila acknowledged with a head bob.

Beverly sighed. "This town is run by fools. Handing out parking tickets is no way to fill the coffers. Handing out violations only serves to deter those who would otherwise be spending money at your quaint stores. Anybody with a brain knows that." Beverly spun on her heels and, in the process, collided with Leila. "I'll fight this ticket. You can be sure of that. Sherry, please tell your father I've been in. He'll know what that means."

Leila stepped aside, and Beverly marched out the door, leaving it ajar for someone else to close.

"Sir, does the sedan in front of the store belong to you?"

Truman patted his pants pocket before pulling out his car key set. He dangled the collection of metal in front of Leila's face. "Yes. I thought there was enough time on the meter, but I can run out and put a quarter in."

"No problem. Done and done." Leila held up a shiny quarter. Her grin warmed Sherry's heart as quickly as a spoonful of her slow-cooker chicken soup. "Have a good day, ladies and gentleman." Leila let herself out.

"Mr. Fletcher, what can I help you with? And, by the way, welcome to the Ruggery. Is this your first visit?" Sherry walked a few steps beyond the counter to move him away from the door.

"Please, call me Truman. I was in maybe two weeks ago. Your father helped me. You must not have been working that day. It was the lunch hour, but I don't recall the exact day."

"No problem. I'm surprised my father didn't mention knowing you after we saw you at the cook-off, but that's beside the point. What can I help you with?"

Amber walked to the Rolodex file.

"Over there. That's what I need." Truman pointed to the demonstration table.

"That's very exciting that you hook your own rugs. Such a wonderful hobby," Amber said.

"No, no. As much as I'd like to say I'm that creative, the metal tool is what I'm interested in."

Sherry trotted over to the frame on which a canvas was tacked. Nearly half of the canvas was hooked with colorful yarns depicting an idyllic scene of grasses and summer flowers intertwined with patterned trim. A feast for the eyes. The portion of the canvas that sat in wait for completion held only an imposing punch tool that was fed with an inviting daffodil-yellow ball of yarn. Customers were tempted to poke the tool through the canvas then pull back slightly, to create a loop. More pokes equaled more loops until eventually a rug was created Sherry had seen everyone from instant experts to the total incompetents attempt a stitch or two, and she enjoyed every moment, every time.

Sherry picked up the punch tool and unthreaded the yarn. "This one?"

"Exactly," Truman said. "I bought one from your father, lost that, borrowed a second with every intention of returning it, and promptly misplaced that one. The problem is, I take the thing back and forth with me to work, and sometimes I lose track of it. Let me pay. I can't ask you to lend me another. Your father insisted on lending not selling, but I've made a mess of his kindness." Truman's lips curled up on one side.

Sherry's hand trembled as she held up the tool. "If you don't mind it saying, 'do not remove from O.R.,' this one's all yours." She put her hand back down by her side to quell the shaking.

"Not a problem. That's what was written on the one I lost. If I lose this one, strike three, I'm out."

"What do you use the tool for if you don't hook rugs?" Amber asked in a near whisper.

Sherry sucked in a breath. She sank her hand into her pants pocket and gripped her phone.

"If you had asked me a few weeks ago, I wouldn't

have answered you, but I'm ready to share because I'm so fully invested that there's no turning back," Truman explained.

Sherry pulled her phone from her pocket and hovered her finger over the number nine on the keypad. "You don't have to share if you don't want to, Mr. Fletcher. No one is forcing you."

Truman plunged his empty hand inside his blazer. Sherry tapped her phone's keys. Truman's hand surfaced clutching a cylindrical contraption that was not unlike a policeman's bully stick.

"Nine-one-one, what's your emergency?"

"Truman waved his hand. "This is what I've been working on." He held up his hand. "It's a prototype of an invention to get kids to eat their vegetables. This is the eighth reincarnation, and I think I'm finally at the stage where I can apply for a patent. Truth be told, you were my inspiration, Sherry."

Sherry placed her phone next to her ear. "I'm sorry. I pocket dialed you. All's safe and well here. Sorry for the inconvenience."

"Your creative recipes have inspired me to get my nieces and nephews to eat better, so I invented what I lovingly call The Peas and Corn Rolling Pin. Your father's punch tool was key to getting the perfect holes into the roller. That spells the difference between success and failure. Let me demonstrate." He pinched each of the two handles on either side of the roller. He unscrewed one of the handles. "A hungry child puts some melted butter or cheese sauce in the core of the roller. He replaces the handle and rolls the pin over his peas, carrots, or corn niblets. They get trapped in the meshy screen. The butter seasons the veggies by drizzling out of the punched holes. The child eats the veggies like a corn on the cob. No fork required and lots more fun."

Sherry thought she saw tears welling up in Truman's eyes. "That's genius. What a sweet idea." Sherry secured her phone in her pocket and handed Truman the punch tool.

"I asked your father not to mention I purchased the tool until I had a model I was proud to show you. I wasn't sure I could get it completed, what with all the turmoil over at the station. I've been very distracted."

"I'm so impressed. I'm sure it'll be a big hit with kids and parents. Wouldn't you agree, Amber?" Sherry noted Amber's stunned expression. I'm not the only one in shock here, she thought. "Please, take this store model. I'll bag it for you. The point is very sharp, as you probably know."

"I would also like to buy this oval rug for my mother. Her birthday is next week, and she adores squirrels, so this would be perfect by her back door. Did you know acorns can help predict weather?" Truman picked up a rug depicting two squirrels foraging for acorns on a beige background trimmed in green. "This is for sale, right?"

"Of course. I'll have to check the price." Sherry put the punch tool in her pocket and rolled the rug up as tight as a beef roulade. "Come over to the register, Truman. Amber, maybe you can find me some twine to tie the rug up."

Amber went to the back room in search of rope cord. Sherry placed the rug on the counter and bent forward to spin the Rolodex to *r*, where she hoped to find the price of a small, oval area rug. Erno had yet to type up a price sheet, so the trusty Rolodex was the only point of reference. Judging by the time-ravaged index card and absence of any price strikeouts, Sherry was certain prices hadn't changed in forever.

The scream Sherry let out brought Amber racing from the back room. Truman braced Sherry's bent torso with both hands.

"What's going on? Get your hands off her." Amber pounded Truman's arm with her fists. Her voice was as shrill as a fire alarm.

"It's okay; it's okay. I stabbed myself with the punch tool. When I leaned over to read the tiny letters on the index card, that sharp point went right into my thigh." Sherry straightened up and plucked the punch tool from her pocket.

"My apologies, Mr. Fletcher. I might have overreacted." Amber reduced her voice to a soothing apologetic tone.

Truman rubbed his forearm where Amber had pummeled him. "If I could pay, I need to get going. Don't bother with the twine." He reached for his wallet while keeping an eye on Amber. "I'm getting out my credit card. No need to panic."

"Message received." Amber turned and headed to the back room. A moment later she returned.

Truman backed up against the counter.

"Sherry, I found a protective sheath for the punch tool back there. Maybe Mr. Fletcher would like one."

"No thanks," Truman said. "That's one too many things I'd have to keep track of. I only need the tool for a few days. After that, you'll see it right back here. Thank you anyway."

"I'll take the covering. We should have one by the table. Thanks, Amber." Sherry put the clear plastic liner in her pocket. She finished ringing Truman's purchase up and opened the door for him to exit through.

Chutney and Bean bounded over and sat under their leashes, which hung at the ready by the door.

"Thank you again. Come back soon."

"I bet he's not itching for a return visit anytime soon." Amber pointed to the base of the door. "You dropped something."

There, on the wooden floor, rested the protective punch tool covering. "How did that . . ." Sherry stuck her hand in her pocket only to have her finger leak through the hole in the bottom. "These are brand-new pants."

"There's the culprit." Amber pointed to a punch tool propped up on the side of the register. "You had the punch tool that you were lending Truman Fletcher in your pocket."

"The point tore through the fabric before it went straight into my leg. No wonder it hurt so much." Sherry inspected the hole further. "A clean tear, easily fixable."

The dogs eyed Sherry.

"I'll note Truman Fletcher's purchase on his card, and then I'd like to give these guys a short walk."

Sherry spun the Rolodex to *f* and found the sparsely filled index card bearing the man's name. His only purchase was indeed a punch tool. In the lower left "notes and preferences" section Erno had written "emergency tool replacement—no charge. Requires extra-large handle." The date was two days before Sherry had prepared her appetizer for the cook-off at News Twelve. Sherry added the day's date to the card and noted his oval squirrel rug purchase along with a "second emergency punch tool replacement."

"What happened to the first replacement?" Sherry muttered before replacing the card. "Maybe I'll give Truman a call, just to tell him we didn't give him the extra-large handle he prefers and see if he wants to make an exchange. And I'll throw in a question or two about his whereabouts during the blackout. He's in need of a solid alibi."

Chapter 14

"How do I let you talk me into these things, Amber?" Sherry tugged at her tennis skirt. "Why do these outfits have to be so revealing?"

"Helps you get to the ball faster," Amber laughed. "You don't want to get tripped up by excess clothing, do you?"

"First you try to convert me to yoga, and now you're thinking whacking a hairy yellow ball with metal and strings while I'm nearly naked is the way to go. I can't remember the last time I played this game. You're not getting me confused with my sister, Marla, are you? She's the real sports enthusiast in the family. I'm more of a referee than an athlete."

Sherry twirled the bright blue graphite racket she'd borrowed from the pro shop with such force it spun out of her hand and landed on the floor of the locker room.

"A one-hour lesson will get your sporty juices flowing. You'll be on the tennis tour in no time. Plus, have you seen the teaching pro here? He's cute." Amber winked at Sherry's reflection in the full-length mirror.

"If you're talking about the guy hanging around

the check-in desk, he's a good ten years younger than me. But I appreciate your attempt to inspire me to expand my horizons. I'm going to need a hair clip if I'm supposed to see the ball." Sherry extended her open hand, and Amber dropped a hair clip in her palm. "Not sure this is my look, but if it's good enough for Chris Evert, it's good enough for me."

"You do know she's retired, right?" Amber asked.

Sherry shrugged and turned away from the mirror. "All set. If I'm slowing you down during the hour, say so. I don't want to hold you back from your greatest potential."

"I might have played more times than you, but you're such a good competitor in the kitchen I know instinct will propel you to great heights on the court. I'm not worried in the least about your holding me back. Only a lesson, by the way. No scoring involved. Think of it as an hour of adventure after work. If you lose focus, pretend it's a tennis cook-off and you're in the finals. Not sure how that would work, but sounds fun."

Sherry glanced at the clock over the mirror. "We better get out there. Time is money." Sherry unzipped her sweatshirt and tied the fleecy cotton garment around her waist. They trotted out of the locker room and met up with their instructor at the tennis facility's front desk.

"Ladies, my name is Kris, and, in the next sixty minutes, I'm going to transform you from a capable wielder of the weapon they call a racket to a magician whose wand performs feats others will admire and fear simultaneously. Let's not waste a moment. Follow me." The young man picked up a basket of balls and his neon-orange racket and led the ladies to the court.

"Who knew we were going to make magic!" Sherry waved her racket over her head.

When the hour was up, Sherry's shirt was soaked with liquid effort. She collected the sweatshirt she had flung over the mid-court bench and tied it around her waist.

"That was the best," Amber said. "Wasn't Kris great? I learned so much from him."

"I admit I think I improved. I may have found my sport." Sherry paused. "Did those words come out of my mouth?"

"My work here is complete." Amber dusted her palms against each other.

"It was good fun, but after the first ten minutes, I was thinking about the hole in my pocket on and off for the remainder of our time on court." Sherry held the tennis facility's double doors open for Amber.

The new and improved tennis players made their way to the car for the short trip back to Sherry's house. Sherry unlocked her car, and they climbed in, tossing their purses in the back seat.

"So were you talking about the hole in your pocket you made at work today?" Amber took her seat on the passenger side. "I guess the pointy edge of the punch tool has to be that sharp to punch through the canvas, but it really could be harmful." Amber lifted her hand to her mouth. "That was the tool used to kill the woman at the TV station. Now I understand how lethal it could be if it can pass through tough fabric so easily."

"Exactly. As you were crushing killer forehands and backhands, I was reminded of the cook-off at

News Twelve, and that led to the memory of something I witnessed as Dad and I were getting set to leave the station." Sherry backed out of the parking lot and left the many high-end vehicles still waiting for their owners to finish playing their matches. Sherry checked her side mirrors. At the all clear, she merged onto the two-lane road that would take them back to her house, where Amber had left her car.

"You're losing me. You said you were thinking about the hole in your pocket while we were on the court. What does that have to do with the cook-off? And, by the way, tennis is a game of focus. If you let all those other thoughts creep into your brain, you might not have been playing at your best."

Sherry nodded in agreement. She put on her turn signal and made the turn onto her street. "No doubt about that. But now I fully appreciate how exercise can make a clearer thinker out of you. I've been wrestling with where I've seen a hole like that before, and the answer dawned on me, along with what the missing ingredient in my Spinach Lentil Curry was. I'd have thought that recipe would have won the taste-testing party vote, but now I realize it was missing a key ingredient."

Amber shifted in her seat. "Holes, pants, curry, ingredients. I'm trying to follow along. Keep going."

"You know how Kris said if you're playing your best tennis, you see the ball as the size of a watermelon? It's so easy to hit an object that size. You're completely in the zone. On the other hand, today I saw the ball as being as small as one of the roasted chickpeas in my cook-off appetizer recipe. Needless to say, that could have been one of the reasons I wasn't as good as you."

Sherry threw her hands up in the air for a split second before returning them to the steering wheel. "Hold that thought. We've arrived. To be continued." Sherry parked the car, retrieved her purse from the back seat, and got out.

"Want to come in for a bit?" Sherry asked as Amber emerged from the car.

"Of course. I've got to see where you're going with those roasted chickpeas."

Once inside, they tossed their purses on the front hall table and went to the kitchen for water. Chutney waited by his water bowl with a suggestive posture that Sherry knew all too well meant he was thirsty.

After thoroughly rehydrating, Sherry continued. "When the tennis ball reminded me of chickpeas that would have made my Spinach Lentil Curry perfect, that, in turn, reminded me of the cook-off. It was held on live TV. If the contest lasted for more than thirty minutes, Truman Fletcher felt he'd lose audience interest. Most of us had recipes that required more time than that, but since the cooking process is the least camera friendly, we were asked to accelerate the time in the oven if possible. There wasn't much choice. We either roasted at high heat or risked not completing our recipes in thirty minutes and suffering probable elimination."

"Okay, but the hole?"

"Stay tuned. I'm almost there." Sherry drained the last sip of her water. "Roasting my chickpeas was beneficial for me in the short term because the spices took on an intense, smoky quality that baking at a lower temperature can't bring out. The judges got a nice burst of flavor, along with a satisfying crunch when they were served. By the time the judging was over, I noticed the chickpeas were drying out. Still edible, mind you, but, as time passed, they approached the consistency of BB pellets. Potential tooth breakers. I didn't want to be seen throwing my food in the garbage. That might send the wrong message. So I was bound and determined to get them home before I disposed of them."

Amber relocated a few steps toward the chairs and set herself down in one. "Sorry, but my legs are giving out. I didn't want Kris to think I wasn't putting forth my best effort, so I went a little overboard trying to get every ball he hit."

Sherry followed Amber's cue and sat down. "Problem came when I was on my way out of the building. I was trying to balance my equipment bag in one hand and the tray of leftover goodies in the other. With every gyration I made, the almonds stayed put, but those hardening chickpeas jostled for position like football fans around a tray of buffalo wings. Turns out they'd been raining down in the studio like a hailstorm. Walking over them would have been like trying to keep your balance on a floor covered with ball bearings."

Sherry promenaded her index and middle finger across the table surface. She flung the same fingers forward and landed them flat on the table, splayed out and motionless. "I watched Brett Paladin go down hard after stepping on the chickpeas I spilled. When he got back up, I was embarrassed to see he had ripped his pants. Completely my fault."

"So, you're saying Brett had a rip that was similar to yours?"

"The hole was more than similar. It was the exact match. A very clean tear in the fabric that could only be made by a sharp edge." Sherry made a fist and punched downward. "A fast clean tear, not a slow, yanking one you might get if your car key caught on the pocket lining. No jagged, frayed edges. Those kind of rips are the devil to mend."

"I think I know what you're getting at, but you said Brett fell as you were on your way out of the building. By that time Carmell Gordy was already dead, and the murder weapon was on the scene. Brett must have had scissors or something with a cutting edge in his pocket when he went down in front of you. That was a good correlation you made, though. Details just don't add up to his being involved in the murder, in my opinion." Amber shrugged. "I'm going to head home. I need to walk my little Bean. Thanks again for splitting the tennis lesson. I think I'll continue at least once a week, no matter where I end up living. I really enjoyed myself."

Sherry blinked hard to sort her racing thoughts. "I'm sorry, what did you say?"

"I said I had a good time today."

"Whether I continue or not is yet to be determined, but, me too."

"Time to call it a night. Don't get up. I can let myself out. I'll see you Monday morning." Amber asked as she rose to her feet. "Have anything exciting planned for tomorrow on your day off?"

"I have a Founder's Day volunteers meeting. I'll be assigned my tasks for the big day."

Amber laughed as she headed toward the door. "Good luck."

After Amber left, Sherry took a much-needed shower, walked Chutney, and set about planning her dinner. As often happened, she was sidetracked by a reconsideration of how to improve her recipes. The ballot vote from her dinner party had come out a tie amongst her guests, but the Peanut Butter Chicken Curry had won the most enthusiastic praise in the written comments. She agreed the rich, luscious sauce the chicken was bathed in was complex with its many layers of flavors. The cubed sweet potatoes swimming alongside the chicken bites played perfectly off the toasted coriander and smoky cumin. The addition of mango chutney countered the spices and challenged them to complement the gingery condiment. The final presentation in a royal-blue casserole dish with a sprinkle of chopped peanuts and a shower of fresh cilantro leaves as garnish was a knockout. A warm blanket of satisfaction wrapped itself around Sherry, only to be usurped by prickly discomfort when her next thought drifted to the losing dish.

Sherry picked up the pile of papers she'd set aside from that night. What else had gone wrong with the Spinach Lentil Curry? If the recipe wasn't a clear winner with her friends, her ingredients and preparation were failures. She should have included chickpeas to give the dish more substance, but her father had expressed his dislike for the legume. She had let that sway her decision to leave them out. As a result, the consistency had been as uninviting as that of a refrigerated tomato. The flavors were nice, but the feel was lackluster. Of course, her guests' comments had been much more diplomatic than her self-criticism, but what Sherry read between the lines was the need for recipe rehab.

"I'm putting all this aside until after dinner." She waved the printed recipe copies and ballots at Chutney, who wagged his tail with such vigor he lost his balance. She set the pile on the counter and opened the refrigerator. She pulled out the covered container of Peanut Butter Chicken Curry and proceeded to the microwave. With a punch of a button, the tiny food molecules were zapped by magical heat energy, and seconds later the proper level of warmth was reached.

Even eating alone, Sherry would never consider eating directly from the container. As was her nightly ritual, she arranged a floral place mat and silverware for herself. She plated the food, poured herself a glass of wine, and sat down. A moment later, Sherry rose from her seat. She gathered the stack of papers and laid them beside her plate. She separated out the recipes and moved them to the bottom of the pile. She picked up the first ballot. The looping, freestyle letters written with a noticeable tremor in the penmanship were a dead giveaway as to the author. With a forkful of curry in her mouth, she ran her eyes over her father's comments.

"My choice is the Peanut Butter Chicken Curry. Pros: flavor that never quits. Cons: sticky on the tongue. Made me thirsty. Had a sip of Ruth's Merlot. Hard to hold a conversation while eating it. Food aside, Steele is no longer a suspect, right? Someone tried to kill him, so he can't be guilty. Carmell needed a favor I wasn't willing to do for her; that's why she was angry with me. What about that Truman

Fletcher fellow? He seemed kind of peculiar. Like I always say, 'odd plus odd only evens out for numbers.'"

Sherry shook her head. "Not exactly an anonymous ballot, Dad." She licked the excess sauce off her fork and plunged the prongs toward a sweet potato. She put Erno's ballot at the bottom of the pile and reached for her phone. She crafted a short text and sent it. Setting the phone aside, she studied the next paper.

"Both so good! Do I really have to choose? I have two graduate degrees and years of helping others out of dire circumstances, but I can't seem to make this simple choice. . . . Okay, Peanut Butter Chicken Curry. Ahhh!"

"I would've thought Amber would go for the lentils." Sherry tucked the ballot under Erno's and raised the next one to eye level.

"Spinach Lentil Curry wins. Reasons: unusual, healthy, saucy, spicy, luscious. The other curry was good too, dear, but this one spoke to me. And have you noticed the new neighbors three houses down aren't cleaning up after their designer pooch? I mean, the pup must have cost a pretty penny. Maybe the owners can't afford bags now? Don't they know rescue dogs are only the cost of a donation?" The comment was illustrated with a heart.

Sherry filed Eileen's ballot at the bottom of the pile. She picked up the next ballot in the pile. Sherry squinted and rotated the paper. The words she hadn't been able to decipher last night were still open to interpretation, but the brighter kitchen light made them somewhat clearer.

"Spinach Lentil Curry wins by a slight margin."

Sherry tried but she could only make out two out of five words in the short phrase that followed.

". . . Rich, scrumptious . . ."

Sherry smiled. There was a blank space that separated an additional section of comments at the bottom of the paper, as difficult to read as a doctor's handwriting. Sherry could put two blocks of words together.

"Your father should proceed with caution" and *"relationship with Van Ardans will blow up in his face."*

Sherry shuddered. She noted Ruth's, or was it Frances's, pen stroke had torn through the paper in what seemed an attempt to punctuate with an exclamation point. Sherry handled the ballot as if it were the flesh of a Scotch bonnet chili pepper, discarding it as soon as she was done reading so the burn wouldn't linger. She filed it at the bottom of the pile.

Sherry poked a hefty portion of chicken and sweet potato. She dragged them across the mire of curry sauce on her plate. Her gaze settled on the next ballot. The first word was *"Spinach,"* slashed by a diagonal line. Below the stricken word, *"Peanut Butter Chicken"* was written with a light touch. Sherry pursed her lips. Her brow rose and fell.

"Reason—loved both but big fan of sweet potatoes. The deciding factor."

Sherry cocked her head to the side.

"Great pickle sales numbers this week. Ruth knows more than she's letting on."

Sherry's attempt to swallow her last chew failed, and she coughed until Chutney appeared at her side with a twitching nose.

"Sorry, boy. I forgot I'm not good at multitasking." She slipped Frances's ballot underneath the previous one she deduced had to be Ruth's.

The next ballot simply read *"Spinach Lentil Curry is the winner; it's what I want for dinner. And if Eileen can't make the recipe as well as you, the delicious memory on my taste buds will have to do."*

A low-pitched warble emanated from Sherry's throat.

"Peanut Butter Chicken Curry" headlined the next ballot, written in all capital letters, no less. *"Best meal I've ever eaten!"*

The corners of Sherry's mouth curled up before she continued reading.

"Trivselbit *means leave the last crumb on the plate for comfort and security. If Augustinians don't* trivselbit, *no one is safe. All we hold dear is vulnerable."*

Sherry sighed. Larson was still on his soapbox. She straightened the pile of papers and read the final sheet. *"Brett"* was dead center in the middle of the otherwise blank sheet of paper.

Sherry squared the papers up and laid them on top of the two recipes. She gave Chutney a pat on the head. "Here's the final tally. Out of the eight voters, four votes for Peanut Butter Chicken, four votes for Spinach Lentil. In non-recipe-related election results, one vote for Brett Paladin and one for the Van Ardans. One for *trivselbit* and one for Truman Fletcher. Seems to have gotten a bit off track, but I'm grateful for the opinions on every topic."

As Sherry rose to bring her plate to the dishwasher, her phone rang. "Hi, Dad. How're you doing?"

"Very well, sweetie. I'm dangerously close to returning to work. I'm getting a bit stir-crazy here. You texted me a message. What can I do for you?"

"What was the favor Carmell asked of you?"

"All I can say is she wanted me to use my influence on some of my dearest friends, and I refused. Case closed."

Sherry rocked on her heels before sitting back down. "Truman Fletcher bought a punch tool from you."

"That's right. And when he lost it, I lent him a store model."

"He was in yesterday asking about another replacement because he lost the loaner. That all adds up to things look pretty bad for him."

Erno sniffed. "I sense a 'but' lurking."

"But, he has an alibi. Truman spelled it all out when I called him to offer the punch tool with the extra long handle. As delicately as I could I mentioned the detective had questioned me about who might have recently purchased a punch tool. As the conversation progressed Ray told me he had solid proof Truman was not in the studio when Carmell was murdered." Sherry sighed when she heard her father's prolonged exhale. "Truman's made an invention, inspired by me, no less, and he's using the punch tool to engineer it. He's even applied for a patent. He was submitting his patent application at the moment of the crime. He couldn't get an Internet connection while the power was out, which was lucky for him, because he was forced to save his e-mail attempts as drafts, offline, and they were time-stamped. Can't get any more concrete an alibi than that."

"I was afraid you were going to say that. And Damien Castle? Is he still on your suspect list?"

"Nope. He's off the list, too. Damien was at a Gamblers Anonymous meeting at the time of the murder and can prove it. That's a whole other story, but it boils down to everyone has his or her vices, and betting was his." Sherry heard an extended puff of air crackle through the phone. "Steele Dumont is no longer on Detective Bease's radar because he was Damien's driver, plus it's evident he was the intended target of the unscrewed falling shelves that took Lucky's life."

Erno moaned, reminiscent of the time he had eaten one too many slices of his mother's decadent pecan pie at Thanksgiving when Sherry was very young. She let the subsequent silence linger until Erno began clicking his tongue on the roof of his mouth.

"Dad, do you have something you want to tell me?"

Chapter 15

"Charlie, I watched the video of the cook-off, and I have a few concerns." Sherry punched on her phone's speaker setting so she could better hear her ex-husband as she continued getting dressed for her meeting.

Chutney jumped up on her bed and curled up next to her pillows.

"Wait a minute! You said we could watch together."

"Check your facts, counselor." Sherry slipped a pink blouse over her head. "You're the one who said we should watch the tape together. I made no such statement."

"Okay. Duly noted. What are your concerns? Before you proceed, may I remind you, I don't know anything more about cook-offs than what you taught me."

Sherry fastened her skirt, sat on the bed, and stared inside the open closet door. "No cook-off issues. My first question is about something I saw before the event started. The video caught a shot of Carmell Gordy seated at her set desk. She had a travel mug to the side of her notes. The cup had the logo 'MediaPie' on it. I was surprised the station would allow such blatant branding in the camera shot. Is that legal?"

"Ah, yes. The Van Ardan enterprise. I'm familiar with a branch of the company because they bought a radio station in the neighboring county, and our office did the legal work on the environmental impact of the upgrades they applied for. As for the cup, displaying a company logo most certainly is legal. MediaPie might pay a good price for that product placement. If they didn't, News Twelve is doing a disservice to themselves by being the cow that gives away the milk for free."

"So MediaPie has its fingers in lots of pies, so to speak? No pun intended. Well, maybe some intention." Sherry lifted the corners of her mouth.

"They're a growing media company in the Northeast and recently have begun acquiring small television and radio stations with key audience demographics."

"What do they do with the stations after they acquire them?" Sherry stood and put the phone in the palm of her hand.

Chutney jumped off the bed and parked himself by the bedroom door.

"I can only speak about the radio station we represented. The papers we filed for them indicated MediaPie wanted to bring the station under their broadcast umbrella, which would broaden their listening audience but, on the flip side, the outcome is that any local feel the station was known and loved for may get phased out. I assume that's their plan for the other stations, both radio and television, they're targeting to purchase. Sounds like News Twelve is in their crosshairs."

"Did you know Brett Paladin's father owned the

station at one point?" Sherry stepped inside her closet and slipped her feet in a pair of flats the color of butternut squash pulp. A moment later, she kicked them off and shimmied her feet into brown suede driving shoes.

"A man named Damien Castle is the majority shareholder now, if I recall correctly. He uses a lawyer in the firm for business dealings, but I'm not at liberty to go into detail. I can tell you, the man has his work cut out for him trying to salvage the station on his own. May not be the worst thing to sell out while he can."

"Was the station on solid footing when Damien bought it from the Gadabees? Did you know that's Brett Paladin's real last name. He took on Paladin when he applied for the job at the station."

Charlie exhaled at length, an indication she was over-probing him. "The station was very successful for a local cable channel. That was evident in the substantial amount Damien Castle had to pay to Ruth Gadabee. But that number, too, is confidential. I didn't have any idea the Gadabees had a son, namely Brett Paladin. He was never part of the purchase agreement. If I remember correctly, Ruth Gadabee was a second wife, so I'm guessing, because of his age and hers not being too far apart, Brett is Ruth's stepson, not biological son."

"That's right." Sherry lifted the phone to eye level and checked the time. "One more question before I leave. This one is going in a completely different direction."

"Why am I not surprised?" Charlie responded.

"I'm off to a final Founder's Day organization meeting, and I want to arm myself with some knowledge."

Sherry shut the closet door with her knee. "If there isn't a public record of a town's founder, but instead, hearsay and/or folklore passed down through the generations, is that strong enough evidence to be irrefutable?"

"There are settlers, founders, town incorporators, and more, any number of whom can lay claim to being a town's founder. Depends on the fine-tooth comb you're using to pinpoint the exact person. I would think there would be, at the very least, a diary artifact, a travel log, or a financial transaction record book that verified the answer. Sometimes it boils down to the largest landholder wins. Which individual held multiple jobs when the town was in its infancy? Important question. That person was often considered the founder because he put himself in those jobs before anyone else was in residence to claim them. Not unheard of that the same person was the mayor, the town realtor, the general store proprietor, the justice of the peace all at once. On the other hand, bear in mind, it's rare one single person is credited with founding, rather than a few families or a religious group of some sort, with reasons to make the effort to found a new settlement. Very unusual that no records would remain, even if they were simply in a trunk in someone's attic. Does that help? And yes, you've gone in a lot of different directions in one phone call."

Sherry clicked her phone off speaker mode and held it up to her ear. "Thanks, Charlie. Next cook-off I promise we'll watch the replay together if it's televised. Bye, bye." Sherry ended the call.

Trailed by Chutney, Sherry bounded down the stairs. She dropped her phone in her purse and gave her dog a pat on the head. "I hope this won't take long, boy. I'll be back to get you, and we'll join your friend Bean at the store this afternoon. Keep an eye out until I get back." The soothing tone of voice Sherry used seemed to reassure Chutney his owner would return soon because he plopped down by the sofa without any prodding.

The drive along the shoreline to the town beach clubhouse remained one of Sherry's favorites. She might have paid a premium for her small house and tiny parcel of land, but she never regretted her choice. For the same price she could have gotten twice the square footage and double the acreage in a location farther from the Long Island Sound, but that wasn't an option, in her mind. The proximity to the town center, the natural beauty of the serene salt water, a river snaking through the county and hills to the north, all within a two-mile radius, made living where she did priceless. Overhead were hawks, sea birds, and the state bird, the robin, along with dozens of other winged creatures of every color. Prowling around covertly through the neighborhoods, hills, and riverbanks were otters, coyotes, bear, and wild turkeys, to name a few of the animal inhabitants. Unless the season was midwinter, whenever Sherry drove, she insisted the windows of her car be cracked open to invite fresh air to brush her cheeks and paint them with a radiant glow. Augustin was a town worth fighting for. She gripped the wheel so hard her nails dug into the palm of her hands.

Sherry arrived at the town beach with a jaw sore from clenching. She checked her face in the rearview mirror, but was distracted by the reflection of a car maneuvering into a parking spot behind hers. A moment later, Larson Anderson was at her window.

She waved to him in hopes he'd step away from the door so she could wedge herself out of the car.

He pulled the door handle and bowed from the waist. "Welcome, Ms. Oliveri. I'm happy you could attend."

Sherry smoothed her skirt and swung her legs out of the car, while keeping a hand on the hem so as not to flash anyone. "Thank you, sir." She shimmied out of the car, locking it behind her. "Another glorious autumn day. Such a nice idea to have the meeting down at the beach. Everyone's mood will be sky-high."

"I'm not too sure about that," Larson said as they strolled down the wooden walkway to the town beach clubhouse. A few yards away, the gentle waves lapped against the sandy shore, providing a steady, churning murmur. "The ambiance may be serene, but we're having a visit from someone who insisted on showing up and stirring the pot, so the slop might be hitting the fan very soon."

"I hope you're not talking about me?" Beverly Van Ardan caught up to the duo from behind.

Sherry spun her head around. "Mrs. Van Ardan, so nice to see you."

"Yes, Beverly, I was talking about you." Larson turned to face the woman wrapped in an oversized silver silk scarf. Without waiting for a response, he picked up his stride until he reached the weathered wooden building.

Sherry pumped her arms to keep pace. Once inside, they found others from the organization committee seated at a round table in a small room with no windows. The serenity Mother Nature provided outside the doors was walled out.

"Thank you for coming, ladies and gentlemen," Larson said before Sherry was able to sit. "I'm happy all eight of us could make it here." He eyed Beverly, who was descending onto a chair along the wall. "Mrs. Van Ardan will be joining us for the first few minutes as she wishes to address the committee."

Chatter began amongst the attendees, with the exception of Sherry, who lowered her head and studied the backs of her hands.

"What is it you would like to say to the committee, Beverly?" Larson asked.

As she stood, Beverly's extensive scarf caught under the leg of the chair and unfurled in its entirety from around her shoulders. The silk rectangle cascaded to the floor. She scanned the room. Sherry detected a blush on the woman's cheeks that boiled up through her thick concealer. Sherry stood, gathered the scarf, as well as the glares of everyone in the room, and handed the garment to Beverly, before returning to her seat.

"Thank you, dear. You are your father's daughter. So kind and generous." Beverly tied herself up in the scarf and fluffed the underside of her hair with her fingers. "And thank you, Larson, for giving me a moment of your committee's time. I wanted to address you all concerning my time to speak at the event. I have been advised that we can give a ten-minute presentation during the Trivselbit presentations. That extremely brief time will give the family a chance to present concrete evidence of my great-great-great, I think it is, grandfather's role in founding this town. If it weren't for Knut Eklind's selflessness, this town most likely wouldn't exist."

A robust man with blood-red, bulging cheeks lifted from his seat. "Dirty money. He exploited people's weakness for alcohol and nearly ruined the community. If it weren't for Andre August Dahlback, this town's history would be a black hole of debauchery."

"Harry, please, let the woman say her piece." Larson used his hands to suppress the turbulent air until the interruption was quieted.

"The point I'm trying to make is, while I realize what's done is done, I feel a strong obligation to present the facts. So, I'm asking for table space to lay out photos, an unopened bottle of decades-old Knut Eklind Gin, and a deed from a land purchase here in Hillsboro County dated in the eighteen hundreds." Beverly paused. "I have also arranged for News Twelve to cover the event, although they insist a member of this committee meet with them prior to iron out details."

A volcanic breath erupted from the direction of the previous outburst. "Give her what she wants so she'll leave us alone. The truth will come out in the end."

"You'll have to pardon Harry," Larson said. "He, like most of our citizens, wonders why a family with no current connections to Augustin, other than your patronage in our stores, which we fully appreciate, bothers to want a relative recognized for a deed he might or might not have done. To this day, the man has no lasting influence on our town in any way. Seems more self-serving to his present-day relatives than a tribute to the man. So, yes, fine. You will be provided with a display table. There's a vacant table next to the Augustin Society for Roadway Beautification table. That's a very prestigious location, Beverly.

The local chapter of Safeguard the Groundhog was forced to forfeit the spot for lack of volunteers."

"Thank you." Beverly tipped her head slightly.

"Who can I entice to meet with representatives at News Twelve to arrange their schedule?" Larson peered around the room.

Sherry raised her hand as if Larson had asked for volunteers to try a scoop of her favorite butterscotch ice cream.

"Ms. Oliveri, you're kind to volunteer. If you're available later this afternoon, I'll arrange for you to meet up with a crew from the station to go over details. Here's a handout of all they need to know." Larson walked a stapled set of papers over to Sherry, bypassing Beverly on the way. "Are there any other issues at hand, Beverly? Because you can excuse yourself if not."

Beverly fingered her scarf. "That's it. I hope everyone has a nice day." She gathered her purse and left the room.

"You made that too easy for her, Larson. The Van Ardans have their foot in the door, and soon they and their corporate machine will suck this town dry. We might as well rename the place MediaPie-town." Harry covered his face with his hands.

"Okay, folks, we're moving on before we lose track of our mission." Larson sighed and picked up his cell phone. He used his thumb to scroll down the screen. He pointed to a woman seated next to Sherry. "Cora, you'll be our roving Comfort Ambassador throughout the day."

The woman giggled. "That's a polite way of saying the person who points out the porta potty locations."

"A very important duty," Larson added.

"Good pun, Larson," Harry shouted.

Larson's cheeks lifted, then lowered. "Wyatt, as publications director, the only task left for you is to pick up the maps, brochures, and table identification signs." Larson nodded to the man seated across from Sherry. "Vivienne, you have done an outstanding job coordinating the youth of Augustin. Their parade will go off without a hitch, I'm sure. Sherry, I've taken you off the cleanup taskforce and reassigned you as food vendor chairwoman, for obvious reasons. We're using all the same vendors as last year, so you merely need to give them a location on the town square to set up. I remind you, do not put Grassroots Grub next to Caveman Carnivore. Last year the wind was fierce and blew straight down the row of tables. All the vegans and vegetarians complained their food tasted like grilled steak sandwiches."

Sherry smiled. "Understood."

"With that business settled, I would like to read you my introduction to the Trivselbit ceremony." Larson pulled his reading glasses from his shirt pocket. He adjusted the screen of his phone to eye level before clearing his throat. "The Town of Augustin was officially incorporated on June second, eighteen thirteen, with lands from three existing villages. Andre August Dahlback led seventy-three people living in the territory that is now known as Augustin to petition for Augustin's incorporation. The driving force behind the petition was to assist their village's economic viability that was being overshadowed by surrounding towns' farms. For more than a decade, Augustin was a prosperous agricultural community and the leading onion-growing center in the U.S. Unfortunately, a blight then destroyed the entire crop, leading to a brief era of, shall we say, uncertainty, as to the future of the town, especially after the death of its inspirational leader, Mr. Dahlback. Records show the history of a successful town was already written, and this period of misfortune was a tiny blip on the radar. The foundation of a town with strength and character had been laid by Dahlback, and, thanks to him, we all live in peace and harmony today."

"You never go into details about that rough period and how the town emerged from near devastation. Is there any reason for that?" Sherry asked.

"Best to keep the day light and positive," Larson said.

"After such a compelling story, how can the Van Ardans lay any claim to their ancestor's being Augustin's founder?" Harry asked. "They don't have a pot to pee in. No offense, Cora."

"None taken." Cora giggled.

Larson lowered his phone. "I wish I could say that's true, but fact is, when the town was in its darkest time, Knut Eklind purchased a large percentage of the town's land with his gin fortune and kept the town from falling into the hands of those whose intentions weren't the best. He wasn't a very popular guy because of how he made his money. The movement toward temperance was in its infancy in early America, and the young town of Augustin was at the forefront of promoting healthier lifestyles. Along came Knut, a savior to a few and doing the devil's work. Ironically, his money was welcomed, but he was not. The town that might have gone bankrupt was prosperous again in the short term until the farmers could get back on their feet. Turned out they never really did, but commerce in other forms took root, and Augustin prospered once again. No one would ever wish the town to be renamed Knutville, as the man himself had once petitioned for. Thank goodness for his personal unpopularity, if you ask me, or we'd all be known as Knuties."

"Now, centuries later, the family is back to claim what they feel is theirs?" asked Cora.

"Looks that way. But we can keep this little nugget of historical information to ourselves, can't we? No sense rocking the boat now," said Harry. "As I heard Erno Oliveri once say, 'history without the *s-t-o-r-y* is just a short hello.'"

"Agreed. Let's finish up here, people. It's going to be a great day, thanks to all your hard work," Larson said.

After the meeting's business was concluded, Sherry drove home to change her clothes and pick up Chutney to bring to the Ruggery. As she parked her car at the curb in front of her house, which she did when she knew she was only staying for a brief time, her phone rang.

"Sherry, this is Detective Ray Bease."

Sherry smiled at the man's formal tone. "You must have ESP. I was about to call you."

There was a gurgle from his end of the call. "I'll go first since I made the call. I'd like to follow up with your father about the e-mail threat he received. Our tech team has traced the message's origin to a computer at News Twelve. Not too difficult a task; the station hasn't upgraded their computer security in years."

Sherry slipped out of her car. "Ray, someone over there is mad enough to kill, possibly twice, and my dad is on that person's radar. Are you moving as fast as you can?"

A groan assaulted Sherry's ear. "I appreciate your desire for speed. From your perspective, I'm sure the investigation is moving like molasses in February, but, keep in mind, not too long ago your father was a prime suspect, so be thankful fact gathering, sorting, and deciphering is our top priority."

"So, if you're suggesting he's no longer a suspect, what do you want to talk to him about?"

"See, that's where your investigative skills are lacking. Your father may, without knowing, be holding onto information of value in this case. It's a matter of my asking him the correct question."

Sherry's turn to groan.

Sherry thought back to her father's comment about not considering himself completely innocent. What had he meant by that? "If you want my blessing to talk to him, I'll give it on one condition."

"Sherry." The detective raised his voice, and Sherry recoiled. "No bargaining."

"I didn't mean it that way. I meant, can you run the questions by me first?" Sherry opened the door to her house and was greeted by Chutney.

"Your father told me there were four people at the station he knew prior to the day of your cook-off. Carmell Gordy, Brett Paladin, Truman Fletcher, and Steele Dumont."

Sherry's voice raised an octave. "That's right. Brett was a customer at the Ruggery many years ago, and Steele Dumont has ties with our family, so that's how my father knew them. Truman Fletcher made a purchase at the store a few weeks before the cook-off.

Brett Paladin's stepmother is a close friend of Dad's, which came as a surprise to me, but their acquaintance doesn't raise any red flags, for me, at least." Sherry visualized Damien Castle's voting ballot.

Detective Bease hummed a single baritone note. "Okay. What I would like to ask your father is could he recall any detail about any of those four individuals that may be of use. My feeling is, before we have to formally question him, I may be able to coax a recollection or piece of overlooked information out of him in a more relaxed atmosphere. Some recollection he doesn't recognize as relevant or possibly isn't sure he wants to share."

Sherry's cheek muscle twitched. "I've tried." She pressed her hand to her face. "Would you consider Brett Paladin a suspect?"

"You know I can't go into investigation specifics, Sherry. I'll say he's not at the top."

"I'm heading over to News Twelve later this afternoon for some Founder's Day business." Sherry waited, but there was only silence and possibly a pen tap. "Is there more? I need to keep moving and get over to the store."

"That's all." The detective paused. He lowered his voice. "If you do see or hear something pertinent to the case when you're at the station, please call me. But, under no circumstances are you to put yourself at risk. Do you understand me?"

Sherry began an eye roll, reconsidered, and slammed her eyelids shut instead. "Yes, sir."

Chapter 16

Sherry bundled up the eight by ten-foot rug as tight as a jelly roll and bound the colorful canvas with twine. "In all the years Patti Mellitt has lived in Hillsboro County, this is the first time she has made a purchase at the store."

"She picked a sensational rug. I know she's a foodie, so this apple, purple cabbage, and winter squash motif will keep her inspired for a long time to come."

Sherry waved a fresh index card in front of Amber. "Would you mind filling the card out with her information? Last name, first name, purchase description, and price will suffice. We'll let Dad do the preferences section, if he wants, to get him back in the swing of things." Sherry walked the rug over to the sales counter.

She turned her gaze back to Amber. "While you're in the files, would you mind pulling Brett Paladin's card?"

Amber squinted. "Sherry? What exactly do you

have in mind?" She began spinning the carousel of cards. "Here you go." Amber handed the card to Sherry.

Sherry lifted the card high to catch the light. "Dad's handwriting is fading on this Paladin card. I can barely make it out. 'Preferences: do not contact him by phone, avoid talk of family and business.'"

"Your father's notes are an enigma all their own." Amber put out her hand to receive the card. At the same time, the front door swung open.

Sherry's gaze darted toward the incoming customer.

Patti Mellitt, dressed in a beige linen pantsuit, brown flats, and a pink baseball hat, shut the door behind her. She lifted her sunglasses and set them on the rim of her cap. "Good afternoon, ladies. I'm so excited to pick up my rug. I feel like a true Augustinian now that I'm about to lay a famous Ruggery objet d'art in my front hall. I'm not sure why it took me so long to join the party."

"Right here. All ready for you." Sherry patted the rug as if it were a perfectly risen mound of pizza dough waiting to be rolled out. "Anything else you need?"

"No. Ring me up, and I'm on my way. I'm reviewing a bakery down the street, and my stomach's been barking at me to hurry up and get there since an hour after breakfast." Patti slipped her wallet out of her purse. "Any breaks in the murder investigation over at News Twelve? I believe, the last time I saw you, a second murder had occurred, although they had the unfortunate victim's identity wrong." She handed Sherry her credit card. Patti pointed to the punch tool next to the register. "A tool like that was used to take Carmell Gordy's life, if what I read was correct."

"Unfortunately, yes." Sherry's smile melted to a frown.

"As I recall, I told Detective Bease two details stood out to me that morning," Patti said. "One was how Carmell Gordy refused to try even the smallest bite of the contestants' food. She sipped her green drink, which I suppose is how she maintained her svelte figure, but I thought a good move would have been to try a bite. Makes the cooks feel appreciated. Carmell hovered over me while I judged the appetizers in the room off the studio, but declined every morsel I offered her. The second detail was when I saw Brett Paladin fall hard as he rounded a corner a few minutes after you were awarded first prize. His face turned fire red, and he let out a yowl that sent shivers up my spine. He was as adamant about refusing help as Carmell was about refusing solid food. It's amazing how stubborn people can be. His pocket contents scattered because I think he ripped his pants. He swam across the floor, very undignified, spread-eagle, in a panic to grab all the items up, including a smashed cookie." Patti accepted her credit card back from Sherry.

"Strangely, that's a relief to me that you saw him fall because I thought I caused him to rip his pants when he skidded on my spilled chickpeas."

"I think it was round beads on the floor that tripped him up. Ball bearings best describe them." Patti rubbed her index finger and thumb together. "Small, but they did the trick."

"Okay, now I feel guilty. Those were escapees from my appetizer platter."

"Couldn't have been. I would never have awarded you first prize if they had been so overcooked," Patti sang out.

"They really were my chickpeas. You tasted them fresh out of the oven, but, an hour later, they were as hard as cherry pits. I'll offer again to pay for any mending Brett might have had done, when I see him later. I'm heading over there in a few hours for a meeting."

"Thanks for the rug, and please give your father my best regards."

"I will. I'm just about to call him."

Patti gathered up her purchase and left the store.

Chapter 17

"I don't think the meeting at News Twelve will be very long, so I'll bring Chutney with me and leave him in the car. Weather's cool, so the car will be a perfect temperature for him. Are you okay closing up?" Sherry lifted Chutney and tucked him under one arm.

He went limp, as he always did when he was in his owner's secure embrace.

"Of course," Amber replied.

The door swung open.

As Sherry rotated to greet the customer, she jerked her neck back and blinked hard. "Dad? What are you doing here?"

"Hello to you too. It's my store, you know. You shouldn't be that astonished when I show up." Erno unzipped his windbreaker. He rubbed Chutney's head and was rewarded with a vigorous tail wag.

"Hi, Erno. So nice to see you." Amber made a quick scan around the store. "I hope everything is in order, the way I was taught you like it. I've kept that in mind every minute I've worked here."

"That's why I made a special trip over. I'm thinking tomorrow morning is my day of return."

Sherry shifted her gaze from her father to Amber. Her friend's shoulders slumped forward.

"Are you sure, Dad? Do you think you're feeling strong enough?"

"I'll come in for one hour, tops. I've got to get my toe dipped in the pool."

Amber's smile capsized. "Of course. I should figure out my next move anyway. It's been so much fun, Erno. I can't express my appreciation for the time you've given me here. I couldn't have foreseen how much I was going to enjoy it."

"Whoa, Amber. I hope you don't think you're done working here. You can't get off that easily," Erno said. "I was only considering returning part-time, but that's solely based on your availability to stick around. I know you have your column to write, in addition to working here, and, unlike my daughter, you probably would like to enjoy a full social life too. So, I want to make sure you're able to accomplish all those goals."

Sherry opened her mouth to speak, but only managed a choked whimper.

"Say the word, and I'll stay on." Amber's smile returned. "My townhouse rental is month by month, so that's no problem. As soon as the landlady heard I was working for you, she sweetened the deal in every way possible."

"Consider your job secure." Erno held out his hand. It was met with Amber's grip. "As I like to say, when a bluebird comes a callin', don't hide the birdseed."

"I agree, and now I've got to get to my meeting. See you two tomorrow." Sherry reached her free hand out to find the doorknob while keeping her eyes on her father.

"I don't suppose we'll be needing you tomorrow,

sweetie. I mean, unless Amber needs you to come in after I leave."

"I certainly have lots of errands to do. If you're okay flying solo, would you mind if I knock a few items off my to-do list tomorrow?"

"I'll be fine. I'll call you if the unforeseen arises, but I doubt I'll need you."

"Great." After she made her way around the building to her car, Sherry came to a dead halt. Chutney stared at his owner.

"I forgot to ask Dad if Detective Bease called. I'll call him later. I don't want to disrupt the good mood Dad's in. Let him enjoy a moment of peace."

Sherry arrived at the News Twelve driveway, then she circled the parking lot twice before deciding on a spot she had overlooked on her prior laps. It looked like a tight fit, but, since she had no human passenger needing to leave the car, she shoehorned the car in with no margin for error on the side opposite hers. Leaving Chutney asleep in the back seat, Sherry carried a batch of home-baked butter pecan cookies to the station lobby.

Sherry approached the receptionist stationed behind a makeshift partition.

The woman leaned toward an opening. "Good afternoon. May I help you?"

"This is new." Sherry tipped her head toward the partition.

"Management's attempt at heightened security after Ms. Gordy's murder. I can't say I feel any more secure in here." The woman shrugged as she leaned into the opening between her and Sherry. "How may I help you?"

Hi. I'm Sherry Oliveri. I have an appointment."

The woman checked her computer screen. "Sherry Oliveri? We've been expecting you. Your meeting with Mr. Paladin and Mr. Fletcher is in the break room. Mr. Castle will join in, but he has a prior commitment, so his attendance may be brief."

"I brought some cookies to share. Would you like one . . ." Sherry squinted and read the woman's name tag. ". . . Elsa?" Sherry plunged the container of cookies through the opening.

"We have a new policy about no external food being allowed in without proper documentation. But I know you're a remarkable cook, so I'm willing to, you know, make sure they're not contaminated in any way." Elsa snickered and shot her hand toward the bag, extracted a cookie, and popped it in her mouth. Her red lipstick-glazed lips pulsed forward and sideways with each chew. She pinched her eyes shut and sniffed in a rush of air before exhaling a column of sugar-laced breath. "The best. If you'll leave me one more, I'll be sure of my decision."

Sherry laughed and reeled cookies back in, not before Elsa plucked out one more.

"Steele Dumont will be right over to escort you in. Sign the log, and pass through the metal detector first, please. Remember to power down your phone. Have a seat if you like." Elsa pointed to the sign-in book and tethered pen on the ledge outside the partition. The phone on Elsa's desk rang, and she turned her back to Sherry.

A few minutes later, Steele Dumont, with short, disheveled hair, appeared at Sherry's side. "Ms. Oliveri, so nice to see you again. I keep hearing accolades about your pickle-selling skills from my grandmother." Steele swept the unruly bangs from his eyes.

"She's exaggerating. It's her pickling expertise that's doing the selling. I'm just the middleman woman." Sherry stood and scrutinized Steele's trimmed hairline. "I can't help but notice your new look. Or is it flavor, you called it? What happened to all the long hair you used to put up in a bun?"

Steele lowered his head. "After Lucky died, wasn't as much fun to sport the style. My twin was gone. In his honor, I cut it off." Steele raised his head, and his eyes were glistening. "We better get going. Brett's on the air in thirty minutes."

Sherry trailed Steele to the break room, where they found Brett and Truman Fletcher seated at a small rectangular table. Damien Castle stood behind Truman, holding his cell phone in one hand and a clipboard in the other. As Sherry entered the room, Damien handed the clipboard to Truman.

"Good afternoon, Sherry," Damien said.

Sherry set her cookies on the table. "Hi, Damien." Sherry accepted his hand, but let hers go limp as he shook. "I brought cookies."

"Please, have a seat." Damien pointed to a vacant chair, but remained standing. He reached over Brett's shoulder and grabbed two cookies. He handed one to Steele. "Dumont, could you please pick up Ms. Oliveri in twenty minutes?"

Steele nodded and shut the door behind him as he left the room.

"I have to leave in a minute, so if you'd give me the time frame and location of the Founder's Day live remote, we can discuss the logistics." Damien crossed his arms and sent a side-eye glance toward the back of Brett's head.

"I thought Beverly Van Ardan was in charge of how the day unfolds." Brett raised his chin.

Sherry's forearms began to swelter, despite the cooling breeze the overhead vent sent her way. She pushed up her shirtsleeves. The frigid metal table surface shocked her flaming skin, and she broke out in goose bumps. She tugged at her sleeves to extend them again.

"Are you comfortable, Sherry? I could raise or lower the thermostat," Truman said.

"We have a lock on the system now, remember? A real money saver, right?" Brett rotated his torso toward Damien.

"I'm fine." Sherry's reply clumped in her throat as if she were trying to swallow a spoonful of tahini paste.

"To address your belief, Brett, Beverly Van Ardan did approach the station about live Founder's Day coverage, and, frankly, I think it's a great idea," Damien said with an air of confirmation.

"Seems like she's full of great ideas." Brett wiped his lips with the sleeve of his blazer, as if his words had left a bitter residue on them. "I don't see why the usual post-celebration wrap-up we've done in the past isn't sufficient."

"I brought a diagram of the exhibit locations. We finalized it at a meeting this morning." Sherry held the picture up in the air and waited for one of the men to take the paper from her.

Each peered at the others until Truman stood and pinched it from Sherry's grasp.

"We'll be at the location for two hours with a camera operator. We should speak to the table representatives first. Isn't there a ceremony at some point on the town green?" Truman clipped the diagram to his board.

Sherry straightened her posture. "That's right. The Trivselbit presentations follow the August-Tinies parade, which is the cutest parade you'll ever want to see. That only lasts about ten minutes, depending how cooperative the kids are. Getting them all lined up and marching in somewhat of an order, youngest to oldest, is about as easy as getting fresh coconut out of the shell."

"I don't know, is it hard or easy to get fresh coconut out of the shell?" Damien asked.

"It's hard to do." Brett said. "The cook knows her metaphors."

"What else do you need from me? I need to keep moving." Damien tipped his head toward Truman and Brett. "These two are fully capable of finishing the meeting without me."

"Speaking of metaphors, sharks need to constantly move or they drown," Brett said. "We're all getting used to Castle's not being around much anymore. No one really knows where he constantly swims off to."

Damien huffed a mighty exhale.

"Thank you for your input at my taste-testing." Sherry held an unblinking gaze on Damien.

Damien peered at the ceiling for a moment with a finger on his temple. "I think what I wrote on my ballot is worth chewing over." He took a bite of one of Sherry's cookies and left the room.

"That sounded cozy," Brett said. "Back to the business at hand. After we talk to the exhibitors and commentate on the parade, the ceremony will take place, correct?"

Sherry nodded. "Would you be interested in opening the first ever Trivselbit ceremony with a few words, Brett? We'd be honored to have you. Larson Anderson will introduce you. Then we promised Erik Van Ardan a few minutes, followed by acknowledgments onstage of Augustin's wealth of talent. My dad and I are among the citizens being acknowledged, but I'm pretty sure our role is as fillers."

"My family's ties to Augustin go way back, you know," Brett said. "People may not be aware that my father's father opened the first seafood eatery in town. All local fish and shellfish. Place was called Gadabee's Seven Seas. I'm told it was very popular with the upper crust in town, but fell out of favor when the competition grew. That wasn't all bad because his next venture led him to reporting the town's news in print. Ultimately, journalism became the family business." Brett cracked his knuckles, one finger at a time.

Sherry cringed with each popping sound.

"Yes, I'd be honored to open the ceremony."

"Perfect." Sherry handed Brett a piece of paper. "Here's the list of event times. If you would be at the podium five minutes prior to the ceremony, events should all run smoothly. Thank you very much." She stood, hands on hips.

"Is that all?" Truman asked. "If it is, I'd like to show you the final version of my invention to get kids to eat their vegetables."

Brett rose from his chair. "I was going to ask if you'd try my improved breakfast cookie." He extracted a small plastic bag from his blazer pocket and waved it in front of Sherry.

Truman produced a paper bag from under his

chair. He thrust his orange and green, mesh-wrapped rolling pin in front of her face. "I have two companies interested in The Peas and Corn Rolling Pin. The days of clipboards and counting the seconds down until broadcast may, fingers crossed, be over soon."

"I know if I were a kid, I'd have fun using your invention to gather my humdrum veggies off the plate to eat them like corn on the cob. You've got yourself a winner." Sherry held up an imaginary corncob and nibbled across it while rotating the invisible cylinder in her fingers.

Truman pumped his fist. Brett's shoulders drooped.

"And you brought a breakfast cookie sample, Brett?" Sherry enunciated, as if she were speaking to a five-year-old.

Brett broke off a piece of cookie and handed it to Sherry. She inspected the surface with the same attention to detail she used when washing sand from leeks, after having once served the vegetable halfheartedly rinsed and listening to her guests crunch their way through what was supposed to be a velvety smooth cream of leek soup. She placed the cookie in her mouth and said a silent prayer. *Please let this cookie be okay, in taste and every other way.* She used her tongue to roll the bite around in her mouth before biting down. "Very nice."

Brett's mouth dropped open. "Really? Do you mean it? I took all your suggestions to heart."

"Really. This is the one." Sherry swallowed. She coughed, in hopes of clearing her throat of a stubborn crumb that wouldn't go down.

"Sounds like you might have baked up your ticket out of here." Truman pointed to Brett's baggie remains.

"This is a side project. I'm not going anywhere. They'll have to pry my cold, dead fingers off the anchor desk to get me to leave." Brett laughed through closed lips.

With an unsteady hand, Sherry collected her cookie container and purse off her chair. "Do you think Steele is in the hall? I should get going."

Sherry left the room and followed Steele back to the building entrance.

The woman behind the glass panel slid open the window and called out, "Any cookies left?"

"They're all yours." Sherry frowned and handed the remaining cookies over. "This wasn't a popular day for cookies. I usually don't have any left. I'm glad you like them."

Elsa winked. "Come back soon."

Sherry made her way to her car and opened the door as quietly as she could, so as not to startle sleeping Chutney. As she slipped in undetected, her phone rang. Chutney leapt to his feet and barked. Sherry answered the call.

"Hi, let me pull out of the parking lot. Hold on a minute." Sherry drove out of the television complex and pointed her car toward home. "I'm back. What can I do for you, Ray?"

"Did you know your father was a minor investor with Damien Castle over at News Twelve?"

Sherry steered her car to the side of the road and parked. She stared out her windshield as cars whizzed by her before increasing the volume of her phone. "Are you sure?"

Sitting in her car on the side of the road, her stomach churned from a combination of hunger and unease.

"I can't claim I know much about his finances, but I would have thought that nugget of information would have come up in conversation over the last few days, given the recent events." She rubbed her turbulent tummy. Maybe Brett's cookie contained too much fiber. It was a breakfast cookie, after all. He might have loaded the recipe with stick-to-your-ribs substances. When her stomach didn't respond positively to her core massage, she reached over in search of the cookie container on the passenger seat. When her hand returned empty, she silently cursed her generous spirit for coming up with the idea of donating all the cookies to the receptionist.

"The legal and financial documents were at the station, under very lax security, I might add, and Erno Oliveri was listed among those who invested with Damien Castle when he took over the station from the Gadabee family," Ray said. "Erno's share was a small amount of money, relative to the other five investors; in fact, his was the smallest amount. He might have even sold his share at a later date to one of the other investors because a subsequent document doesn't list him at all. This information is interesting for a few reasons. Number one, your father now dates Ruth Gadabee, if I'm not mistaken, correct?"

Sherry watched a well-worn green station wagon roll by. The car was the same relic her family had driven for years. "They seem to be more than friends, yes."

"At the time of the transaction, Mr. Gadabee had recently passed away. Brett, his son, was too inexperienced to take over as owner, and his wife, Ruth, wanted to liquidate her deceased husband's holdings for financial security. Your father and the other investors did her a big favor. The station was doing well at that time, and she made quite a profit. If she'd waited much longer, she would have never realized the amount she did. There was even a bidding war with a fledgling company, the MediaPie Corporation, but they backed off early in the game."

"Maybe Dad got out at the right time, too. Possibly at the urging of Ruth. I can imagine, if their friendship was blossoming, he thought his holdings were a conflict of interest of sorts." Sherry put her hand up to shield her ear as a group of motorcycles thundered by.

"Here's interesting reason number two. Damien Castle says he bought the station as fulfillment of a dream to control the local broadcasting in the Augustin and immediate vicinity's market. Your father began advertising his store on News Twelve the same year Castle purchased the station. There's no record of payment from your father for advertising time, so I deduce he got ads for free in some sort of deal he struck up."

The corners of Sherry's mouth lifted. "Again, I'm surprised. Dad never mentioned he knew Damien before the cook-off. Sounds like a shrewd business move on Dad's part."

"His connection to the station appears to have a long history."

"I'm not sure what you're getting at." Sherry squinted as the lowering sun pitched brilliant rays through her side window.

"Your father may not know who killed Carmell Gordy and even the young man Lucky, but I'm betting he knows *why* they were killed."

"Detective, I mean, Ray, I'm not sure . . ."

"I have to go. Someone's trying to call me."

The line went silent.

Sherry set the phone down, checked her side mirror for oncoming traffic, and began her merge. She pushed the accelerator to the floor and merged into the fast lane.

Chapter 18

"Tomorrow is the big Founder's Day celebration. How excited are you?" Sherry unhooked Chutney and stored his leash on the peg next to the door.

Bean emerged from the back room to greet his friend, and they scampered off toward the display rugs.

Amber rubbed her hands together. "I'm excited to be manning the Ruggery table while you and Erno are receiving honors on the Trivselbit podium."

Erno carried a hand towel from the yarn storage room. He used the cloth to wipe the sales counter after he applied spray-on wood polish. "Hi, sweetie. Did I hear my name being mentioned?"

"Amber was saying how she didn't need us tomorrow. She's doing well on her own." Sherry winked at her friend. "I dropped Chutney off. He's over there with Bean." She pointed to the two canines sniffing a newly hooked area rug depicting a fawn in a forest setting. "I'll be back for him after the farmer's market. I fed him already, but any snacks are always appreciated."

"Did you tell Sherry about the tennis social?" Erno asked Amber.

Amber produced a gasp that turned Sherry's head. "Sorry, was that a secret?"

"Dad's way of letting the cat out of the bag is more like releasing a raging bull out of a shoot. So be careful what you say to him." Sherry let out a hearty laugh. "What's the tennis social all about?"

"I wanted to ask if you'd join me in a tennis happy hour at the indoor facility where we played, next Saturday," Amber said. "No rush on your decision, but I need to sign us up by midweek."

"Let me think about it. I have to tweak my curry recipes before the contest's entry deadline, and I'm running out of time."

Erno tapped his shoe on the floor. "Tick, tick, tick. Hear that? It's the time of your life passing you by. Get out there and do some cooking outside of the kitchen, if you get my meaning. Stir the pot; get wild. Skip the main course, and jump right into dessert."

"Okay, Dad. Message received. I should branch out. Marla must have gotten to you." Sherry sighed and raised her arms as if waving the surrender flag. "I'm off. I'll see you later, Amber. Thanks for watching Chutney. Dad, I'd like to have a discussion with you, so if I don't see you here later, I'll call you." Sherry waved to no one in particular and left the store.

Sherry's morning at the farmer's market was a human smorgasbord of casual browsers, pickle connoisseurs, impulse buyers, and foodies. There was a lull in the action after the noon hour, while most patrons were seated at picnic tables enjoying their lunch. Seeing them enjoying their purchases, Sherry's stomach began whining, so she emptied the thermal lunch bag she had brought from home onto her table.

She peeled off the lid of one of the two containers she had set on her table.

"You mean to say you don't exclusively eat pickles at every meal?"

Sherry peered up from the table. Mrs. Dumont was repositioning a misaligned pickle jar on the table in front of her.

"Frances, hi." Sherry popped the lid back on her lunch.

"Two lunches?" Frances pointed to both containers. "Are you expecting someone to join you? And, if that person doesn't show up, I'd be happy to eat whatever remarkable edible you've concocted."

Sherry's cheeks tingled as a warm breeze wafted across them. "I brought my two recipes from the taste-testing party. The guests' votes came up dead even, so I'm performing my own tasting to make a final decision. I'm having a devil of a time with this contest."

Frances stepped to the edge of the table and leaned in. "You do have trouble making up your mind on a number of matters, dear. The Peanut Butter Chicken Curry was the better of the two. I have no doubt about that. There wasn't quite enough going on in the Spinach Lentil Curry. Maybe adding some chickpeas would elevate the dish if you want to stay meatless."

"Thanks. I take all comments to heart."

"Please, go ahead and eat before the crowd wakes up from their lunchtime food coma." Frances pushed a pickle jar a smidge to the left.

Sherry pulled the lid off both containers. She forked a bite of the chicken curry.

"While you eat, can we talk?" Frances lifted the end curl of her hair with the palm of her hand. With a toss, she let the locks bounce back in place. "Your party reinforced the idea that I miss this place. The work you put into your cooking contesting hobby is truly inspirational. I'm not happy with all the free time I have. I think I want my hobby and work back."

Sherry chewed her chicken until every poultry fiber was obliterated. On the last chomp, she bit the edge of her tongue. "Ah!" Her eyes filled with tears, and her nose dripped until she was able to subdue the leak with the back of her hand. "Funny. People keep telling me I inspire them, but I think I'm the one who needs inspiring."

"What I'm asking is, after this season, would you be willing to give up the Perfect Storm pickle table?"

"Frances, it's rightfully yours in every way. I don't even have to finish out the season if you'd like to take over immediately." Sherry plunged a scoop of Spinach Lentil Curry in her mouth.

"No, no. I'm busy for the immediate future, so please finish out this season," Frances said with an airy tone. "That's settled. Now I'd also like to discuss my grandson, Steele." Frances paused and waved her finger at Sherry. "You have some spinach in your teeth, dear."

Sherry bowed her head and ran her tongue around her mouth. "A hazard of the hobby."

"It's no secret there's most likely a connection between the two deaths, Carmell Gordy and Steele's friend Lucky, over at News Twelve. What I was told, much to my horror, was that Steele was the intended target, not his friend. When Steele was a suspect, I was in shock. Now I'm in a constant state of worry that whoever did this will try again and won't make a mistake the second time around. And to compound my worry, your father has been on the receiving end of a threat. Good lord!"

"Of course, I understand your concern, Frances. Detective Bease is doing his best to solve the case."

"Steele continues to tell me how chaotic the situation at the TV station is."

After a few slow, deliberate bites of food, being careful to avoid irritating her tender tongue, Sherry set down her fork. "I've seen it for myself. The atmosphere is rough over there. I met with Brett, Damien Castle, and Truman Fletcher to firm up the TV coverage for Founder's Day, and the takeaway was that two of them seem to have one foot out the door and the third says he wouldn't leave what seems to be a sinking ship for all the tea in China."

"You're referring to Brett Paladin as the one who'd go down with the ship."

"I have a question. Has Steele ever mentioned Brett's obsession with his breakfast cookie recipe?" Sherry watched the woman who brined one of the most delicious pickles in the region let her usually perky cheeks sag like a bulldog's.

"As a matter of fact, he has. Why in the world would you ask that?"

"Frances Dumont. What a coincidence of the highest magnitude to see you here today. Perfect timing because I have a burning question to ask you."

Sherry jerked her head around and came face-to-face with Beverly Van Ardan in a quilted barn coat and tall English garden boots, with the largest tote bag Sherry had ever seen. The carryall had a stitched monogram across the face.

"Beverly Van Ardan. What brings you so far out of your urban oasis?" Frances asked.

"There's a good chance I'll be spending a lot more time in this town, and I'm trying to familiarize myself with its intricacies. The farmer's market is on the not-to-be-missed list I got from the chamber of commerce. The Perfect Storm pickles were listed as a must buy." She cradled a jar of dilly delights. "I couldn't help but overhear Brett Paladin's name mentioned a moment ago. Do either of you know what some of his favorite pastimes are? Frances, you must, being as close to his stepmother as you are. Where is your partner in crime? Quite unusual to see one of you without the other."

"Ruth is shopping with Erno." Frances smiled at Sherry. "He needs a new television. You're right, though. I feel as if a part of me is missing when we're not together. To answer your question about Brett Paladin, I remember Ruth's mentioning that, when they were living together, and granted that was many years ago, he loved reading history books, biographies, and cookbooks. She said he didn't really have hobbies, but he once helped her finish a rug she was hooking."

Sherry took a step back and caught her heel on a tuft of grass. She steadied her balance by grasping the edge of the table. "Why do you want to know what some of Brett's favorite pastimes are?"

Beverly's hand disappeared into her bottomless tote bag. Her arm was swallowed up to her bicep. A MediaPie mug emerged in her grip. "I want him onboard with my husband's buyout offer, and he's rebutted every attempt made thus far to win him over. I thought of appealing to a yet undiscovered softer side of the man."

Sherry held her gaze on the mug. "Did you give other employees at News Twelve mugs similar to that one?" She knew the answer, but hoped for the specifics, much like knowing how a recipe should end up tasting before figuring out how to get the ingredients to cooperate.

"At the meeting where the contracts were presented, we encouraged people to accept a mug. Carmell, bless her heart, was the first taker that day. She did seem to live on smoothies, so I'm sure she made good use of our gift."

"Is the sale of the station a done deal?" Sherry scanned the shoppers milling about behind Beverly. Many were disposing of their recyclable lunch containers in the collection bins. Others were dispersing toward the vendor tables.

"Hardly. There are holdouts, and we're respectful of that, but I think the chips will fall the right way eventually. The promise of timely, appropriate paychecks and an updated, improved working environment will be too alluring to turn down. Now, if we could clear up the murder mystery that's casting such a dark shadow over the place, moods would elevate. I have a theory about who may be behind all that."

"Beverly, since when did you become a detective?" Frances's tone was as sharp as Vermont cheddar. "Why don't you let the professionals do their job and stop muddying the water? The only amateur qualified to give advice on the matter is our Sherry. She's been solving the town's murders for years."

Sherry's cheeks burned. "That's not exactly the case. I gave a bit of information that led to a conviction in one murder, but I appreciate your confidence in me. Let's hear what Beverly has to say."

"Thank you, dear." Beverly set her mug on the table

next to the pickle jars. "I wouldn't be surprised if the camera operator, Kirin, I believe her name was, was behind all the shenanigans. She had such an attitude when I was there. Everyone bothered her, and her temper seemed hair-trigger. When Brett was doing a weather forecast, he made a slight error, and they had to reshoot. She slammed her soiled baseball cap to the floor. She tripped on the camera cable when she went to collect her hat, hitting the camera and knocking the rubber grip off the controls. She had to ask Steele to go to the supply closet and find her a new one. The entire incident cost them so much time Brett couldn't finish the weather. The poor man's closing words were 'for today's forecast, check back in a few hours.' The camera's red light was only off for a second before Kirin announced, 'You all are making me look so bad. Why didn't I accept that job offer in San Francisco?'"

"You have to go on more than the appearance of anger to convict someone for murder, Beverly. Motives, lack of alibis, etcetera. But if I talk to Detective Bease, I'll mention what you've told us. Or you could contact him yourself." Sherry separated the MediaPie mug from the pickle jars and slid the cup a substantial distance away. "Would you like a sample of our spears?"

"Yes, please." Beverly pinched a toothpick and pierced a pickle. She held the green-dimpled chunk in front of her face. "Swedes are famous for pickled herring. My ancestor Knut Eklind was said to have eaten the sour fermented fish six out of seven days of the week. On the seventh day lore says he drank a lot of water, thirsty from a week's worth of high salt consumption." She sucked the pickle off the tiny wooden stick. "Fantastic. I'll take a jar."

"From what I hear, your ancestor Knut Eklind pickled himself with plenty of alcohol. You know that's not the reputation the citizens of Augustin want for their founder, so why don't you give up that fight?" Frances's tone was firm but respectful.

Beverly handed Sherry some bills and gathered up her pickles. She placed the jar in her bag. "Come by my exhibit table tomorrow and judge for yourself. I think the items displayed will be eye-openers. Which way to The Spice Trap? I need some Italian blend for dinner."

Sherry pointed across the market.

Beverly hoisted her bag onto her shoulder and strutted away.

A woman with an infant in a sling filled the spot left vacant by Beverly. She picked up a jar of Perfect Storm whole baby pickles. "I love anything associated with 'baby.'" She stroked the only body part of her child that was visible, the crown of her head. "I'll take this jar, please."

"Your baby's precious," Frances cooed as the woman and her bundle left the table. "Dear, why did you ask me about Brett Paladin's breakfast cookie recipe?"

Sherry set out a jar of petite pickles to replace the one purchased by the woman with the baby. "The three times I've set foot in the station, he's been after me to taste-test his baked good. He solicits my opinion and makes the changes I suggest. But the baked good is becoming my cookie, not his, and I'd like to get out of the role of his personal cookie designer. In the contesting world, I've learned to keep my recipe secrets to myself or I'm more than likely to see my ideas with someone else's name attached to them in the next contest I enter."

"Oh my. That's a quandary," Frances said.

"I don't like the position I'm put in. His success or failure shouldn't be dependent on my tips. But he's so insistent, and I have some sympathy for the spot he's in over there. Hard to say no."

A group of mothers and infants in strollers wheeled toward Sherry. One of the babies was crying so hard a woman had to park her wheels and scramble to get a cuddle under way as quickly as possible. As she cajoled the squirming screamer, Sherry's gaze locked with hers. "My friend was right. The one over there with the baby sac. She told me you're the woman who won the News Twelve appetizer contest. We watched you compete on TV. It was such an exciting event. Would you mind holding my baby, and I'll take a picture?"

Before Sherry could open her mouth to respond, the hyperventilating wriggler was in her arms.

"Can you stand close to your Perfect Storm sign, please?"

Sherry took two steps toward the large banner draped behind her table.

"Great. Hold still." The woman snapped some shots with her cell phone. Leaving the baby in Sherry's arms, the woman proceeded to peruse the items on the table.

"I'm going to move along, dear." Frances stroked the gurgling baby's scalp fuzz. "You may have found your calling. She's very happy now. Bye, bye. I'll be in touch."

One of the women slid two jars across the table

toward Sherry. "Excuse me. I'd like these two jars please."

The woman with the empty stroller reached across the pickle table for the baby. Peering at Sherry's name tag, she asked, "May I call you Sherry? Or do you prefer Ms. Oliveri?"

"Sherry, please. Ms. Oliveri makes me sound ancient."

"Sherry, I was wondering why investigators are taking so long to unravel the murders," the young mother said. "You must have been there for at least one of them. It was right after the cook-off. I'm the same age as Carmell Gordy, and the incident disturbs me to no end. I didn't know her, but I did go to school with Lucky Pannell, and what happened to him is even more disturbing. I know you were involved in gathering clues in a murder that occurred at a recent cook-off, so I had an idea I wanted to share with you."

The baby's eyelids fluttered before drifting shut. The pint-sized human began to purr as sleep blanketed him.

Contentment tugged at the corners of Sherry's mouth. There was an aura so peaceful and innocent around an infant napping. "What's your idea?"

"This may seem farfetched and straight out of the movies, but can a trap be set to catch the murderer? I mean, maybe bait him or her somehow? It's obviously either someone who works at the TV station, has full access to the facility, or is able to clear security because presumably he or she is a frequent visitor. I was there recently when I was interviewed about my book *Life Improvement Through Veganism.* I know there's a procedure to getting past security, and, unless you're on the appointment book, you're going to run into a roadblock." The woman snuggled her baby nose to nose.

"I've been watching the morning show on News Twelve since Brett Paladin was the sole anchor, so I feel like they're my family over there, and I'm concerned."

"You and a lot of others." Sherry shook her head. "Everyone has an opinion; that's for sure. The culprit could be anyone at this point. Just when I think I've narrowed down the options, the person I have in mind comes up with an alibi."

"I'd think recipe invention is a little like gathering evidence in an investigation. Once you start second-guessing yourself, details can get overworked and watered down." The woman kissed her baby's porcelain white cheek.

"That's exactly where I am right now, in second-guess mode. But my main concern is I don't want anyone else to get hurt, and that especially means my father."

Chapter 19

"When we set up the Ruggery exhibit table, why not put a few jars of Perfect Storm pickles out?" Amber asked. "More proof of your family's industrious entrepreneurial fortitude."

Sherry lowered her phone and grinned. She raised the phone back to chin level. "You're overselling us a bit, but I understand what you're getting at. I'll bring some with me. I should be there in a half hour after I make a quick trip to the bank. It's about time I cash the check I won at the appetizer cook-off. I hope I can find the envelope in the equipment carryall I brought to the cook-off, otherwise I have no idea where the darn thing is." Sherry put down her blush brush, checked her made-up face in the bathroom mirror, and picked up her phone. "Did Dad do a good job of picking which rugs to display today? If not, feel free to substitute your favorite."

"You know I can hear you, right?" Erno called from a distance.

"Oops, didn't know I was on speaker." Sherry lowered her voice to a breathy whisper. "Amber, seriously, feel free. You're the one manning the Founder's

Day table today, so we should represent your tastes as well." She raised her voice again. "I'll see you two in a bit down at the town center. And bring Bean because Chutney's coming."

Sherry went to the closet in search of her small suitcase on wheels that served as her easy-driving cook-off supply locker. She rolled it out and lifted the flap. Chutney bounded from the bedroom and stuck his nose in the case's empty hollows while Sherry examined the crevices for the envelope containing the check. On the brink of abandoning the search, Sherry tried pulling back the stitched seam of a pocket. There, wedged deep inside, was the bent, but recoverable, envelope. As she fondled the paper, Chutney recoiled with a yelp.

"What's the matter, boy? I hope you didn't surprise a spider with an attitude in there." Sherry put down the envelope, grabbed Chutney's collar with one hand, and pushed his backside down with the other. "Just sit. You're okay." She removed her hands and stared at the glistening red spot on her thumb. "Are you bleeding?"

Sherry lifted her dog's snout and saw a streak of blood on his nose. She reached inside the suitcase and felt around the pocket. She ferried a cold, hard object to eye level. "Dad's tool. He didn't misplace it at the station. It was lost in my bag all this time. That'll teach you to blindly follow your nose, right, boy?"

Sherry held the punch tool up to her face. The image of Truman Fletcher's Peas and Corn Rolling Pin invaded Sherry's brain. "Dad wasn't the murderer because, well, because he's my dad and I know he couldn't do such a heinous act. And when I prove who did, Dad'll be solidly in the clear. I need to connect the dots between Truman Fletcher's punch tool leaving his possession and eventually landing in the hands of the killer."

Sherry left the bag open on the floor and set the punch tool in the middle of its cavernous belly. "Let's go, Chutney. We've got a stop to make at the bank, then we're off to the Founder's Day celebration. Just one quick phone call first." Sherry trotted back to her bedroom, collected her phone, and placed the call.

Chutney and Bean scampered around the grass before settling on a sunny patch to the side of the Ruggery's Founder's Day exhibit table.

"Amber, the display's so pretty." Sherry circled the rugs that lay side by side on the table. "Dad, you made great choices."

Two rugs depicting outdoor picnic scenes rested on the grass in front of the table.

"We swapped one or two of my choices for Amber's favorites but, all in all, I think we both did a fine job." Erno held his chin high. "You know what I always say, two heads are better than one as long as one is twice as smart."

"Dad, I've never heard you say . . ."

"Good morning, Oliveris and Ms. Sherman." Truman Fletcher cast a shadow over the rug display. "Sherry, I got your message, and I brought my invention."

"Mr. Fletcher . . ." Sherry paused.

"Truman, please," the man said.

"Truman, thanks for bringing your rolling pin. I'm putting it right next to the pickle jars." Sherry held out her hand to receive Truman's colorful vegetable trapper.

Sherry caught her father shaking his head. "Do you have any literature or contact cards to leave?"

"No, I'm sorry. Your call caught me off guard, but I could write my phone number on a piece of paper. That's the best I can do on such short notice."

"No problem. We'll take names of everyone interested. Amber is manning the table all afternoon, so we've got it covered."

"Much appreciated. I'm off to meet Castle and Paladin for our live remote. We'll be by for an interview later." Truman turned and walked away.

"Did we discuss displaying Truman's invention?" Erno asked his daughter. "I don't mind, but I don't remember making that decision. I'm giving myself partial credit if the contraption takes off in the marketplace since he used our hooking tool to create the perfect butter drip holes." He repositioned the rolling pin on a cloth napkin. "Doesn't look half bad, if you ask me. Another example of Augustin ingenuity."

Her father's joy yanked at her heart. She took a step back to admire their display, only to find herself within arm's length of the neighboring group setting up the Scapegoats Weed Eaters exhibit. "How perfect. We're all about gorgeous lamb's wool, and you're all about clearing weeds with goats. And who do we have here?"

Sherry stepped closer to a parti-colored baby goat with tiny horn buds sprouting on its forehead. She held out her hand and was greeted with a head butt. "Oh, not out of your teenage years I see."

A woman in overalls and a straw hat arranging bales of hay straightened up and nodded to Sherry.

"This is Billy the Kid. He's a pygmy goat. Only six months old. We'll have to make sure he doesn't eat your beautiful rugs. He's bred to clear-cut, and to him anything not nailed down or otherwise secured is fair game."

A muted gasp flew out of Sherry's mouth. "We'd appreciate that. I'm sure he'll behave like a proper gentleman. I'm Sherry, and these two are Erno and Amber." Sherry gestured toward her table, and Erno and Amber waved.

"I'm Sally, and this is my husband, Garrett. We live on Four Leaf Cloven Farm out on the northern border of Augustin." The woman nudged her hat with her knuckles.

"You must be neighbors with the Dumont farm. I work with Frances Dumont. These are her pickles, as a matter of fact." Sherry pointed to the two jars on her table.

"She's a great person. Couldn't ask for a better neighbor. I'm so glad she decided not to sell her farm." Sally fed Billy a bunch of greenery that resembled cilantro.

"You must be mistaken. Frances would have told me if she were trying to sell the farm." Sherry's tone exuded confidence, while her stomach fluttered with a passing chill.

Garrett emerged from behind Sally. "To that couple, as a matter of fact." He pointed down the row of exhibitors to a woman dressed in a pantsuit, donning a floral wide-brimmed sun hat. Next to her was a man in a business suit, arms crossed, legs set in a rigid stance.

"Excuse me. I need to finish setting up. Very nice to meet you." Sherry left the couple and raced back to her father. "Dad, did you know Frances considered selling her farm to the Van Ardans?"

Erno spun his head toward his daughter. "She didn't, so there's nothing to know."

"Dad, you're so aggravating." Sherry's cheeks prickled with heat as she watched her father continue unloading small rugs. "I'm running to the ladies' room. Amber, want to join me?"

"Sure. Erno, will you be okay?" Amber handed Erno the last rug to be displayed.

He nodded.

"Chutney and Bean will keep you company."

"Beware, only portable potties are provided. Not the most elegant, but it's the solution the committee came up with to satisfy the crowd's natural urges." Sherry led Amber down the rows of tables featuring an assortment of Augustin's offerings. With her eye on her destination, Sherry kept her pace brisk as she passed each exhibitor.

On their return trip, Sherry slowed when she reached the Van Ardans' table. Beverly was adjusting a sign that read "Knut Eklind, once Augustin's largest land owner, first mayor, and distilled grain entrepreneur." Her husband, Erik, still doing his best imitation of the letter *A*, stood behind her.

Sherry's legs ground to a halt. "Mrs. Van Ardan, your table's so inviting."

"Thank you, dear. I haven't had a chance to visit yours, but we will, right, Erik?"

"Of course. I've prepared a few words, concerning Knut Eklind, to address the attendees of the Trivselbit ceremony. I think the audience will be enlightened." The silver streaks in Erik Van Ardan's hair shimmered in the morning sun. He was dashing in his dark suit, so out of place in the casual atmosphere of the day, yet he wore it as if it were his second skin.

Erik picked up two tattered, leather-bound books from a huge tote bag and set them on the table in front of his wife. Next to the books he supplied a pair of white cotton gloves. One book was titled, *Good Kettle Cookery: An Onion In Every Pot.* The second book had a burgundy and gold cover emblazoned dead center with three capital letters and a word. Sherry squinted to make out the letters written with a flourish and was able to decipher EDK DIARY.

"Beautiful books. They're so delicate; is that what the gloves are for?" Amber reached for the hand protectors, but then retracted her hand.

"Yes. The oils from human skin can destroy these relics. There are only two of these cookbooks known to remain." Beverly gazed at the books. "This copy here is missing a page, which was torn out today by a visitor to our booth. Brett Paladin thought I didn't see, but he had a reason to deface one of my treasured heirlooms. He put the page in his blazer pocket, and I have every intention of getting it back."

"I think I understand what he wanted it for." Sherry trailed her finger across her lips.

"I'll come by later and have a closer look-see, Mrs. Van Ardan. Right now, I better go join Erno," Amber said.

She and Sherry locked glances. "I'll meet you back there in a few, Sherry. Nice to see you, Mr. and Mrs. Van Ardan." Amber trotted away as Sherry returned her attention to the book.

"What does the *D* stand for?" Sherry's finger hovered over the gold letter between the *E* and the *K*.

"I think you know, dear."

"So it is true the Eklinds and the Dahlbacks are related? Why haven't you made this public knowledge?" Sherry searched Beverly's eyes during the elder woman's dramatic silence.

"There's a reason Erik and I don't live in Augustin. The town wasn't welcoming for our Eklind ancestor, and we took it quite personally. The man made his fortune bottling gin, and that was frowned upon by this community. Hard work afforded him the ability to become the area's largest landholder, but he was also quite a humble man, as many pages of his diary attest to. He quietly helped many citizens in need, often anonymously, asking nothing in return. Where I have placed a bookmark in the diary is the page where Knut spells out the financial assistance his ex-brother-in-law Andre August Dahlback refused to accept when the onion crop couldn't recover from the persistent blight. Months later, Dahlback came begging Knut to extend a second offer, and this time funds were accepted on the terms that the arrangement remain a secret. That way the very popular Dahlback could save face. Knut's sister was married for a short time to Dahlback, but died young. She being Knut's only close family connection, he left town, turning his landholdings over to be used as the town green, library, and river walk spaces, all under the name Augustin not Dahlback. Families have secrets, and this is a big one about a selfless man." Beverly picked up a glove and used it to reposition the book farther from the Knut Eklind Gin bottle.

"You say Dahlback was his brother-in-law? And

Dahlback was Knut's middle name? That sounds a little too close for comfort, in the familial sense."

"From what we could trace on the family tree, they were distant enough relatives. The families settled here together intentionally. They came from the same town in Sweden, and their intention was to move overseas to broaden opportunities. So, I would wager, if you found yourself related to one of these men, you were somehow related to the other."

"It's not a new concept that Augustin celebrates Founder's Day every year, so why are you choosing this year to unveil the Eklind family's involvement in the town's history?" Sherry studied the woman. She was sure Beverly was about to tell her of MediaPie's plan to acquire News Twelve in order to revamp the way the town got its subdued local news and entertainment spoon-fed to them.

Beverly leaned in. "If I tell you the reason, will you promise to keep the source secret?"

"Okay, sure, I promise. Seems a bit silly, though." Sherry shrugged.

Beverly lowered her voice. "The time has come for the misunderstood and underrepresented Eklinds to reclaim their place in Augustin's history. The Van Ardans are here to stay, and we want to be accepted as the contributors our family has always been. MediaPie's move to acquire News Twelve is moving along on schedule with only a few hiccups. The one most opposed to the acquisition is a certain member of the Gadabee family, Brett Paladin. That man has done everything in his power to undermine the Van Ardan good name. Unbeknownst to Brett, his stepmother, Ruth Gadabee, has worked tirelessly to accelerate the acquisition process because it's what's going to preserve the station, not undermine it. Ruth puts on a show that Knut Eklind shouldn't be recognized as a town founder. For heaven's sake, her best friend, Frances Dumont, was about to sell us her farm so we had a home out here. That is until she realized she'd miss it dearly. Both ladies are all for the change. Your father, too, has been instrumental in providing strong networking connections for Erik and me here in town. Ruth's wish is that Erno appear as if he's against our efforts so he doesn't suffer the backlash we have been going through, but he wants what's right in the end. And, may I add, Erno has a vested interest in seeing Ruth happy if they're going to spend the rest of their lives together."

Sherry's mouth dropped open.

"Beverly!" Erik placed his hands on his wife's shoulders. "It's not your place to talk about people's personal business." Erik softened his tone. "Forgive my wife. She's a hopeless romantic."

Sherry's scalp prickled as a rush of cold blood flowed just beneath the surface. Bright dots danced across her vision until she realized she had forgotten to breathe in. "I have to get to work. Good luck today." Sherry spun on her heels, whacking the edge of the table with her knee in the process. She fell forward, avoiding performing a full cartwheel by clinging to the side of a dolly the Van Ardans had used to transport their items from the car to the table.

"You've shocked the poor girl senseless, Beverly. You really must be careful what you say," Erik said as Sherry dusted herself off.

Sherry trotted past the neighboring exhibits. "Where's Dad?"

"Well, after we cleaned up the remains of the casserole you brought in to display on the local talent table, Mrs. Gadabee and Mrs. Dumont showed up and kidnapped him. I didn't ask where they were headed. Should I have?"

"Did you say remains of my casserole? What happened?"

Amber pointed to the animal tethered to the adjacent table. "Billy the Kid's not pregnant; that's just a belly full of smoky steak fajita casserole. That contented creature over there might lose his job feeding on weeds now he's tasted your cooking. He now knows the grass is literally greener on the other side. We turned our back for a moment, and the damage was done. Let the record show Bean and Chutney didn't lift a paw to ward off the invader."

Sherry's gaze locked with Sally's. The woman in the straw hat threw up her arms, surrender style. "Sure looked delicious. Wish I'd gotten a chance to try a bite. Sorry!"

"No problem. These things happen. Not the first time I've cooked for a goat, that's for sure. . . ." Sherry's face collapsed into a pout. She shifted her attention back to Amber. "I'm glad I remembered to bring some cook-off aprons for the talent table."

Sherry surveyed the surrounding area. "Wonder where Dad went. He's got some explaining to do when he returns, and I don't mean about the four-legged raider."

It wasn't long before Erno returned from his jaunt with his lady friends. The morning became a blur of out-of-town visitor questions, instructional lectures on everything having to do with rug hooking, pickling, and inventions, and explanations of the ins and outs of contest cooking. If Sherry had received a dime for every time she was asked what she was making for dinner that evening, she could have bought the new ceramic knife set she'd been craving but felt she couldn't afford.

As the time ticked closer to the noon hour, Sherry made mental preparations for leaving Amber so she and her father could head for the August-Tinies parade. There they would meet up with the others who would be honored at the Trivselbit ceremony. Lost in thought, Sherry didn't see the man dressed in business attire approach.

"Sherry and Erno Oliveri, may we interview you for our live broadcast?" Brett Paladin asked.

Kirin and her camera were at his side.

Sherry checked the time. "I have to head over to the parade in about seven minutes."

"We do, too. A quick discussion of your table contents is all we need. Kirin, are you set?" Brett offered up his empty hand, and Kirin filled it with a microphone.

The camerawoman hoisted her equipment up to her shoulder while she backed away from Sherry and Brett.

"Brett, are you getting a sunburn? I hope the camera doesn't amplify your blazing complexion next to Sherry's pale, I mean, muted coloring," Kirin said.

"A flare-up. Can't be helped." Brett put the back of his hand to his cheek.

"Would you like some water?" Sherry reached under the table for a bottle. "That might calm the redness. You said stress triggered a flare-up when you had the same symptoms at the cook-off. Are things not going smoothly here?"

Brett stepped toward the table. "What's this doing here?" He set the mic down next to Truman's rolling pin. He held up the invention until Sherry made her way over.

"I thought the opportunity was there to showcase one more smart idea from an Augustin citizen. So much time and effort was put into its development. I think the concept's quite inspirational. Truman has two companies interested in marketing it as soon as he can patent it."

Brett groaned, set the rolling pin down, and scooped up the mic. He turned toward Kirin, who was shoulder to shoulder with Truman Fletcher and Damien Castle. "Good job, Fletcher. This day seems less about the town's founder and more about capitalism. I should have had you display my breakfast cookie. Now there's an idea whose time has come."

"Have you visited many of the other exhibits?" Sherry curled her words around a core of saccharin sweetness. "I was very interested in the MediaPie table. The Van Ardans have a compelling argument in favor of Knut Eklind's having founded Augustin. They're beginning to win me over."

"That's an appropriate display? A gin bottle? A diary of questionable origin? They had some land deeds, but I'm sure they were bogus. That family needs to get a hobby and leave the town and TV station alone."

"You're back on in thirty seconds, Brett," Damien called out.

Brett inched closer to Sherry. "I brought you something." He passed Sherry a cookie. "Save it for later."

When Truman gave the thumbs-up sign, Kirin's camera light bloomed red.

Brett's face was enveloped in a broad grin. "We've traveled down the row of tables from the fantasy world of a family who wants to lay claim to something that's not theirs to a real-life success story involving a blank canvas and some lambs' wool. Erno Oliveri is the patriarch of the Ruggery, and we're also joined by his daughter, Sherry. Behind them is an impressive sampling of rugs and one of the store managers . . ." Brett paused.

"Amber Sherman," Amber called out.

"Right. Erno Oliveri, may I have a word with you?" Brett sidled up to Sherry's father.

Sherry inched closer to Erno until there was no space between the threesome.

"As a loyal Augustinian, your business means more than financial gains for your family. It lends support and strength to this community." Brett picked up a punch tool that lay on the table. "Not unlike the necessity of this tool in the rug-hooking process, without one you can't have the other."

"Thank you, Brett. You're very kind. We value opinions like yours," Erno replied.

"But, I've heard your loyalties may be shifting." Brett's inflection sharpened. "Can you substantiate the rumor that you're supportive of outsiders buying up Augustin's homespun businesses and transforming them into pawns of big business? Will this town be able to survive the change from a slower pace of doing business, one where shopkeepers know their customers by name, to an environment in which the only goal is to add to big corporations' coffers?" Brett thrust the mic toward Erno's lips.

"Brett, we need to get over to the parade," Damien called out as he made slicing gestures across his neck.

Sherry yanked Erno's shirt from behind, sending him stumbling back a step. "I'm sure we'll see you over there."

"That's the report from the Ruggery," Brett announced. "We're going to break for commercials now. Be sure to join us as we follow the youngest citizens of Augustin parading around the town green." Brett handed the microphone back to Kirin, who shoved it in her belt.

"Paladin, stay on script," Damien Castle barked. "Follow me, everyone."

"We better go, too, Dad. Amber, are you sure you'll be okay here? We could close up shop and all go to the ceremony together."

Amber pursed her lips. "I wouldn't mind that, actually. I'm feeling a bit unsettled right now." Amber laid a cloth over the display table, shrouding its contents from view. "Is this going to work?"

"That's fine. Come on, Dad. Let's get over to the green." Sherry's quivering hand rested on her father's back.

Chapter 20

When the future men and women of Augustin finished skipping, giggling, marching, and roughhousing in semi-formation, people began to file toward the folding chairs that had been set up facing the deluxe stage in the middle of the town green. The news crew was clustered on the side of the stage, along with those being honored. Sherry and Erno stood beside Remington, the past Olympian, Lonnie, the fitness instructor and published author, and Colton, the dog trainer, whose graduates included two canines with lucrative movie careers.

With the seats full, with the exception of a few in the front row, Larson Anderson positioned himself center stage. "Ladies and gentlemen. Welcome to Augustin's Founder's Day celebration, and thank you for attending the first ever Trivselbit ceremony. We're joined by a special group of Augustin citizens this afternoon. It's my honor to award these folks with Distinguished Citizen medals for their service to our community and for upholding the high standards expected of an Augustinian."

Sherry nestled closer to her father as Larson engaged the crowd with his history of the town's founding. Amber was in sight, seated at the end of the third row with Chutney and Bean's heads protruding into the aisle. Standing a few feet from her, under an expansive oak tree branch, was Detective Bease.

"Andre August Dahlback laid the foundation for this town with his hard work and strong values, and it's in his memory we give these awards out each year to individuals we feel personify the man's legacy. Before we hand out the medals, I've invited one of our local celebrities to say a few words," Larson said.

Sherry's breath caught at the base of her throat as she watched Ruth and Frances take their seats in the front row. She turned her attention to her father, who she caught winking. She touched his side with her elbow, and he let loose a soft murmur.

"Brett Paladin, please come join me." Brett accompanied Larson at center stage. Before Brett had time to put his microphone up to his lips, Larson continued, "I led you to believe I asked you here to give the Trivselbit its proper introduction, but that was a ploy."

Sherry guided her father back a step as she leaned across him for a better vantage point. Brett's face screwed up into a scowl as he dropped the mic to his side.

"We'd like to present you with an honorary lifetime achievement award. On behalf of the Founder's Day nominating committee, let me call up our representatives Frances Dumont and a woman you know very well, Ruth Gadabee. Come on up, ladies, and don't forget the medal."

Ruth and Frances made their way from their seats

and brushed past the Trivselbit honorees to reach center stage.

"Welcome, ladies." Larson shifted to give the women room on either side of Brett.

"This is unnecessary, Mr. Anderson. I'm merely here to introduce the festivities." Brett attempted to ooze out of the center of the lady sandwich, but his exit was blocked.

"Brett's my stepson, as many of you might know, and it gives me pleasure to award him with the Lifetime Achievement medal this year," Ruth announced. "Frances Dumont, someone I would consider *my* lifetime achievement award, has your medal right here." The audience rumbled with laughter.

"Lifetime achievement awards are for people who have one foot in the grave. That's not me." Brett thrust his hand up, putting the brakes on Ruth.

"Your father would be so proud of you and how far you've come in the business he loved so much." Ruth raised her hand and swiped Brett's away.

"Please accept this and wear it with pride as the bearer of the Gadabee legacy, if not in name anymore. The way you conduct business here in your hometown of Augustin would make your ancestors proud." Larson plucked the medal out of Frances's possession and hung the hardware around Brett's neck.

The audience clapped while Brett kept his head bowed.

"Do you have any words you'd like to say, Brett?"

Brett took a step forward and raised the microphone to his mouth. "There is something I'd like to say."

Sherry sucked in a deep breath. Erno turned to face her. She put her finger up to her lips.

"Some people may think I'm at the end of my career." Brett scanned the audience until he pinpointed a destination for his searing glare.

Sherry followed his line of sight to Beverly Van Ardan, who was standing a few feet from Detective Bease. She matched Brett's intense expression with a return leer so heated it could have melted the shaved ice sold at the Frozen Fantasies concession stand.

"Those same people seem to want to hijack the town's reputation for their own personal and financial gain. But neither will happen any time soon, and I'll tell you why. Two murders have taken place at our beloved News Twelve, and I'd like to use this opportunity to place the blame on the Van Ardan family."

The audience gasped. Sherry spun her head around toward Mrs. Van Ardan. Detective Bease had his arm extended, blockading her at the waist.

"Brett, I'm sure you don't mean that," Ruth chirped. "The Van Ardans aren't the villains they've been portrayed as. As a matter of fact, their relative Knut Eklind saved this town from ruin when Andre August Dahlback had nowhere else to turn." Ruth leaned into Frances's arm.

"It doesn't seem odd to investigators that every time the Van Ardans called a meeting at News Twelve, a murder followed soon thereafter? For all I know, I was next on their hit list because I refuse to let the station my family built from scratch go up in smoke." Brett lowered his chin and wrestled the medal and its thick red ribbon over his head. He chucked the shiny medallion in the air, and Larson snagged it. "And your friend Erno Oliveri was most likely an accomplice, Ruth. All evidence points to that. You may want to make better social choices."

"Brett, why are you fighting the truth so hard? You know you're related to the Eklinds." Beverly called out from the audience.

Brett pivoted around toward Ruth. With his nose by hers he shouted, "This is all your fault. No one is supposed to know that. If you hadn't taken up with this murderer, everything would have remained as it was meant to be." Brett hurled his pointed finger at Erno. "Yes, my father and plenty of others in this town can be traced back to the Eklind family. They seem to have been prolific breeders and had plenty of marriages and lots of children. But I'm not one of them. I'm my father's son, and I want what he wanted."

Frances snatched the microphone from Brett's hand. "Brett, your father was on the verge of selling out before he died. Take a look at the set of papers on the Van Ardans' table, and you'll see his signature on the seller's line of a MediaPie purchase contract. After he died, the document was never filed out of respect for his widow."

Sherry nodded toward Amber before whispering in her father's ear. When he tipped his head, she stepped forward, urging one foot in front of the other until she got her muscles to fully cooperate. Despite the quivering in her legs, she managed to reach center stage with only one misstep.

"May I say a few words?" Sherry was handed the microphone. Her trembling hand lifted it to her parched lips. Her paralyzed tongue, secured to the top of her mouth with dry saliva, thickened her words. "I think Brett should be recognized for his cooking prowess, too. He can follow a cookbook recipe perfectly." Sherry lifted a cookie high in the air.

"When I said save the cookie for later, I meant after

the ceremony," Brett hissed. "And what do you mean, 'follow a cookbook recipe'? Those cookies are made from my own recipe."

"Amazingly, the same recipe exists in the *Good Kettle Cookery* cookbook, page twenty-six in the 'hearty way to start your day' chapter. I'm very familiar with the cookbook, and I recognized the recipe for your breakfast cookies, better known back in the day as Goodly Oat Hand Cakes. I made them once, but they were a bit too hearty for me. You might want to be advised that changing the name of a recipe doesn't make it yours. Cooking contesting one oh one. And changing your last name doesn't sever the ties to your ancestors, either."

"That's impossible," Brett said. "It's one hundred percent my recipe for Breakfast Energy Boost Cookies, before you forced me to make changes, that is."

"If that's true, what's that piece of paper in your coat pocket?" Sherry patted Brett's blue silk blazer, and the mic broadcast a crackling. "May we see? Beverly Van Ardan saw you rip a page out of her cookbook when you thought she was distracted. Maybe you were afraid someone would discover your recipe was plagiarized? Lucky for you, not many people read cookbooks cover to cover like you do. Unlucky for you that I do. And doubly unlucky my father has the only other existing copy of the very same cookbook; he received it as a gift from your stepmother. When I first tasted your cookie, I knew it seemed awfully familiar. They're not the tastiest cookies, but cookies in the old days meant something different than they do today."

"Is there a point to all this because you're boring the audience to tears," Brett scolded as he pulled the paper from his pocket and crumpled it up.

"No, it's fascinating," a baritone male voice called out.

"You can make me cookies any time, Brett," a woman shrieked.

"I'm with Brett. I think the Van Ardans are the evil empire," a gravelly voice exclaimed. "This town is better off without their money and booze."

"Thank you," Brett acknowledged the audience with a nod. He faced Sherry. "That's what I've been trying to tell you people. You have to take what Sherry and her father say with a grain of salt. She may be trying to deflect attention from her actions by bringing up this cookie issue, which is truly a nonissue. Ms. Oliveri chooses to play favorites by using her amateur celebrity status to promote whomever serves her needs. Right, Fletcher? Your kid-friendly veggie-eating invention is a pretty good idea, but how do we know that wasn't plagiarized? You might want to investigate that, Sherry." Brett turned his attention to the side of the stage where Truman stood motionless, mouth agape. "If we're done here, I need to get back to the station."

"Oh, and one more thing, Brett." Sherry cleared her throat. "The morning of the News Twelve cook-off, you ripped your pants when you slipped on some chickpeas I spilled on the studio floor. Do you remember that?"

"I have a very busy schedule. I can't be expected to remember every trivial detail of my day." Brett's hand traveled down to his pants pocket.

"Something very sharp pierced a hole in your tropical weight silk and wool blend slacks. It was an expensive repair. One hundred and seventy-five dollars, to be exact. I know all this because Steele Dumont was the one who searched out a tailor who could perform such a hurried repair, and he shared the story when I asked him if I could pay for your pants to be mended. You guys use Steele for your personal errands way too much, you know. At least he gets to drive your nice cars. That's small pittance for the overworked, underpaid intern."

"Are we getting our awards?" Colton, the dog trainer, barked from the side of the stage.

"When is someone going to explain what *trivselbit* means?" Lonnie, the fitness instructor asked as she performed a sun salutation.

Sherry forced the edges of her mouth up into a smile. Her parched lips remained stuck to her teeth. "Very soon."

"Has anyone ever told you a road map is needed to figure out where your point is headed, Sherry?" Brett remarked with a sneer.

Detective Bease sidestepped toward the center of the stage. "Her point is that the fabric fibers that made up that custom patch matched fibers found imbedded in the punch tool that was in Carmell Gordy's neck. Brett Paladin, I'm here to arrest you for the murder of Carmell Gordy. Officers, right this way."

"Stop right there. This is ridiculous. Why would I kill my co-anchor?" Brett scanned the audience, his cheeks swelling red. He reached inside his blazer and yanked out a plastic bag filled with brown discs. He took aim and hurled the bag point-blank at the detective, who clutched his assaulted face. "See if you like those cookies," he shouted. As Brett made a move for stage right, Sherry rifled her cookie across the deluxe wood planks that made up the stage. Brett's smooth-soled dress shoes were no match for the unforgiving nuggets of overbaked Hand Cakes, and he went down.

Damien and Truman followed the officers onstage and formed a human barricade around Brett, Sherry, and Detective Bease.

"With Carmell gone, you had a hope of holding on to the way things used to be," Damien said. "You couldn't handle her ambition and her forward thinking. You couldn't handle her growing alliance with MediaPie's vision for the future of News Twelve. It's the right move, Brett. They have our best interests in mind. Why would you throw it all away to stay stagnant?"

"Give it up, Brett. Time has run out," Truman said. "You borrowed my punch tool the day of the murder to open your breakfast yogurt and never returned it. Now the proof is in. We know what else you used it for."

The detective snapped handcuffs on Brett's flailing wrists.

"You're making a big mistake," Brett yelled. "Everyone here is guilty except me. This town is headed for disaster."

Brett was shuffled off stage toward a waiting police car.

"Now, will someone please explain *trivselbit*?" Lonnie asked.

Larson watched the squad car pull away just beyond the audience. "The custom is that the last piece, morsel, or crumb be left on the serving plate. You do not want to be the one who takes the last morsel. Whether the taker would be cursed, as some mythology suggests, that's hard to say, but leaving the last morsel is said to represent comfort and security. That's the ideal we think our town best represents. A place of comfort and security."

"The way his luck is going, Brett must have taken the last piece of something," Erno whispered to Sherry as she took her place beside him.

Chapter 21

"Amber, remind me again what's fun about doubles tennis." Sherry executed an aggressive forehand with her racket as they proceeded down the hallway.

"Hey, watch where you're swinging that." Amber ducked.

Sherry held the door open for Amber as they entered the tennis facility's locker room.

"It's social. That's its redeeming value," Amber suggested.

Sherry parked herself in front of the changing room's expansive mirror. She fiddled with her hair clips, adjusting the hair holders to show more forehead, less forehead, more ear, less ear, before settling on an arrangement that best showcased her new golden highlights.

Sherry squinted at her reflection. "Not bad. Not as cute as Chris Evert, but not bad."

When she was done prepping her hair, Sherry reached for an abandoned tennis ball that lay on the counter beneath the mirror. She rolled the fuzzy yellow orb back and forth across the slab of faux marble.

Amber joined Sherry at the mirror. She smoothed

down a strand of flyaway hair. "If you were any more lost in thought, I'd have to send out a search party."

"I was thinking about what Ray said when he called to tell me the case against Brett Paladin appeared to be airtight."

"What did he say?" Amber slipped a pink sweatband on her wrist.

"He said if I hadn't recalled my chickpea cooking error, the case could have taken much longer to solve. When Ray used the word *error* in association with my cooking, it stung like lemon juice in a paper cut, but a direct result of my goof-up was the over-roasted mini cannonballs tripping up Brett Paladin, leading to his fall, in more ways than one. When Patti Mellitt described how Brett reacted when she saw him go down, red flags were flying all over the place." Sherry held the ball still and backed away from the mirror.

"Brett slipped on your appetizer, went down in a heap, and the murder weapon punched a clean hole through his pants. But his mistake was sending Steele Dumont out to have them mended." Amber practiced her backhand stroke.

Sherry bobbed her head in rhythm with her pulsing thoughts. "One too many personal errands for the intern. Ray went on to say Brett confessed to trying to silence Steele because he thought Steele suspected him of Carmell's murder. What was the chance Steele would have Lucky go in the supply closet for him that morning?"

Amber pinched up her forehead. "Did Ray tell you the motive that pushed Brett to the point of no return with Carmell Gordy?"

"Carmell was being wooed by MediaPie, and she was convincing other employees to join her when she switched teams. Dad finally told me that the day of the cook-off when many believed he had argued with Carmell what was being observed, in actuality, was her exuberant reaction to his delivery of a message from the Van Ardans. Carmell was being offered a lucrative position in the MediaPie family. Beverly convinced Dad to deliver the written offer since he was coming to the station for the cook-off. With Carmell's transfer secured, the station changing hands was a done deal. Those employees that didn't care to make the move, like Truman Fletcher and Kirin, had other career options. Brett's world was shrinking to nothing. When Carmell placed the mug on her anchor desk and spun the MediaPie logo toward the camera instead of hiding it, Brett recognized it as a pronouncement that time was up for the News Twelve he knew and loved. Unfortunately, his young coworker was the one he took his anger out on."

"Is the station going off the air after all that's happened?" Amber leaned down and tied one of her sneakers tighter.

"On the contrary. The Van Ardans vow to make improvements, but keep the local flavor, with a dash of national interest sprinkled in for good measure."

Sherry bent her knee, raised it, and hugged it with one hand into her chest. She repeated the stretch with her other leg. She lowered herself into a squat, using her racket for balance. She groaned as she straightened up.

"Ray took the time to apologize for keeping Dad o the suspect list for what seemed like forever. But turned out to be a good thing because Brett thou all the evidence he had planted against Dad made case cut-and-dry. Truth is, Brett relaxed too m and it was only a matter of time before mistakes did him in." Sherry turned her backside to the mirror and peeked over her shoulder. She flung her hand at her reflection.

"I have a feeling Ray knew what he was doing all along."

"And Dad's lady friends, too. But I admit I thought Dad had gone to the dark side the more he seemed to be siding with the Van Ardans and MediaPie. Apparently when Ruth shared her suspicion that her stepson had gone off the rails and could be guilty, Dad jumped at the chance to test his acting skills by playing the innocent victim. Beverly, too, gave a great performance, convincing everyone she was the town's scapegoat."

"They're a tricky bunch, your Dad and his lady friends." Amber winked. "Don't underestimate them."

"It took some convincing to get Ray to believe I wasn't in on the ladies' master plan to test Brett's innocence. The detective's not one to choose reason over fact. My own suspicion of Brett heightened when he kept after me about the cookie recipe. Unbeknownst to him, he was showing me an unsavory side of his character when he kept calling the recipe his own. I knew it came from that old cookbook. Cooks have ethics too, you know. At the same time, Dad and the ladies were swooping in from another angle. At Trivselbit, we had Brett cornered from all sides. Thank goodness Ray believed me when I told him he might want to attend, because we had no plan B when the situation escalated, let alone handcuffs."

"Ray Bease isn't a bad guy. He does his job and does

it well. With a little help from you, that is." Amber winked again.

"Yeah, he's okay. Maybe I'll eat out with him next time he asks. While we're on the subject of who's not bad, I wanted to mention Damien Castle's a nice guy. I prejudged him due to circumstances, but he's trying to improve himself, and you can't fault anyone for that. Ray gave Damien credit for giving all the News Twelve personnel ample opportunities to join the new reorganization, wanting to leave no one behind, including Brett."

"Agreed. I'll keep that in mind when he and I are at dinner this weekend," Amber said.

"Well, aren't you full of surprises." Sherry clicked her tongue on the roof of her mouth. "It's time to go kick some tennis butt."

"Let me ask you something." Amber stared at the racket she had a grip on. "Was that Founder's Day controversy concerning the Dahlbacks and the Eklinds legitimate? Or was that some sort of public relations stunt?"

"It was so real that next year's Founder's Day will include the first annual Gone Knuts recipe cook-off in honor of the town's newest co-creator. I'll be one of the judges, so you may want to enter."

"Hey, ladies," bellowed a woman in a striped sweat suit as she burst through the locker room doorway. "If you're signed up for the doubles social, it's time to get out on the court and make it happen."

"We'll be right there." Sherry gripped her racket with both hands.

"Hey, aren't you the lady who was onstage with that crazy Brett Paladin at the Founder's Day celebration?

I was watching from the audience. That was quite a show." The woman clapped her hand on the strings of her racket. "You're quite the cook. You know, my Panko Crispy Onion Chicken Strips with Apricot Dipping Sauce isn't half bad. It's my post-exercise recovery recipe. If you come again, give me a heads-up; I'll bring you a sample. I could use your improvement recommendations." She disappeared out the doorway.

"You're a mentor, whether you like it or not," Amber said as they climbed the steps toward the courts.

"Hope you're ready to mentor me while we're playing. I'm getting nervous. Is it too late to back out and go home to work on my bucket list?"

As she set foot on the dusty clay surface, Sherry caught sight of a familiar face. Her head snapped back as she double-checked her sighting. "Leila? I didn't know you played tennis. How fun to see you outside of work." Sherry sidled up to Leila, who was dressed in all-black tennis attire. Sherry leaned in. "Hope I parked between the lines out there."

"I'm off duty, Ms. Oliveri. But, now that you mention it, you didn't, and the guy next to you was forced to park so close you'll never get back in the driver's side. This isn't my jurisdiction, but if it were, I'd advise adherence to the designated markings. They're there for a reason." Leila brandished her racket as an instrument of affirmation.

"Yes, ma'am." Sherry lowered her head.

"Want to be partners?" Leila asked with a sudden lightening of her tone.

"I'm sorry. Amber and I were going to give it a try together tonight. Maybe next time?"

Amber's elbow poked her spine.

"But we'll see you at cocktails afterward."

"I have to skip that. I have a dinner date," Leila said.

"That's exciting." Sherry's eyebrows lifted. "Anyone I know?"

"Ray Bease, the detective fellow I always see you with at your father's store. It's our first date, and I'm hopeful I've met my soul mate," Leila stated as if she were reading a criminal the Miranda rights. "Good luck in your game." Leila strutted to the neighboring court.

"Come on, girl. Pick up the jaw you dropped, and let's get social," Amber said.

"I'd much rather be at a cook-off," Sherry said as two men twirling their rackets approached.

Please turn the page for

Recipes from Sherry's Kitchen

Farmer's Market Chicken and Couscous

2 tablespoons olive oil
1 cup peeled sweet potato, cut in small dice
1 pound boneless, skinless chicken thighs, cut in 1-inch cubes
1 package (5.8 ounces) Roasted Garlic and Olive Oil Couscous mix
1½ cup diced farm fresh tomatoes
½ teaspoon ground cumin
⅛ teaspoon ground cinnamon
1 teaspoon minced jalapeno pepper
1 teaspoon sea salt
2 tablespoons apricot preserves
¼ cup freshly squeezed lemon juice
¼ cup smoked almonds, chopped

Preheat oven to 400 degrees.

Heat olive oil in a Dutch oven over medium heat on stovetop. Add the sweet potato and chicken pieces and cook until chicken is no longer pink, stirring occasionally, about 6 minutes. Add the couscous package contents, water amount per package directions, tomatoes, cumin, cinnamon, jalapeno, salt, preserves, and lemon juice. Stir gently to combine. Cover and bake for 15–20 minutes until bubbly and couscous is tender. Sprinkle with almonds and serve.

GRILLED HAM STEAK WITH SOFRITO RICE

Serves 6

¼ cup apricot jam
4 tablespoons fresh lemon juice, divided
2 tablespoons smoked paprika
1 boneless ham steak, approximately 2 pounds, or 2 1-pound ham steaks
3 tablespoons cooking oil, divided use
1 garlic clove, minced
½ cup chopped onion
½ cup chopped green bell pepper
2 cups diced tomatoes
1 tablespoon dried oregano
1 teaspoon each coarse salt and black pepper
⅛ teaspoon dried red pepper flakes
½ cup grated Asiago cheese
Cooked brown rice, 3 cups, prepared as per package instructions
¼ cup cilantro leaves
2 tablespoons Spanish olive slices

Combine the jam, 2 tablespoons lemon juice, and paprika, and rub onto both sides of ham steak(s). Heat a clean gas or charcoal grill to medium hot. Rub grill lightly with 2 tablespoons cooking oil to prevent sticking. Grill ham until grill marks appear; flip and grill other side similarly.

Prepare sofrito sauce by heating a large sauté pan to medium. Add 1 tablespoon oil, garlic, onion and peppers. Sauté until onions are soft, then add the tomatoes, oregano, remaining 2 tablespoons lemon juice, salt and pepper, red pepper flakes, and ½ cup diced grilled ham and heat 1 more minute. Remove from heat.

Divide ham steak pieces between 6 plates, top with sofrito sauce, and sprinkle with cheese. Serve with hot rice topped with extra sofrito sauce. Sprinkle with cilantro and olives.

Crab Sliders with Avocado Tartar Cream

1 pound lump crabmeat, picked over
¼ cup crushed flaky butter crackers, such as Ritz
2 shallots, finely minced
¼ cup mayonnaise
1 tablespoon grainy mustard
1 egg
1 teaspoon Worcestershire sauce
1 teaspoon plus ¼ teaspoon sea salt
1 teaspoon black pepper
1 ripe avocado, peeled, pitted
2 tablespoons sour cream
2 tablespoons fresh lemon juice
1 tablespoon grated horseradish
2 tablespoons chopped dill pickle
1 tablespoon fresh dill
Cooking oil
8 split small ciabatta rolls

Preheat clean grill to medium heat.

In a large bowl combine the crabmeat, crushed crackers, shallots, mayonnaise, mustard, egg, Worcestershire sauce, 1 teaspoon salt, and 1 teaspoon pepper. Form 8 crab patties the size of your ciabatta rolls, and lay them side by side on a parchment paper-lined tray. Refrigerate for 15 minutes.

Prepare avocado tartar cream by mashing the avocado with a fork in a medium bowl. Stir in the sour cream, lemon juice, horseradish, pickle, dill, and ¼ teaspoon salt.

Brush crab sliders with cooking oil and grill them until golden and grill marks are visible, flipping once. After flipping the sliders, toast the rolls on the grill, cut side down. Assemble sliders by placing a crab patty on the bottom of each roll and placing a large dollop of avocado tartar cream on patty.

Place top of roll on next and serve!

GRILLED MAPLE CORN CHOW CHOW SALAD

4 ears fresh corn
2 tablespoons cooking oil
2 ripe plum tomatoes, diced
⅓ cup red onion, diced
½ cup red bell pepper, diced
1 cup finely chopped green cabbage
2 tablespoons olive oil
1 garlic clove, minced
3 tablespoons apple cider vinegar
3 tablespoons maple syrup
½ teaspoon cumin
½ teaspoon smoked paprika

Preheat clean grill to medium heat.

Brush corn ear with 2 tablespoons oil and grill until golden, turning to cook all sides. Remove to a plate and cut off kernels with a sharp knife, discarding husks. Combine corn, tomatoes, onion, bell pepper, and cabbage in a salad bowl.

Combine olive oil, garlic, vinegar, maple syrup, cumin, paprika, and salt to taste in a large saucepan over heated grill or stove top and bring just to a simmer. Remove from heat. Pour immediately over salad bowl contents and toss to coat. Serve at room temperature.